39 SIXTY

THOMAS JOHNSON'S NOVELS

39 Sixty

Their Last Chance

Shattered (SERIES) - #1 How will he Recover?
Shattered - #2 Seeking a new Life

Escape Perfection (SERIES) - #1 William Rises
Escape Perfection - #2 William Takes Flight
Escape Perfection #3 Milo Pursues
Escape Perfection #4 Race to the Barrier

Battle for Dóchas (SERIES) – #1 Encountering Aylin
Battle for Dóchas – #2 Warfare at Shepherd Lake
Battle for Dóchas – #3 Sovrano's Revenge

39 SIXTY

A NOVEL BY

THOMAS JOHNSON

Kepha Press

39 SIXTY

KEPHA PRESS

Author Email: tpjohnson@kephapress.com
Publisher website: http://kephapress.com/
Twitter: https://twitter.com/tpjohnson11
Softcover: ISBN: 978-1-950950-15-7
Hardcover ISBN: 978-1-950950-14-0
eBook ISBN: 978-1-950950-16-4
Library of Congress Control Number: 2015905285

CONTRIBUTORS:

General Editor:	Randal C Powers
Contributions by:	Wendy Johnson, Edmundo Martinez
Designed by:	Jesus Cardenas
Cover and layout by:	Kepha Press

10 9 8 7 5 6 5 4

To Wendy, my wife, and to my children: Rachel, Nicole, Lauren, Sean, Joseph, and Patrick, for giving me love and hope when I needed it most.

AUTHOR'S NOTE

Thank you for purchasing **39 SIXTY**. If you enjoy this novel, please leave a five-star review online and spread the word about my work. You can learn about my books at the publisher's website: https://kephapress.com.

I hope you read many terrific books,

Thomas Johnson

39 SIXTY

CHAPTER ONE

BROKEN ANGEL

Aedan O'Beirne's life was about to take a painful turn.

While clutching a pink heart-shaped note, he walked into the kitchen. He searched the room, his eyes settled on Ciara, his wife, placing a baking sheet into the oven. He sneered as he marched toward her, his sweaty bare feet made slapping sounds on the cold ceramic tile.

Why is she awake, and why's she baking?

His left foot came upon a glass Christmas tree ornament lying on the tile floor. He bore down on the tiny angel. The decorative piece shattered; glass shards carved painful cuts in his left arch. Pain consumed him as he took the weight off his foot. A slight scream escaped his mouth.

Ciara looked at him. "Are you okay?"

"That's a stupid question." He shook his head.

"Dad, you broke the angel." Five-year-old Colin cried; tears flowed down his cheeks. "Mom, Dad smashed the angel. Look, Mom."

Aedan folded the pink note and shoved it into his pocket. He hopped on his right foot to a chair. He tripped and tumbled toward the floor; his head struck the island counter. He dropped in a painful heap onto the ceramic tile. A baking sheet, filled with fresh-baked Christmas cookies, fell from the countertop, crashing onto his back; the cookies jettisoned across the room. The heat from the tray penetrated his t-shirt, resulting in a burn to his skin. He rotated away. The cookie sheet crashed to the floor. He grimaced as pain flooded his senses.

Ciara slammed the oven door shut. She hurried to him.

He thrust his right hand toward her in anger. "Stay away from me." Pain consumed him as he looked at her. "Why are you up? Why are you baking? Colin should be sleeping. I enjoy having the house to myself in the morning." He glared at her; his eyes narrowed. He grunted through the pain.

She never understands I have a life and that I have needs of my own.

Ciara ignored him. "Are you okay?"

Colin cried as he retrieved pieces of the crushed angel ornament from the floor. "Dad, why'd you smash it?"

"I didn't break the stupid ornament on purpose." He sat in a nearby chair. Blood ran down his nose and into his mouth. He coughed, the blood and spittle mixture jettisoned from his mouth, landing with a splat on Ciara's Christmas pajama pants, creating a stain.

"Oh, gross, Dad."

"Aedan," she shouted. "What's wrong with you?" She handed him a towel to clean his forehead. "Go to the hospital."

He shook his head in defiance. "No chance, I will leave for work and soon." Aedan's foot continued to bleed. His wounds caused him to spread blood across a five-foot-square section of floor close to the island. His cuts transformed the kitchen into an injury and blood splatter zone. He sneered as he took calming breaths.

This can't be happening to me, not today.

"I'm not cleaning this mess," Ciara said.

He frowned. "I don't have time; I have to get to work."

"Why are you going to work today?"

He stared at her. "Do I have to remind you, again? It won't be a good day for our family."

"You worry too much. The firm won't fire you."

Irritation caused his jaw to clench. "Whatever, you've no idea what you're talking about." He glared at Ciara. "I can't take a chance that you're right. Do you understand how hard it is to find a job in this economy?"

"They won't fire you. Stop worrying," Ciara said.

"Ciara, I have to keep my job. I don't want to go to work today, but I have to protect my job."

Colin cried as he climbed onto a counter stool while clutching pieces from the broken angel. He placed them in an empty bowl on the countertop. After climbing down from the seat; he continued filling the container with the smashed ornament.

Aedan raised his eyebrows. "Colin, get to bed."

The boy's eyes flooded with tears. He ran into the living room, seeking comfort from the bright Christmas tree lights.

Ciara's eyes bore down on Aedan. "Stop yelling at Colin; he did nothing to you. If you're working today, go now."

"First, I must wrap these wounds." He wrapped the towel around his foot. "Leave me alone ."

"You're so mean. Maybe I should stay at my parent's house for Christmas. You'd love it if I did that."

He glared at her. He groaned from the pain emanating from his wounds. "Are you trying to start a fight with me?"

What does she want from me? She knows I never wanted kids.

"I don't understand. What's your problem?" Ciara said.

He reached into his pocket and extracted the note. He raised the pink heart to Ciara. "I read your message. You're pregnant again. How? And why?"

Ciara removed fresh cookies from the oven. She laughed.

"Why are you laughing?" He took in quick and shallow breaths.

"Oh, please, do you need me to tell you how I became pregnant? You were there, remember? And you know I love having a family."

Silence filled the room. He struggled to find the perfect response to put her in her place. "Well, I blame this newest pregnancy on you."

"Okay genius, how do you figure it's my fault?"

His response had failed. "I blame this mess on you."

"Mess? Now you're calling our second child a mess?"

"Stop that; you know what I meant," he said. "You know I don't want another baby. Are you trying to ruin our marriage?"

She glared at him. "You think another baby will ruin us?"

"Yes, how are we going to support another baby if I lose my job?"

She never understands. What's wrong with her?

Colin returned to the kitchen. "Mom?"

"Yes?"

"Will Santa still come to our house?"

"Colin, you belong in bed," Aedan shouted.

"Leave him alone," she said. She turned to Colin. "Yes, Santa will stop at our house. But Christmas means more to us than gifts and Santa."

"I know Mom. But maybe Santa won't come to our house this year." Tears covered his face.

"Look at what you've done." She glowered at Aedan.

"Don't say that, you know I'm not trying to hurt him."

"What's your problem? We're having a second child; the news is an excellent Christmas gift." Her face softened as she focused her eyes on him to pierce his outer mental armor.

Since the day they had met, her eyes had a near hypnotic impact on him. Aedan loved her so much and could never say no to her when she focused her eyes on him. Her gaze weakened him. Refusing to release his anger, he shook his head in defiance, rejecting her effort to lessen his foul mood. "I'm angry because you're pregnant again, and I'm worried about my job. Your eyes won't work this time."

He walked away in a childish pout, stopping to look back at her. "Why do you want more children? One kid is enough." He strode to the back stairs and dragged his wounded thin frame to the second floor before she could respond.

After limping down the back stairwell, Aedan surveyed the kitchen. Colin sat on a counter stool, giggling as he pushed cereal pieces onto the floor; with each one dropped, he laughed with delight. Ciara continued working with the cookie dough.

He pulled a business card from his right pants pocket. A friend, an attorney, specializing in family law, had given him a batch of the cards after he moved to an office in Chicago's Loop. He returned the card to his pocket. As he walked to the front door, his mechanical movements revealed his anger as he attempted to understand why Ciara wanted more children. He frowned as he moved away from the kitchen.

She saw him creeping away. She walked to the hallway. "We have a three o'clock consult with the pediatrician."

He glared at her with anger. "You know I can't make that appointment today."

"We have to be careful this time. I want you there. Please, Aedan, be there."

He gazed at her. He sighed.

She doesn't get that I deserve a life of my own.

Aedan ran his right hand into his pants pocket and fidgeted with his friend's business card as he offered her an angry stare. He ignored her pleas. "The meeting is today." His eyes narrowed. "You remember the meeting?"

"How could I forget? You've reminded me fifty times," she said.

"Then, you know I can't make it to the consult," he said.

Her face reddened. "Your meeting is this morning. It's an afternoon consult." She forced a smile. "Please, I want us to meet at the appointment. It's important to me. I'm worried about the baby."

He sighed. "Whatever, you don't need me there."

"I want you there. I'm worried."

He sneered at her. He marveled at her ability to ignore his words as if they never reached her ears.

She crossed her arms over her chest. "Take your car to work. Don't take the train. I called Frank and told him to go alone. We have the last appointment before the doctor's office closes for Christmas."

"Do you listen to what I say?" He watched her as she returned to the large bowl with cookie dough mixture inside. She tossed eggshells into the trash with exaggerated intensity.

He frowned when he saw tears flowing down her cheeks. He could not stand hurting her. It broke his heart.

"Why can't you be the person you used to be? You were so much fun, and filled with joy," Ciara said. Her expression betrayed her sadness. "I used to ache to have you home with me. I want that person back."

His expression betrayed his surprise. "I'm still the same person." He yanked his hand from his pocket. He looked at Colin. "You know I love you both." His voice trembled. "How can you doubt my love for you?" He groaned. "I'm the same person. You know that I'm having trouble now."

Ciara looked at Colin. "Not, you're not the same. Not close. I want the real you back; the man I married."

His head sank in a sign of pain and guilt. "You know that I love you and Colin."

"Do you?"

"How could you ask that? How can you doubt how much I love you?" He looked into her eyes, pleading for her to understand, and hoping she would offer him patience. He found nothing in her stare.

She crossed her arms. "Whatever. You should leave. You'll miss your precious meeting. Don't forget the consult."

He looked away from her, his expression set in an angry scowl. He tried to grasp why she did not recognize that he had needs of his own.

And, why doesn't she understand that I love them both?

He refused to look at her as he walked to the rear. He slammed the door closed as he headed to their detached garage.

CHAPTER TWO

HAIL OF A TIME

They lived in Oak Valley, Illinois, a suburb forty miles northwest from Chicago. Aedan wanted to live in the Loop. Ciara insisted they raise their children in the suburbs. He enjoyed the city with its sports, excellent restaurants, and museums while she preferred a simpler life in suburbia.

Aedan entered the detached garage through a side door.

She took everything away from us. Now's she's pregnant again. How many kids does she want? And how can she doubt how much I love her? I'm in a rough spot now — that doesn't mean I don't care for them. What's wrong with her?

He flung the garage door open; it sped toward the overhead stops; the force caused it to bounce against the rubber blocks at the end of the tracks. He refused to release his foul mood as he entered his car, a black eighteen-year-old sedan with two hundred and fifty thousand miles on the odometer. The black outer body had such an extensive layer of rust, his neighbors refused to accept its original color. They had nicknamed the car, Crumbly, an accurate name to describe its horrible condition.

Ciara had begged him to buy a new car. He refused. He intended to drive the sedan until it reached three-hundred thousand miles or higher. Eking out the miles and saving money had become a mission.

Why should I buy a new car with number two on the way?

He shoved the manual transmission into reverse.

I'll let her close the garage door; serves her right.

As he moved toward the street, his friend and neighbor, Frank Ausio, approached, causing him to slam on the brakes.

"Hey bonehead, good luck taking Crumbly downtown."

"Get out of my way," Aedan shouted. "I've got to get to work."

"Hey, what crawled up your keister?"

"Shut up." He sent the car backward in a rush.

Frank leaped away to avoid having his right foot run over. "Hey, what's your problem?"

He shoved the transmission into first gear.

Can't the idiot tell I'm not in the mood for small talk?

Aedan sped away.

In a swift, angry move, he cut in front of several cars as he entered the ramp leading to the interstate. As he moved through traffic, large hailstones thick with slushy water began plummeting onto his windshield, blocking his view.

Oh, man, not now, and not today.

He dropped his speed, expecting the caution drivers ahead would take. Soon, a raging downpour shrouded the hail as side winds of over sixty miles an hour buffeted his car. Lightning and thunder crackled around him. The morning light disappeared under the sudden storm's onslaught.

Excellent, a thunderstorm and hail in Chicago, in December. What else will get in my way?

He slammed the dashboard with his right hand. He slowed further.

The storm became a squall, and in an instant, the roadway filled with large hail balls. Several cars had pulled over to the shoulder. Aedan dropped the car's speed further, to fifteen miles per hour.

Great — why is this happening today? I have an important meeting. Give me a break, I must be there on time. The weather report predicted a sunny and mild day.

He pounded the steering wheel.

I should've taken the train. Ciara doesn't need me to attend that stupid consult.

He inched through the hail-filled slush while moving in the right lane. His frustration swelled with each passing second, the minutes crawled. The wind increased again; his car shook from side-to-side. He slowed to a near stop as a massive trailer truck slid along the road close to his left side.

The truck, moving in an uncontrollable slide across the icy mixture covering the road, glided toward the guardrail. The trailer swung toward Aedan's car; it contacted the left front of the aging sedan. He entered a fast spin; the car's tires had nothing to grip while sliding across the ice.

The vehicle came upon an ice-free spot, which stopped the car from spinning, causing him to lurch forward — his head bounced off the rearview mirror. Blood rushed from underneath the bandage covering his kitchen wound, making his eyes sting with pain, and it blurred his vision.

This is getting ridiculous.

His face filled with concern as he aimed the car toward the shoulder. Seconds later, the sedan slid against the guardrail. The truck bounced off the railing two-hundred feet in front of him.

He took deep breaths. Blood continued to flow from his re-injured head wound, dripping off his chin and onto his white dress shirt. Aedan jerked the glove box door open and extracted a box of tissues, grabbed a handful, and pressed them against his forehead. After cleaning the wound, he moved fast to cover the gash with a bandage from an emergency kit. He placed a second bandage over the first. The bleeding stopped; his face remained a mess. He tried to remove the blood — he failed.

I'll clean-up in the bathroom when I get to the office.

He looked at the blood trail on his shirt.

That looks bad, but my suit coat will cover the blood long enough to get through the meeting.

The storm came to an abrupt halt. In seconds, the clouds had cleared. Aedan squinted his eyes against the sunlight blasting through the windshield; the sun's warmth radiated through the glass. Searching the sky, he could not see a cloud in sight. In seconds, the slush and hail mixture began melting under the heat of the solar rays pounding the roadway.

What the — I've seen nothing like this.

Aedan put the car in gear and with caution pulled back onto the interstate. The gleaming downtown Chicago towers came into view as he approached his exit into the loop. He wondered how he had proceeded so far on the road.

It seemed minutes ago I was close to O'Hare Airport — it's so weird.

The bandage covering his head wounds had become blood red, unable to stop the flow; a slight trickle ran down his face. He did his best to wipe it away as he continued to his exit.

He took Ohio Street.

I mustn't miss the meeting. The vultures are out to get me.

His palms oozed with sweat as he entered the Loop. He drove through the crowded downtown streets.

Why does she want more kids?

He tapped the steering to the beat of a song on the radio.

She knows I love her and Colin. Why isn't that enough?

He grimaced when blood escaped the bandages.

Our problems have nothing to do with money. It all started when Ciara pushed hard to start a family. Children are expensive, and I hate spending money. She's won all battles in our marriage. Now another kid is on the way. For most people, one child is plenty. I don't want more children.

An image of the pink note filled his mind, causing him to feel sad at the realization that he had left the house in the middle of a fight.

I wish I would have been kinder to them. But when will the baby-making stop? When do I get to have a life?

He tapped the steering wheel with greater force.

Before they had married, he had promised to have children with Ciara. For years, he had said no; he realized his reluctance did not sit well with her, and he felt terrible about that. At thirty-eight years old, he had a hard time dealing with his own troubles. Aedan knew additional children would make his struggles more difficult. He often felt as if life would swallow him whole, and his dreams of living in the city seemed more distant with each new day.

He wiped the blood from his forehead while moving around a truck.

She never considers my feelings. I don't want more children.

He pulled into the parking garage several blocks from his work building. From behind, a blaring car horn drew his attention. He pulled into a parking space, clearing the narrow road for the car behind him. He left the sedan.

His clenched jaw revealed his anger as he left the garage.

We already know the drill. We have sex. Ciara gets pregnant. We wait until she is ready to have our baby, and we get to the hospital. Then, we start another cycle, and who knows how many more cycles before our family is large enough for her. She doesn't need me at that stupid consult.

Several people looked at him. He offered them angry stares; most turned away from his blood-filled countenance. Ciara's pregnancy had caused him to cease treating others well.

Aedan came to a mid-block newsstand, a rare sight in a digital age. While sneering at the people, he pushed through heavy foot traffic.

Aedan's usual routine would include a stop at the newsstand to speak with the owner, Charlie, seventy years old and a lifetime Chicagoan. Thick age lines covered the older man's face exposing the five decades he had spent serving customers and selling his wares. He was a stout and humble man. He offered an intriguing personality to a town once named the *City of the Big Shoulders*, as Carl Sandburg, famed winner of the Pulitzer Prize, wrote in his poem, *Chicago*. Many Chicagoans enjoyed that reputation.

That day, as Aedan approached the newsstand, he watched Charlie serving the people milling around his business. Sidewalk merchants could write encyclopedias about the many people they encountered over the decades. Newsstands, years in the past, were a familiar sight in cities across the nation. Chicago contained several hundred newsstands during the pinnacle of printed multi-edition newspapers. Yet, those numbers dropped to well under one hundred.

He pondered the many times he watched complete strangers stop to chat with his old friend. Those people felt comfortable spewing forth with their problems and personal issues. Charlie would smile and listen, a sidewalk counselor to the masses, and he often received no sale for his efforts, with many people taking time to chat with him.

He never heard his friend complain. Charlie had a smile and a kind word for everyone he met, including people who walked by his stand without stopping. His open and warm personality attracted people to his business daily. That is how Aedan and Charlie had become close friends; a chance *hello* from the newsstand owner began a years-long friendship.

He ignored the stand. He did not say a word to his friend.

"How are you this morning, Mr. O'Beirne?" Charlie called to him. He smiled as he took money from a customer.

Aedan ignored him.

"What happened? You're a wreck. Do you want me to call for help?"

"Don't bother me today, Charlie." He continued walking.

"Stop, Mr. O'Beirne, you're bleeding, and the wounds look severe. If you hit your head, you might have a concussion. I am offering help." He took money from another customer.

"Mind your own business. I told you not today."

"Ciara's pregnant again, huh?" Charlie called.

Aedan stopped, glared at him. "Why did you say that?"

"You had the same pained and sour look after your wife's last pregnancy, which blessed you with Colin." He laughed. It was a kind and warm chuckle. He seemed incapable of unkindness. "You become unhinged when your family grows."

"Family grows?"

"Yes, your wife is having another baby. Your family is growing."

He grunted. "Whatever, I can't talk with you today. I have to get to work for a critical meeting; it's important to my growing family."

Charlie smiled. "I understand. No newspaper today?"

"Stop talking to me, and you can shove the paper." He walked and then jogged, away from the newsstand and toward his office.

"I thought we're friends?" Charlie chuckled.

"We are friends, but everyone needs to get out of my way today. I have zero patience, and I'm in a hurry to get to a meeting. It's critical for my future at the firm. So, leave me alone."

"Mr. O'Beirne," shouted Charlie. "Congratulations."

"Shut up, Charlie, just shut up." He did not look back.

Aedan stopped walking after hearing a horrific crash emanating from behind. He looked at his friend's business. A large delivery van had backed into traffic, causing a sedan to swerve to avoid a collision. The red car crashed into the left side of the newsstand; pieces of metal and wood, along with magazines and various products covered the ground.

Man, it looks like the stand exploded. I hope Charlie's okay.

He watched Charlie open the door to help the driver.

What a chump. His stand sits ruined, and he worries about the person who did the wrecking.

Seeing his friend remained unhurt, Aedan continued to his job, not giving Charlie, or his business, any further thought.

His attitude improved; time was short, but it seemed a certainty he would not miss the meeting. His pace quickened. He paid no attention to the sirens reverberating in the manmade canyon of concrete, steel, and glass walls as Chicago police squad cars and an ambulance approached the accident site. The Loop brimmed full of the sounds of many emergency vehicles, yet nothing entered his consciousness.

He turned left and walked to a forty-nine-story building at the corner of Wabash and Adams. He worked as an accountant for Metric & Inch, an engineering firm. After finishing college with an impressive academic record, he received their offer of a lucrative starting salary. Later, the company paid for his MBA at a prestigious downtown Chicago business school. The practice occupied the thirty-ninth floor. Every workday he entered on the Adams Street side, a creature of habit.

He stopped before entering the building, attempting to calm his thoughts and to energize himself for the meeting. A blood trickle continued flowing down his forehead. He walked to a large window and grimaced after seeing his reflection.

I'm already sick of this day. I'm a mess.

He tried to clean his face with the sleeve of his coat. It did not work. He sighed as he pushed through the revolving door.

I'll make it — and that's good because Williamson will try to take me out.

While deep inside his own concerns, he no longer heard the loud wailing sirens outside. He did not notice the ambulance moving toward Michigan Avenue. He did not know his friend, Charlie, laid unconscious on a gurney in the ambulance as the paramedics rushed him to a nearby hospital.

CHAPTER THREE

SLAMS AND OUTAGES

Aedan walked toward the elevators; his computer bag in his left hand. He saw a mature man, Harold, sitting behind a lobby desk. He was the head of building security; Aedan had known him since joining Metric & Inch. He respected Harold for his low-key profile, the man never acted or dressed as though he held a vital security position. With olive skin and a hearty weight of two-hundred and twenty pounds, Aedan thought of him as a tough human fireplug. His seasoned, though not old face revealed he was not a person to challenge — his many years spent in the United States Marine Corps heightened his awareness that security problems come in many shapes and sizes. Aedan considered him a friend.

"Good morning, Mr. O'Beirne."

He frowned. "Whatever, Harold, leave me alone today."

Harold laughed. "Your wife's pregnant again, huh?"

"How'd you know that?"

"You only get that look when your wife's pregnant." Harold became serious. "One day, you'll know how lucky you are."

"Whatever, Harold, what do you know?"

"I know that you look a mess. What happened to you?"

"That's a long story," Aedan said.

Harold stared at him. "Well, go to the bathroom, clean and inspect your wounds. You might require stitches."

"I have an important meeting. I won't stop to get stitches."

From under the counter, Harold pulled out an emergency kit. "Here, take this and try to stop the bleeding, after you clean the wound. You should go to the hospital and have those cuts examined by professionals."

"I told you, I don't have time for that."

"You don't have a difficult choice, Mr. O'Beirne. You can choose either your health or a meeting. Which one is more important?" He frowned and walked away while shaking his head.

"Whatever, what do you know?" Aedan shouted. People around him looked his way. "Oh, mind your own business."

Aedan walked to the men's restroom, pushed through the door, and walked to the long counter and mirror. After grasping paper towels, he cleaned his head wounds with soap and water, groaning under the pain emanating from the deep gashes. He pressed the paper against his forehead, hoping to stem the bleeding.

He placed the fresh bandage over the injury, combed his wavy dark hair and buttoned his suit jacket to hide the blood on his shirt. In the full-length mirror, he examined his six-foot-tall image. "That's better. I have to get to the board meeting."

Aedan walked to the security desk to thank Harold, but the security chief was across the lobby, helping a person with a floor kiosk. He shrugged his shoulders.

He walked to the elevators. The left door opened, and an imposing woman, with olive skin and silver hair, traditional pulled-together beauty, walked from the unit. As she walked toward the desk, she slipped on a coffee spill and slammed into Aedan. She grasped his left arm, which knocked his laptop bag from his hand.

A painful electric jolt raced through his left arm. He froze in horror, as his laptop sprang free from the bag's unzipped top pouch. The computer slid, with high speed, across the waxed floor. Seconds later, the device slammed into a post. The laptop casing split, several plastic pieces flew away from the unit. The PC spun to a stop close to a pillar. Pain and shock consumed him. "No, not now, not today, my account information is on my computer," he shouted. He glared at the woman. "What's wrong with you?"

"I *am* so sorry. I will replace your computer." She smiled.

"That will not do any good, I've lost my work." He sulked.

"I am sorry." She smiled.

"What good does an apology do now?" He scowled at her. Aedan knew that he had seen her smile before but couldn't recall where.

"Aedan, I apologized, and I offered to replace your computer. What else do you expect from me?" She smiled.

He frowned as he pondered her smile. It seemed robotic and had the same appearance each time she flashed it at him.

He glared at her. "How do you know my name? This has already been an exhausting day for me. I hate your smile and your attitude. Tell me how I'll provide the firm's partners what they require at the meeting," he sniped at her.

Aedan retrieved his laptop and attempted to turn its power on, nothing. He stared at her. "Nice job, lady, you've helped ruin my day, and you might well have contributed to me being fired."

"You're already too late for the meeting. Why are you so upset about a gathering you cannot attend? There are more important issues in your life than board rooms." She smiled.

"Stop smiling at me," he shouted. His voice was cruel. "And how do you know about my meeting?" His anger rose, uncommon for him in his professional life. On most days, he projected the calmest, and most levelheaded, demeanor in every room; however, the news of baby number two had thrown him into an emotional tailspin. He felt as if his life was spiraling away from him, and his dreams of returning to the city became less possible with each child born. He could not understand why no one seemed to grasp that his life belonged to him and not to a baby-making machine in the suburbs.

Harold approached. "Mr. O'Beirne, calm yourself. She did not run into you on purpose. You are treating her with cruel unkindness."

He looked at Harold with frustration. "Harold, you're my friend, I don't want you taking her side."

"Calm yourself, or I will have you removed from the building."

Aedan's eyes tightened as he glared at the security chief. "You'll treat me like a stranger off the street? We've known each other for years; I've never given you grief or problems of any sort."

"I'm sorry, Mr. O'Beirne, but I will not tolerate your irresponsible behavior."

He did his best to cram the smashed computer into the bag. The broken parts overflowed, and plastic sections fell to the floor. He snatched them up while complaining through his low-level groans. He took deliberate, dramatic, and slow movements forcing the pieces into the laptop bag to heap guilt about the woman.

"I am sorry, Mr. O'Beirne. There is nothing I can say or do."

Aedan sighed. "Not unless you can fix my computer."

"My sincere apology is all I offer, unless, you will accept my offer to pay for the damaged equipment." She smiled.

He glared at her.

There are fools everywhere I go.

He sighed as he walked to the elevators without saying a word. He pressed the elevator call button, and the left unit opened; the same one the woman had exited moments earlier. He walked into the elevator alone. In an instant, a stinging sense of claustrophobia bore down on him as he pressed the button for the thirty-ninth floor.

As the door closed, he saw the woman standing at the security desk. She was smiling.

A shiver of anxiety ran through his body. His vision blurred when sweat mixed with blood poured into his eyes. He ignored his injuries, hoping he could make it to the meeting before it ended.

Panic rose within him as a profound sense of claustrophobia consumed his mind. His attack came to a halt when the elevator stopped at the fifteenth floor, where a much older man entered.

The man appeared concerned. "Are you okay, son?"

"You should mind your own business."

"I apologize, son. You look sick." The older man smiled.

He ignored the man, and in an angry, swift move, he spun away. Worry and claustrophobia consumed him.

I'm sure they attacked me at the meeting. After all these years, I shouldn't have to fight for my job.

The older man wore a dark gray three-piece suit. He carried a hat in his right hand, a timeworn black fedora, which men had stopped using after the nineteen-fifties and sixties. The man stood six-feet-three-inches tall, and despite many wrinkles, he had a powerful face, like someone who had spent many hours at sea or in the field working. He had a full head of short silvery hair.

Aedan sensed he knew him. The older man exuded a mature and calm presence, which relaxed Aedan.

The elevator moved upward about three feet, the lights flickered, and the unit came to an abrupt stop.

Now, what's happening?

He pushed the button for the thirty-ninth floor, over-and-over. Panic and claustrophobia gripped his mind.

"Afraid of confined spaces, are you?" The older man said.

"Yes, how did you know?"

"The sweat on your face is a real giveaway." He pulled a handkerchief from his pocket and offered it to Aedan.

He took the white cloth. "Thank you."

"Glad to help. I used to have a problem with claustrophobia, so I understand your situation. Trust me, son, I used to take the stairs in all buildings over one story tall."

A quizzical look came over Aedan. He could not remember the last time anyone referred to him as, *son*. He glared at him. "You don't seem the least bit bothered, despite the elevator not moving, which surprises me."

"You are correct; I am not troubled. I had my fear and anxiety about enclosed spaces driven out of me years ago. Perhaps my story will help you." He smiled.

Aedan glared at him. "How did you get rid of your fears?" His voice shuddered as he stared at the closed doors; the elevator remained stuck on the fifteenth floor. He tried to understand how it was all happening to him, on that day, during one of the most momentous events in his career.

Aedan found the emergency button, pressed it again-and-again. Nothing happened. He looked at the older man. His expression filled with desperation. "How? How did the fear and anxiety leave you?"

"It happened after I married the love of my life, Amelia, at twenty-five years old," the old man said. "And son, she could turn the heads of many men, quite a looker, stunning beyond description, with a pair of gorgeous gams. My heart broke to leave her pregnant in Chicago when I traveled to California. I had to go; a close friend set me up with a well-paying job in Sacramento. In those days, Sacramento held fewer than one-hundred-thousand citizens. Moving there appealed to my youthful sense of adventure. I never made the job interview, and Amelia and I never moved to California; instead, about five years later, I opened a firm here in Chicago."

"Why didn't you attend the interview?" He sensed the man had something important to say; the story piqued his interest. "If you have anything to say that will help reduce my sense of claustrophobia, I'll listen."

The older man glared at him as if to say not to interrupt again. "I recall the trip and the accident well. I made my way to California aboard the Pacific Railroad in June. That was before automobiles dominated national transportation and well before Interstate Highways."

"You can't be that old. Right?"

"Please, son, do not interrupt." The older man smiled. "On that day in June, while moving through the mountains, there were no reported problems or delays on the tracks all the way to California. But without warning an unpredicted hail, snow, and slush storm blanketed the region. I recall sitting alone in the rear passenger car with early morning daylight breaking through the windows. The other passengers rested in their bunks.

"The storm caused a landslide, which triggered a derailment of the train. My passenger car broke free; it slid down an incline and slammed into a series of large boulders, causing it to roll over. The impact sent rocks soaring into the air, the falling material crushed my passenger car, pinning me under two seats and surrounding me with fallen rubble." His face revealed that his memories of the accident were fresh and alive.

"How did you survive?"

The older man glared, making Aedan understand he did not abide interruptions. "Imagine how I felt, with a severe case of claustrophobia bearing down on me as I remained there for longer than two days wedged between the two collapsed seats and the fallen rubble. I did not eat or drink in the tightest of spaces, and I had little hope that they would ever find me alive. It was not a source of pleasure to rest in a puddle of my urine. I lost consciousness several times from fear racing through my body.

"Sixty-six-hours after the crash, a Pacific Railroad crew extracted me after trying for longer than two days to find a safe path through the debris and rubble. No one else on the train required extraction, the others walked away from the wreckage minutes after the accident. No one suffered serious harm.

"After the doctors helped me, I learned the passenger car had stopped five feet from a two-thousand-foot vertical plunge. The boulders saved my life; a scant five feet separated me from certain death. Had those boulders not been there, I would have fallen over the edge while inside the passenger car. After that, I trusted in the good Lord to help me. I stopped letting fear control me. When circumstances push you all the way to the brink, and when you remain trapped at the edge for sixty-six hours, everything changes. Those hours changed my life forever."

"That's an incredible story. The freaky hail, snow, and slush storm." Aedan took deep, relaxing breaths.

Just then, the elevator trembled and began rising to the thirty-ninth floor — the *Metric & Inch* office location. Aedan tried to calm his mind. He recalled the firm had moved into the building and leased the entire floor twenty years ago. Metric & Inch experienced several lean years, which required relocation for financial reasons. The firm moved from its original building in the Chicago financial district on South LaSalle Street. At first, Aedan disliked the move, but over the years, the location began to take feel like home to him.

Aedan continued staring at the floor status display. The unit stopped at floor thirty-nine. The doors did not open.

He waited.

Aedan pressed the open button.

He waited.

"Open, open now," he shouted.

Nothing happened. Aedan pressed the button again. He pounded on the panel and pressed the button again. Panic began to rise in him.

He waited.

Why won't it open?

He pressed the button for the fortieth floor hoping the unit would move. Nothing happened.

"Are you kidding me? Why is this happening to me?" he shouted as he slammed the panel with his right hand.

"Aedan try to remain calm. Did my story mean nothing to you?" The old man frowned.

"How do you know my name? I never told you my name."

"I know," the old man said.

He glared at him while raising his eyebrows. "Well, since we are now such fantastic friends, what's your name?"

"My name is Michael."

"Well, Mike," Aedan began.

He interrupted him. "No. My name is Michael."

"Michael, your story is incredible; however, your experience does me little good considering I will face a mess with the firm in a few minutes. Unless this elevator refuses to open, and, in that case, I will lose my job." He sighed.

"There is nothing you can do at this moment. I counsel calmness in the face of your troubling predicament."

"What the...," Aedan said. He looked perplexed. "Your choice of words reminds me of actors in movies from the forties." He turned to the panel. He pressed the open button, again, and again. Sweat combined with the blood from his head wound caused a bloody mixture to trickle down his cheek.

I wish I could get this bleeding to stop.

He wiped away the mixture using Michael's handkerchief.

He waited.

The doors did not open. Aedan pulled out his cell phone; its battery had drained. He kicked the doors hoping the jarring motion would cause them to crack open. It did not work. "Open — open now," he said, his voice level rose.

Seconds later, the power in the elevator turned off. Aedan found himself cast into darkness. "No, not the lights, please, not the lights."

He laughed — not a joyful sound. The elevator dropped two inches. The unit allowed no light to enter. His breathing quickened. "Well, come on Michael — do some good and get us out of this box?" Aedan said. He received no response.

Aedan pounded on the elevator doors hoping someone at the Metric & Inch reception desk might hear the noise. He realized that he had no chance of someone hearing the racket because the reception area lay behind glass entrance doors.

Aedan pounded over-and-over to create a noticeable noise. He kicked the lower portions of the doors. He realized the elevator sealed him off from the outside world; his anxiety rose.

I'm stuck in this stupid box while the meeting is going on.

He continued pounding the door. His hands ached from the repeated pummeling. He slowed his efforts — soon, he stopped. He waited for the doors to open.

Time crawled. Nothing changed, and no one heard the pounding. Aedan continued hammering the door, but his hands throbbed from the beating. He shifted back-and-forth in-place.

He waited.

His cell phone battery had died. He could not call for help.

He could not detect Michael's presence.

His fear had reached a fevered pitch; Aedan could not force himself to move around the elevator to locate Michael. The reality of the situation was unavoidable. He was standing in a pitch-dark elevator hanging on steel cables, suspended thirty-nine floors above the ground, with no way out. He knew the safety systems would prevent a drop by clamping on to the railings if every cable snapped. That knowledge didn't bring peace. With each passing moment, his fear of heights and enclosed spaces increased — bearing down on him with brute force.

I wonder what Ciara and Colin are doing. Maybe they're still making cookies. If I don't make the consult, it'll be a horrible Christmas in our home. I'll charge my cell and call them. I'll surprise her with the morning I've had.

He continued to strike the doors — they didn't open; the lonesome and frightening darkness continued. Aedan trembled. He sensed the walls were moving, closing in on him, trying to entomb him inside the dark box. He shuddered as he worked to break free from his fear. "Michael, what should I do? You've been in a situation like this before, in the mountains, in that train accident. Help us get out of this mess," he shouted.

No response came from Michael.

"Michael...where...where are you? Help us get out of here," he shouted as he shuddered.

Power returned to the elevator. The lights came back on — Aedan jumped with surprise. As the doors opened, he walked from the unit while shielding his eyes from the bright light emanating from the hallway.

He turned back to the elevator and placed his right hand on the doors to hold them open for Michael. "Okay, old man, get off here and take a different elevator." No reply came. He looked at the empty hallway. No sign of him existed anywhere. "Where did he go?"

CHAPTER FOUR

METRIC & INCH

Aedan walked toward the Metric & Inch office space. Large framed photographs and paintings lined the entrance hallway, a memorial created to honor the many men and women who had managed the practice since its establishment in 1910. The images ran the gamut from the early days, through the modern era, covering the firm's major highlights, including pictures of the three managing partners since its inception.

He stopped at the hallway's midway point, where he looked with surprise at a floor to ceiling painting of the firm's founder. The aging man in the image stood at the railing, on the starboard side, of a large sailboat, his face shined with power and happiness; he wore a black fedora. In the background, the forty-story Trenton Tower stood along Michigan Avenue, dwarfing all other structures, which marked the timeframe as after 1955, the tower's completion year. He knew those paintings well.

The artwork troubled him. He examined the image closer. His gaze fell upon the man on the sailboat.

That's Michael from the elevator. I knew I recognized him. But, it can't be the same person, he died a long time ago. This makes no sense. There must be a reasonable explanation.

He read the information plaque below the painting:

MICHAEL WILLIAMSON
FOUNDING PARTNER – AD 1910
BORN AD DECEMBER 22, 1880
PASSED INTO THE LORD'S HANDS:
AD DECEMBER 22, 1965

He looked at the elevator bank — he felt confused about his experiences with Michael. Aedan struggled to make rational sense of the situation when an object on the floor, about a foot to the left of the elevator, caught his eye. He walked to the article, and with disbelief, he pulled the black fedora from the floor. The hat appeared identical to the one the founder wore on the sailboat and the same as the one Michael carried on to the elevator.

He twirled the hat in his right hand as he contemplated his journey from the lobby to the thirty-ninth floor.

What's going on today? Two strange people coming into my life, the weird storm on the highway, and that fool Michael, he's the most bizarre of all. Who is he and where'd he come from, and where did he go when the power went out?

He returned the fedora to the original location on the floor. He shook his head in confusion and returned to the painting.

That man sure looks like Michael from the elevator.

A large framed photograph hung to the right of the painting. The image showed Michael Williamson in his office, smiling and much younger; he was in the company's old location on South LaSalle Street. In the picture's background was a framed image of towering snow-capped mountains, a Pacific Railroad locomotive stood on railroad tracks. Bold type above the engine read:

66 HOURS – THE IMPOSSIBLE HAPPENS

He could not remember seeing that picture during his many walks along the hallway. He shrugged his shoulders as he turned to the firm's glass entrance doors. As he pushed through the doors, a large group of people walked to him. They began clapping as they surrounded him. His mind filled with confusion as they offered him congratulations for having escaped the elevator. Aedan forced himself to hold back from lashing out at them. He could not understand why they would not get out of his way; he wanted to learn about what happened in the meeting.

A man with bright white hair, James Williamson, walked to Aedan and grabbed him by the shoulders. "Welcome back to the world. You've had a rough morning." He looked at his wounded face. "What happened to you? Are you okay? Did that happen in the elevator? That couldn't have been a pleasant experience."

"No, Sir, I received the wounds earlier today. I'm all right. I assume the meeting's over." He forced a nervous smile.

"Meeting? Oh, yes, the meeting is over. Don't worry about that, your face looks as if you fell into a blender. What happened?"

"But I *am* worried about the meeting. Did you fire me?" He glared at James.

"Why would I fire you? Where did you get that idea?"

"There's been talk going around that I might lose my job."

James looked, with scorn, at the surrounding people listening to the conversation. He looked at him. "You should have trusted me. I had your back in the meeting. Don't forget, I brought you into the firm, and you're an excellent asset. I assume in your rush to get to the meeting, something happened that explains the blood all over your face?"

"Yes, I hit my head in my kitchen this morning and rammed the same spot on my car's rearview mirror while on the interstate. It's a long story." His demeanor softened, relieved he would not lose his job. "Thank you for supporting me in the meeting; after the elevator had stopped working, I had no chance of making it."

James grinned. "We asked Harold, from the lobby, to check the board for errors. He discovered a power loss had struck the elevator shaft between the fifteenth and thirty-ninth floors. He dispatched the maintenance crew right away. We weren't certain when you'd make it to this floor, or we would have met you at the elevators." He ran a hand through his white hair. "Later, after speaking further with Harold, we learned a woman exiting the elevator had attended our meeting, her name is Máire O'Cianain. She told us your wife is pregnant. I assumed you knew her from your work here."

"I've never heard her name in my life."

"Strange. How does Máire know about Ciara's pregnancy?"

"That's an excellent question. How *does* Máire know about Ciara, and who is she?" Aedan said.

"We will discuss this further in my office." James looked at the people milling around.

"You know, that woman — "

James interjected. "Her name is Máire."

He frowned. "Máire slammed into me in the lobby; she knocked my laptop bag out of my hand. The computer slid on the floor and smashed into a concrete post." He lifted his computer bag, the laptop and its many broken parts poked through the top zipper opening. "There isn't much left. My presentation files were on the hard drive."

"The tech guys will retrieve the information."

"That's a clever idea. I'll contact IT later." Aedan sighed with relief. "Sir, I apologize for missing the meeting. I fought hard to get here on time, but that freaky storm and the elevator incident halted my progress."

"Storm? What storm?"

"The storm didn't reach the Loop?" Aedan said with doubt.

"No, the sky has been clear all morning."

"I drove through a horrible ice storm on the interstate. I got through the mess, but not with ease."

James looked doubtful. "It must have been a local event."

"I don't know how it could've been a local event. The powerful crosswinds moved cars. Ice covered the road's surface, vehicles pulled off the road for safety, and the storm covered miles."

"I have no explanation. What matters is that you arrived in the Loop unscathed. We must get together to talk." He grinned.

Aedan shivered as he thought about the events leading up to that moment. "Well, Sir, I apologize again."

"Enough with the apologies; get cleaned up, grab a cup of coffee and then come to my office. I will fill you in on what happened in the meeting. The board room filled with tension today." James grinned and smacked him on the back. "You mean more to us than one meeting."

"Thank you, Sir. I'll see you inside your office in ten minutes." He walked away knowing that he would not lose his job. Aedan had expected a battle at the meeting, and he could not grasp what happened. He recalled his early morning encounter with Ciara.

She was right; she insisted they would not want to lose me.

He walked toward his office in the accounting department. He considered the many personal chapters already completed that morning. Shaking his head, he walked into the men's restroom to clean-up.

CHAPTER FIVE

EXPECTING PARTNERSHIP

Aedan stared in the mirror as he scrubbed his wounds with cloth towels and soap. He winced when he reached the deeper cuts on his forehead.

I can't believe the morning I've had.

He dried the wounds and covered them with fresh bandages. He pondered his boss, James Williamson, the grandson of the firm's founder, Michael Williamson, and the Managing Partner. At six feet tall, one hundred and ninety pounds, and with bright silvery hair, Aedan thought of him as an intimidating figure, imposing and cold.

I was sure he would fire me today.

He recalled, after Michael's death, his oldest son, Gabriel, inherited the role of managing partner. Gabriel, who died at age seventy-five, left the position to his son, James, at age thirty-five. Aedan had heard the stories of his ascension to the top of the firm; many people in the office joked the stress of the position caused James' hair to go white as a sign of internal protest.

Aedan checked his wounds and saw the bandages had stopped the bleeding. He combed his hair and straightened his shirt. He left the restroom and headed to James' office — the largest in the firm, at the northeast corner. The location offered stunning sights of Lake Michigan while also allowing for views of classic downtown structures. He walked into the office. "Sir, is this an appropriate time to meet?"

"Come in and close the door." James grinned.

Aedan walked to a chair close to the desk.

"No, not there, join me at the windows."

He crept to the windows. "Sir," Aedan began.

His boss interjected. "Stop calling me Sir. Call me, James."

"I have a fear of heights, James, and of enclosed spaces. Standing close to windows at this height creates real anxiety for me. I'd rather stand farther back if you don't mind." He grimaced as he stepped back in fear.

James looked confused. "But your office is at the same height."

He forced a smile as he took an additional step backward. "Yes, that's true. I positioned my desk well away from the windows and force myself to ignore the outside views."

"I never knew that about you. How do you fly on business trips?"

Aedan cleared his throat. "Well, Sir, I mean James, I seldom take business trips, and when I do, I book only aisles seats."

James shrugged his shoulders. He grinned. "Very well, stand or sit wherever you're the most comfortable."

"Thank you. What happened at the meeting?"

"Yes, the key elements."

"I'm relieved that I'll keep my job," Aedan said.

"You mentioned that already. Several people wanted you out."

Aedan took a deep breath. He sighed. "I suspected as much. Who was after me, and what did I do to them?"

James grinned as he looked at Lake Michigan. "You know, I pulled my boat from the harbor about six weeks ago. I miss taking her out. I named her Jenny after my wife. She blasted me with a ton of grief after I bought the craft. I told her I loved her so much that I wanted a reminder of her while I played on the lake. Jen didn't buy the contrived line, but she laughed for a long time at my attempts to convince her, but she knows that in the water, I'm a child at heart." He laughed hard as he turned away from the window and looked at Aedan. "But, speaking about being a child, oh man, you're such a naïve one. I've often said, the corporate world is not for the weak of heart and mind."

"Are you saying I'm weak?"

"Yes — you're brilliant, and as Director of Accounting, you perform all your required tasks well, but I never see much else from you. It seems you live in your own world most of the time."

"You sound as if you're not satisfied with me," Aedan said.

"Yes, I am, you're an excellent asset. However, you could rise to partner. You have an incredible talent, but you never extend yourself." He sat at the desk.

"Sir, my wife is pregnant again. I'd find no time or desire to maintain a partner's role. Sorry, Sir," he said, with resignation.

"Congratulations on the new baby. However, you've never strived for anything higher than your current level."

"Sir, I am a director."

"I told you to call me James." He glared at him.

"James, I'm trying to catch up; please have patience with me."

"You're in an important job; however, becoming a partner is within your reach." His voice had taken on a scolding tone. "You're capable of much more."

"Sir, you brought me into the firm, and I don't want to let you down. But I have no desire to be a partner. I have family responsibilities, number two is on the way, and I enjoy my work. My position as D-O-A fits my life and my personality, as long as you're satisfied with my performance."

James ran a hand through his white hair. He sighed. "I abhor witnessing wasted talent. I see much more capability in you. Perhaps I have misjudged your skills all these years."

"I apologize for disappointing you."

"Stop apologizing." His sharp tone revealed his disgust. "You have no confidence; this constant apologizing sickens me. I want confident people on my leadership team."

"Stop saying things like that. I'm a committed leader. I'm the Director of Accounting. Why is that not enough for you?" His jaw set in a tight clench as he glared at James.

"Why did you join this firm if you did not want to grow and advance?"

"I'm the only Director of Accounting." Aedan's breathing quickened.

"I'm an excellent judge of talent — that is why I hired you, I saw you as a future partner during the first interview you had with the firm. You're wasting your extraordinary talent."

"Sir stop this." He glared at James. "I'm the Director of Accounting."

"And that position is beneath your capabilities."

"Sir," Aedan began.

He interrupted with anger. "Call me, James."

"James, there's one Director of Accounting in this firm, me."

"Yes, but you're capable of so much more."

Aedan had grown weary of the attacks. He faced the older man with a fixed stare. "Mr. Williamson, may I be honest?"

"Yes, speak without restraint."

His eyes narrowed as he considered his thoughts. "Sir, I don't appreciate you pressuring me to take on a position that doesn't fit my life."

"Tread with caution, Aedan," James said.

"You provided me permission to speak with freedom."

James stared at Aedan. "Yes, with caution."

Aedan frowned as he interrupted. "No, Sir, you provided me permission to speak with freedom." He glared at James. "The workings and needs of this firm consume your life as managing partner, and through your arduous work, you provide lasting value to our clients. You are carrying forward the mantle of your family name well from my perspective. But, I'm not a mini-you, and I don't care if you believe I'd make a good partner. As an accountant, I'm smart with my money, and you have provided a generous salary for my work, which means I have no financial drive to be a partner. I don't want your life."

"I warn you, again, tread with caution." James frowned.

Aedan glowered. "You berate me because I don't hold a more ambitious personality after complimenting the work I do as D-O-A. I have grown tired of you complaining about my lack of drive. Becoming a partner is not for me. If that is not acceptable to you, I will offer my resignation this moment."

James pulled his hands into a tight clench. "I will not abide by the rebukes from my employees."

"Sir, and yes, I refer to you as, *Sir* because your position deserves respect; you hold authority over me in my role as D-O-A." He sighed and took calming breaths. "I am attempting to have an honest conversation with you, which entails me being forthright about my lack of desire for a firm partnership. You're a brilliant man; however, leading this practice is not for me. I work hard for Metric & Inch so my family and I will have a life away from work. This firm is your life. We are opposites, and I do not enjoy you slamming me after I have worked so hard for this company. Again, if you desire, I will resign now."

James looked at him with an appreciative glare, he laughed. "I am most impressed with you at this moment because you did not retreat or fold after I pressed." He grinned with warmth. "I respect your wishes, and I will remove you from consideration for future partnerships. I will not accept your resignation; you're an asset to this practice."

"Thank you, Sir."

"The meeting today — you owe a debt to Máire O'Cianain."

"Why is that?"

"You burned people in the Design Department; they are the ones out to get you. I cannot discuss individuals because we are taking legal steps to resolve the situation."

"That makes no sense. What did I do to those in the DD?"

"You prevented the D-D from stealing from the firm. They wanted to start new bridge modeling projects that they would have used as a foundation to pull away from the firm. They planned, in secret, to skim money from Metric & Inch to help them establish their own company."

"That comes as a surprise."

"Why do you think I called you naïve?"

"How could I know such plans existed inside the firm?"

James leaned toward him. "You protected the business when you rejected their projects. People in the D-D intended to roll the blame on you and your department. While I was in Europe signing new clients, they presented a case to the board claiming you were standing in the way of executing lucrative contracts with potential new customers. The D-D claimed we would lose millions because of your unfair meddling. They had an ingenious plan in place."

"I am such a fool. I had no clue."

James laughed. "Máire had informed us of the D-D's plans before the situation exploded. She informed us you had nothing to do with the scheme, and she provided substantial evidence though I cannot share that with you. She helped save your reputation and your job. The board did not react well to the

D-D's plans. For legal reasons, I cannot say anything else, and you must keep this to yourself. Is that clear?"

"Yes, Sir."

James laughed. "I will break you of that *Sir* habit." He grinned. "Have you eaten? May I take you to lunch?"

Aedan frowned. "I'm sorry, Sir, may I reschedule? I have work to do, and I will eat a quick lunch across the street. I have to leave early to meet Ciara."

"Yes but do me two favors."

"Anything, Sir."

"Do not, ever again, speak about resigning. I will not react well if you do and stop referring to your new baby in that manner," James said in a scolding tone.

"Sir," Aedan started.

James interrupted. "No, you will listen to me now."

Aedan squirmed in his seat; he braced for the verbal assault he expected was coming his way.

"You infuriate me when you refer to your second child as *number two*. Jenny and I tried for ten years to have children, we never could." He glanced at two framed photographs on his desk. "We adopted Mark and Jennifer, and we love them beyond words; however, we would have considered it a blessing to have at least one biological child to go with our adopted children.

"So, please, stop referring to your newest baby as *number two*. Your baby is a human being, not a number. If you continue in that manner, I will conclude that I have overestimated your character all these years. If that happens, resigning will not be possible because I will toss you out of this firm without a second thought. I assume that I've made myself clear." James glared at him.

Aedan looked stunned by the rebuke. He had no response. In silence, he stood and walked from the room. He walked to his office feeling stung by James' harsh scolding about number two.

CHAPTER SIX

A THORN NAMED MÁIRE

Aedan took the stairs to street level. He needed the exercise, hoping the activity would clear his mind, and he wanted to avoid the elevators after being stuck for so long inside the box. He held no shame in feeling concerned about the strange events with Michael, and he did not want to take a chance at a repeat.

There are too many weird things happening today.

He came through the lobby level doors and walked to Harold, perched in a chair behind the security desk. "Hey, Harold, I'm sorry for the way I acted when I came in today and thanks for trying to help me. I should have remained calm."

"No problem, Mister O'Beirne. Number two is on the way?"

"Yes, number two is on the way, but I'll stop using a number when referring to our new baby." The meeting remained fresh in Aedan's mind.

"Mr. O'Beirne, I say this with all respect. You would do yourself good to appreciate the many blessings you have in your life. You act as if you're entitled to the things you enjoy. I had to scratch and crawl my way through life, and that taught me to take nothing for granted."

Aedan sighed as his anger rose. He stepped closer to Harold. "You've no idea what I've gone through to get where I am. You assume too much. I worked for everything I have — as you have. So, shut up and keep your opinions to yourself. I came here to thank you and to apologize. I did not expect to receive a lecture." He turned from the desk.

Everyone has turned into philosophers, with me as their prime student.

He walked to the exit, and as he peered through the glass doors, he came to an instant halt after seeing Máire O'Cianain.

She smiled.

His jaw set in a tight clench as anger consumed him. He walked from the building at the Adams Street exit. Despite the young hours in the day, his shoulders dropped, revealing his exhaustion. He walked to Máire. "What are you doing here?"

"I will join you for lunch." She smiled. "We must talk."

"No chance, lady. I will have lunch alone. Leave me alone. I have enough on my mind, and I don't want to deal with you right now. Though, I thank you for supporting me at the meeting this morning."

"I attended the meeting to offer an accurate account, nothing more."

"Well, you helped me get out of a rough spot, and I'm grateful for your help," Aedan said.

"You are welcome." She smiled. "We must talk — it's not about your job, and it is not about Metric & Inch. Rather, I want to discuss your personal life."

She unnerved him with her smile; he felt sure he had seen it before. "Lady, we will not speak about my life, ever."

"Aedan — "

He interrupted. "No. I will not listen to you."

She stepped closer to him. With a firm voice, she said, "My name is Máire. Do not call me, Lady. You show disrespect to me and my mission to you by referring to me in such a demeaning manner."

He laughed; it was a most unpleasant sound. "Lady, I don't understand what you're referring to about a mission to me. But I want you out of my life, now." His voice had taken on a biting edge. He walked away.

"You must not avoid me. Your future will be more difficult if you do not speak with me," Máire shouted.

He looked at her. "Leave me alone. Don't bother me again."

She smiled. "We must talk."

"Not here, not at lunch, not today, and never." He trotted away. Aedan did not look back as he turned right onto Wabash Avenue; he walked across the street and strode to a pub situated midway between Monroe and E. Madison Street.

Aedan entered the busy tavern, long a Chicago classic. There were tables for patrons to eat, and a bar at which to sit to enjoy a meal or a drink, with television screens installed throughout the establishment. Photographs of famous Chicagoans, politicians, sports figures, actors, etc., lined the walls. The pub served people from the loop area for lunch, dinner, and well into the night.

He walked to the long bar. He had eaten there so many times his mind directed him to his regular bar stool without conscious thought. "Hey Eddie, toss me a cold one and my usual."

A tall man, dark-skinned, Edward *Eddie* Sherman, walked to Aedan. "Good to see you, Wyoming. How are things?"

"I've spent days feeling sick that were better than this."

Eddie broke into hearty and contagious laughter that caused the others seated at the bar to laugh with him. "Wife's pregnant again, huh?"

"Wow, you're the third person today who guessed my wife is pregnant before I told them. What's with that?"

Eddie leaned closer. "Wyoming, you're my closest friend; I know your expressions and attitudes better than my own." His contagious laughter rushed across the bar. "When's the baby due?"

"Number two is well on the way." He frowned as he recalled James' strong admonition. "Rather, our new baby's well on its way."

"Cheer up pal, having a large family is a blast," Eddie said. "I come from a family with eleven kids."

"Yeah, I know, you tell me that every time I mention children."

"Large families are remarkable. There's always a constant flow of people around. I wish I had ten kids, but I'd have to start with a wife, and I haven't found the right woman, yet." Eddie worked hard to lift Aedan's mood. He beamed. "What's wrong with you? Do you ever act happy?"

"Yeah, yeah, whatever." He shoved the bowl of pretzels away from his place at the bar. Aedan could not understand why no one knew that number two upset him.

Eddie frowned, the smile lines worn into his cheeks reversed, changing his appearance from happiness to sadness. "Okay, Wyoming." He sighed. "One corned beef sandwich and one bottle of beer coming up. I will leave you to your self-induced misery."

"Self-induced, yeah right — how many kids does she want? We aren't getting any younger," he complained into his beer. "I'll never get the life I want, no chance at all." The person seated next to him moved over one chair, to remove himself from Aedan's miserable complaining.

Aedan did not taste his food; he ignored everything entering his mouth as his mind remained focused on the events of the day. Aedan never could handle an unpredictable life.

I hate this day — abhor it.

"Eddie," he called. "I'll take the bill." Aedan smiled as he watched his friend, and the owner of the pub, as he moved back-and-forth — he was ensuring his customers received proper service. They had become friends at three years old when they lived across the street from each other in Oak Valley, Illinois. He recalled their decision to go to college together right after High School. He had always wanted to live in the West — they chose a university in Wyoming. "Do you remember the event in college?" Aedan said as Eddie approached.

"How could I forget? You helped me out of a huge jam. The *Wyoming* nickname sure stuck after that — you've never stopped being a faithful friend to me." Eddie laughed. "Do you remember the time we hiked high into the Rockies?"

"That was an awesome trip," Aedan said.

"The valley between those peaks was gorgeous, and it seemed like we were on the top of the world. I'm surprised no one has built a town there. The trees and the air in that place were incredible. I'd love to build a town there," Eddie said.

"Maybe someday a town will exist there."

"I'd move there in an instant," Eddie said.

Aedan chuckled. "No way. You wouldn't give up your business and leave all the glamor of the Midwest."

"I'd do it without giving it a second thought, pal." Eddie's hearty laugh filled the air. "Hey, do you remember that strange old man in that valley?"

"How could I forget? He seemed to pop-up out of nowhere. I remember him well," Aedan said as images of Michael from the elevator flooded his mind.

"He called the location his *Heavenly Rock Valley*," Eddie said.

"Yeah, I remember — it's an incredible place." He smiled. "So, where's my bill? I need to get out of here."

"No charge. Congratulations. If it's a boy, name him Edward." He released a hearty laugh. Others around them laughed.

"We'll see; Ciara has a top-secret list of names she deems super meaningful to our Irish roots and to our faith histories. I don't understand how she developed the list, but she'll already have the perfect name ready to go," he said with a heavy dose of sarcasm. "I don't care about baby names, I never have, and I don't care about names right now."

"Okay, I understand — but don't go slamming Ciara. Make sure you treat her right. And stop eating on the run; plan to spend more time when you eat here." He walked away to serve other customers.

As Aedan walked from the bar, he ran into a woman trying to take an empty seat. He knocked her over, her purse dropped, and its contents slid across the floor. Déjà vu filled his senses. He bent to help her. "I'm sorry."

Several other men came forward to help her.

The woman looked at Aedan. "I should have known you would try to get even with me," Máire said.

"What is this? Are you following me?"

"Why in Heaven's name would I do that?" She smiled.

Her smile did not convince him.

Aedan sprinted from the pub to distance himself from Máire. He continued to Adams Street. Aedan jogged through walking traffic to the entrance into his work building. As he neared the doors, Máire walked toward him from a standing position next to the doorway. She smiled as he drew closer to her.

"Oh, man, this is too much, how did you," he started.

She interjected as she flashed her annoying smile. "Are you now ready to speak with me?"

"Shut up and leave me alone," he shouted. Several people approaching the entrance stopped and looked at them, attempting to make sure Máire did not require help. He pushed through the revolving door. He walked, with a rapid gait, to the elevators. As he neared the units, the left doors opened; the same one he shared with Michael earlier. To his surprise, Máire walked through the unit's doors, she headed toward him.

In a sign of resignation, he walked to a long row of chairs hugging a wall opposite the elevators. He sat in a tired heap. He looked at Máire. "What do you want from me? How are you doing this? Who are you?"

"Let us take a walk, we will speak in private. I want to help you."

He looked at the elevators and back at Máire. He stood, his shoulders slumping in resignation. "I will follow you."

CHAPTER SEVEN

FATHERS BY THE BEAN

Aedan followed Máire to Michigan Avenue. He enjoyed the cold winter air against his forehead wounds. They walked to Millennium Park, which ran along Michigan Avenue from Monroe Street to Randolph Street.

He sat with her on an empty bench, away from the many park visitors. Most people concentrated their attention on the *Bean*, an enormous sculpture fabricated from 168 polished stainless-steel plates revealing no seams. The surface offered warped reflections of people passing under its twelve-foot arch. From a near distance, the piece appeared as a mirrored bean, resulting in its local nickname. The park created an attractive and peaceful oasis amid skyscrapers filled with businesses bustling with activity, a favorite location for out-of-town people staying in hotels throughout the Loop and surrounding areas.

He frowned with frustration. "There's work I must get done. Tell me what you want from me." He sighed while preparing to take flight from her when an opportunity arose.

"Do you see the father and his daughter under the Bean?"

"Yes, what of them?" Aedan glared at her with anger.

"Do you see the father and his three boys?" She pointed.

"Yes, what's your point?" Aedan filled the air with a growling voice born of his growing frustration. He could not stop thinking about Ciara; he assumed she remained angry with him.

Why hasn't she called? She always calls to remind me about appointments.

"Describe the scene," Máire said.

"I've had enough of this." He glared at her as he stood. "I'm going back to work. You're more than welcome to stay here. But gawking at complete strangers in the park makes me conclude you're off your nut, lady." His voice bit through the air like a cold Chicago winter wind.

While remaining seated, she leaned close to him, and with surprising aggression, she snatched his right hand. "Take a seat." She did not smile; instead, she reflected a grave seriousness that caused him to shiver. "Take a seat and do so this moment."

Her serious demeanor took him off guard. He glared at her with anger. "I don't care what you want me to do. I'm going back to work."

She became intense, grave. She pulled on Aedan's right hand.

A slight electric jolt raced through his arm and with a perplexed expression, he sat on the bench wondering what happened. His arm and hand tingled from the charge. Confused and surprised, his mind cleared as a dark rage began to a boil and simmer within him. "What did you — "

She interrupted him. "Let us not have to go through that again." Her countenance revealed intense gravity, which told him he should pay attention. "I am here to help you. You will soon be able to return to work."

He relaxed, waiting for a chance to break free of her; though, he realized that he could not call the police because time was short. He would miss the consult. He groaned as his mind filled with frustration.

"You are correct. You would miss the consult, and the police would not believe you," Máire said.

"Oh, man, how did you know," he started.

She glared at him. "Stop, enough of this. There are several fathers with their children in the area. Describe what you see."

With resignation, he said, "I see a father with his young son, about four years old. They're walking in circles under the bean."

"What else do you notice about the father?"

"Nothing, he seems the same as any other father."

"Look closer, what are you missing?"

Aedan sighed. "I don't know. He's a father with his kid."

She smiled. "You detect nothing else?"

"He's showing his kid the park. What else do you want?"

"You refuse to open your mind. Find another example."

Her smile grated on his nerves. He continued searching.

"In the distance, there's a father and his daughter. They're walking through the park and holding hands. The girl is about six, maybe seven years old. She's smiling, and so is the dad."

"They are smiling?"

"Yes. So, what?"

"Find another," she said.

They spent the next fifteen minutes watching people in the park. There were no father figures in their view; however, they found many more examples, including entire families with many children. Máire pushed him to expand his descriptions and to look deeper. She wanted him to discover the elements he was missing. However, he found a few additional ways to describe the many fathers they viewed.

"What do you find in common with all these people? Challenge yourself to consider things beyond your comfort zone."

He sighed with frustration. He wanted to get up and run to his office, but he did not want a replay of the electric jolt he experienced earlier. "We saw a bunch of fathers with their kids." He did not know what she wanted from him. He looked away, gathering control over his emotions. "Lady stop this now. You have wasted my time, and I have none left to lose today." He glared at her. "You say you're trying to help me, but you're delaying me from getting back to my responsibilities to my job and to my family. Stop this now."

"We have seen many fathers. You have learned nothing?" She looked disappointed while ignoring his pleas for her to stop. "You will not try to go any deeper?"

"Listen to me, lady."

She interrupted him. "My name is Máire." She smiled. "Have you not learned anything watching those fathers?"

"No, nothing other than I'm tired of wasting my time with you." He groaned. "I have learned you're an idiot. I'm going back to work." He stood. "And, don't zap me again or I will scream for help. You make me sick, lady."

She glared at him. "Mr. O'Beirne, I came to offer you help; however, no matter my efforts, you have no interest in opening your mind. Your lack of gratitude and humility prevents you from seeing prominent elements in the relationships we have witnessed. I hope you gain those traits before it is too late."

He frowned. "I don't care what you," Aedan began.

"Stop speaking," she demanded. "You are not open to change, at least not at this point. I wanted to help you, and you have refused. I will leave you now; however, you now have three-thousand, five-hundred, and forty moments left. Please, remember I attempted to help you make the reason for that number disappear. I do not know what will come from your refusal to open your mind." She walked away, moving under the Bean's arch and turned left.

What a nutcase she is. I must leave work in an hour to make the stupid doctor appointment. And what was that about three thousand, five-hundred, and forty moments?

He took calming breaths as he moved through foot traffic.

She wants me to open my mind — but, to what?

Pain and confusion consumed him.

My life is tearing away from me, and I don't know why.

He plowed through the pedestrians while moving along the sidewalk.

Why haven't I heard from Ciara? She should have called me at least twice to remind me about the stupid consultation.

He turned right at the corner of Michigan Avenue and Adams Street. The entrance to Metric & Inch lied a one-half block away. His mind focused on the projects and spreadsheets he had to complete before leaving for the consult.

He pushed through the revolving doors; he came to a halt when he peered into the lobby. Máire stood inside. In a start, his frustration rose.

I've had enough; she's gone too far this time.

He walked to her. The heavy traffic close to the entrance doors slowed him. He forced himself through the crowd. He glared at her. "Let's take this off to the side and out of the way."

They walked to a corner location where few people gathered. He glared at her — his anger rose. "You said you would leave me alone. I won't tolerate your intrusion into my life."

"Considering your harsh demeanor, and your clear dislike for me, I hold no desire to continue speaking with you; however, I must ensure you understand a most critical point."

"Fine, I'll bite," Aedan said.

"You cannot avoid what is coming your way." She held a solemn expression as she glared at him. "I realize you do not care about my advice, and that is your choice. I must respect your ability to chart your own course. However, denying help and rejecting sound advice is never wise. You must learn to accept information and help from others. Developing that ability will soon become critical to you."

He shook his head in anger and disbelief as he walked across the lobby. Aedan ignored Harold still perched in his chair behind the security desk. He stopped at the elevator bank, he wondered if he should risk using a unit; however, Aedan knew he had to take one to save time. He entered the leftmost lift.

As he rode the elevator to *Metric & Inch*, he contemplated his encounter with Máire in Millennium Park. A shiver ran up his spine upon seeing a black fedora lying on the floor at the elevator's rear.

CHAPTER EIGHT

WANTING OUT

After leaving the building, Aedan sprinted across Wabash Avenue. He pulled his friend's business card from his pants pocket.

I have enough time to make one quick stop.

He ran to the middle of the block, stopped at a narrow building standing between two others. He read the new printing on the wood door:

WILLIAM SHELTON – ATTORNEY AT LAW

He walked through the outer door, and through the interior entrance. An attractive woman, brown hair, mid-thirties, sat at a welcoming desk. "Hi Katie, is he in?"

"He's in the back." She smiled. "It's good to see you. How are Ciara and Colin?"

"They're all right, I guess. Number two is on the way." He winced as he recalled the stiff rebuke he received from James.

I don't care what anyone thinks about her pregnancy. It's baby number two, and I'm tired of lectures.

"Wow, congratulations." She stood and strode to him, hugged him. "Another child; what a joy, I'm thrilled for you and Ciara."

"Hey, don't hug the clients," William said as he walked into the room. Friends often called him *Bill the Bomb* because of his propensity to burst into booming laughter, taking those around him by surprise. His laughter confused many people because they could not understand how such a thunderous sound could emanate from such a soaring and wispy-thin man. He stood six-feet-six-inches tall, and he weighed one hundred and sixty pounds. When he was a boy, his brothers often teased him when they told him he looked like a human zipper from a side view whenever he stuck out his tongue. He enjoyed the image.

"Who says I'm a client?" Aedan said.

"Why else would you be here? Our friendship sure isn't enough." A loud burst of laughter rang through the office.

"You've been my friend for years."

"I know." He smirked. "But I enjoy seeing how serious you get whenever I give you grief. Come back to my office."

Aedan looked at the files and documents covering Bill's deep oak desk surface to two feet high. He grinned while thinking his friend's organizational skills needed some work.

"What's this about?" Bill said.

"I have five minutes to get advice from you." He swallowed hard, his nerves getting the best of him.

"Then, stop wasting time. What's up?" A laugh boom burst forth from his mouth, papers on his desk shook in the breeze created by the thin man's merriment.

"My life is a mess, and I'm not at all sure how to say this." He squirmed in his chair.

"Stop stalling, say what you came here to say."

He took slow breaths. "What's it cost to get a divorce?" Aedan remained calm as Bill released his anger upon him.

The shouts emanating from the office sent Katie running to find out what happened. She rushed through the closed door to find her husband sitting behind his desk, his narrow face ashen, colorless. "What's going on?"

"Katie, this is a confidential meeting," Bill said. He sat straighter to regain his calm. No booming laughter came from him.

"Leave the office, Katie," Aedan shouted. "I have two minutes left."

In defiance, she crossed her arms, "Bill, are you okay?"

"Yes. This is a private conversation. Leave and close the door." Bill remained fixed in a stunned state.

Katie left the office.

Bill glared at him. "What's this all about?"

Aedan raised his eyebrows. "A more professional attitude, please."

"What? You're one of my best friends, you drop a bomb on me, and you expect instant professionalism?" He frowned with disgust. "You have a great life with Ciara and Colin, why would you think about this?"

"Don't start lecturing me." He frowned.

"I'm not lecturing, I am trying to help. You're my friend."

He looked at Bill. "I have a minute left before I have to leave."

"What do you expect from me in a minute?" Bill tapped on his desk with his right index finger, waiting.

"I want to know how much it will cost to get a divorce?" His face drained of blood, and it took on a cold, colorless appearance. "I realize this is a shock to you, but I have to know, in case."

Bill leaned closer. "In case of what? Why are you asking such a stupid question? Ciara's pregnant, and Colin adores you. I cannot fathom why you would consider divorce; it would be a colossal mistake."

"I trust your legal opinion, but, if this is too much for you, I will ask someone else. I have to know how much a divorce will cost, and I need a quick response because I'm in a full out hurry." He paused. "Will you give me an answer, or not?"

Bill took in calming breaths and forced himself to regain an appropriate attorney demeanor. "You must understand every divorce has different issues to consider. I cannot offer a number with so little time and with no pertinent information. The cost to get a divorce is nothing compared to the overall ongoing financial and emotional damage for the couple involved, and that doesn't come close to addressing the carnage it often causes for the lives of the children involved. This is not something one should do without long and considered thought."

He stood and stretched his right hand to Bill.

His friend refused the handshake. "Sit down and tell me what this is all about. Do it now." Bill waited for a response.

"I have no time; I have to leave for an early pregnancy consult."

Bill's laugh filled the room. "You're a fool. If you're so worried about that consult, why are you asking these questions?" He tapped his skinny right index finger on the desk while waiting for a response.

Aedan contemplated his reply; he did not know if he could tell his friend the truth. "Because I want out of Ciara's plans for a large family."

Bill's laugh boomed. "What? That's your reason, too many kids? You're too late; you already have a son and another child on the way, which is only two children—not a lot. What gives with this?"

Aedan pushed his weight into the chair back; he let his body relax in an exhausted heap. "I see my life slipping away. I love Colin I do. But my life never seems to belong to me anymore."

"I noticed that you didn't say you love Ciara," Bill said.

"So?"

"Why are you saying you love Colin, but don't mention Ciara? What's going on with you two?" Bill tapped the desk.

"I'm angry with Ciara. She wants a large family, and I thought I could handle having a bunch of kids. I was wrong and don't want more children and rather get back to the city to do the things we loved to do after we were first married. I'm sick and tired of losing control over my life as if I'm an observer from the outside. Ciara will never go along with me, so, yes, I'm considering a divorce." He took on a strange look of satisfaction as he realized he had launched the topic into the real world with his spoken words to Bill. He felt no regrets, and he held no desire to take it back.

An extra-loud sarcastic laugh boom sounded, powerful enough to knock a large folder pile off the desk. "You're an absolute fool, an idiot, and to think I thought of you as a smart guy. A house filled with life is an absolute joy. Get out of my office. You're a complete tool of a fool."

Aedan stared at his friend. His anger rose.

"I said go." Bill frowned. He glared at him. "You're late for a consult you should go now and stop this nonsense before you do actual damage. Get out of my office and stop talking about divorce; stop thinking about leaving them. Ciara and Colin would feel crushed if they knew you came here asking these questions, and you know I'm right. I will not mention a word of this to Katie but leave now, or I will call your wife and tell her. Go now." Using both index fingers, Bill tapped hard on the desk as he scowled at him.

Aedan stood as anger consumed him. He refused to look at Bill as he turned and walked from the office.

Why am I getting so many lectures today?

CHAPTER NINE

DEFINING CHOICES

Aedan left Bill's office. As he bobbed and weaved through the crowded sidewalk, his eyes caught sight of yellow tape encasing Charlie's newsstand. He stopped at the curb.

What in the world, where's Charlie?

He ran across the street to the newsstand. He searched the area with frantic intensity. Long black tire skid marks ran in a line from the roadway to the stand's left side. An empty concrete pad revealed where the left flank of the newsstand had rested. Fresh plywood boards covered the remaining display cases. A Chicago Police Officer removed the yellow tape from around the business.

Aedan approached the officer. "What happened? Where's Charlie?"

"Who's asking?"

"A friend."

"You're not giving me much," the officer said. He pulled on a long yellow tape run.

"Officer, my name is Aedan O'Beirne; I work for Metric & Inch at Adams and Wabash. I've known Charlie for years; he is my friend. What happened?" His expression revealed his concern.

"Okay, well, a car slammed into his newsstand, the details of which I will not provide. Your friend suffered an injury. They rushed him to the emergency room at Saint John Hospital — about one and one-half miles from here, on Erie Street. The rest is confidential." He returned to his task.

Aedan recalled seeing Charlie helping the sedan driver.

This is crazy. Charlie didn't look hurt. He seemed more worried about the driver than for himself. This makes no sense.

He looked at the cop. "Officer?"

"Yes?" The interruption did not please him.

"Charlie looked fine after the accident. He helped the driver of the car. I saw it from a distance, and he did not appear hurt. What happened to him?"

The officer frowned, did not look pleased. "I told you everything I can."

"Thank you, officer."

He walked from the scene. Aedan sat on a concrete planter running along the curb while pulling his smartphone from his pocket. He pondered his next step.

Should I go to see Charlie in the hospital, or should I go to the consult?

He knew Ciara's anger would increase if he missed the appointment, yet Aedan understood her fury would work to his advantage if he filed for a divorce. He tapped the phone against his right thigh.

His right thigh began to hurt from the tapping of the cell phone. Aedan took several deep breaths as he dialed Ciara's number, no answer. He redialed, no answer. Aedan tapped the phone against his thigh, over and over. He redialed. No response.

Where is she? This isn't like her.

Redialed, no one picked up.

Aedan leaned into the traffic and hailed a cab. Seconds later, a taxi stopped. After getting into the vehicle, he said, "Saint John Hospital on Erie Street."

As the cab headed north, he looked at the parking garage where he had left his sedan.

My everyday life seems far away. It's as if my previous existence has disappeared. This choice will not be helpful for my marriage; I wish she'd answer her phone. Where is she?

He redialed her number, no answer.

The cab driver moved around cars as they made their way along Michigan Avenue, through heavy downtown traffic. Five call attempts later, still no answer.

The taxi driver moved the vehicle over the bridge crossing the Chicago River. They faced bumper-to-bumper conditions as they approached East Grand Street. Aedan had worked in the Loop and downtown areas long enough to know that several blocks separated them from Erie Street. Looking at his watch, he realized the consult would begin in thirty minutes.

Ciara is going alone — this is not good, not good at all.

He looked at the driver. "Let me out here." Aedan paid for his ride and left the cab. He jogged to Erie Street, turned right and walked to the hospital — stopped at the entrance and dialed Ciara, no answer.

Why is she ignoring my calls?

As he approached the hospital emergency room entrance, the automatic doors opened and out walked Charlie.

"Hey, Mr. O'Beirne, what are you doing here?"

He sighed. "That's a stupid question. You look fine. I wasted time coming here."

"I'm fine." Charlie's deep bass voice reverberated off the walls.

"I'm glad you're okay." His shoulders slumped with the realization he made the wrong decision going to see Charlie. He knew that he had given Ciara's anger additional fuel.

"Why are you here? You will miss the consult for number two," Charlie said. He placed his right hand on Aedan's shoulder. "You shouldn't have come here, I am fine. You should join your family."

"I don't care about the stupid appointment. Besides, I already missed it. But how do you know I had a consult?"

"I have learned, over the years, to keep my eyes and ears open." A low-pitched chortle came through his mouth, emanating from his stomach.

Aedan chuckled. He enjoyed Charlie's laughs. "Well, you're okay, so I'm going to take off. I have to get my car and get home."

"Hey, don't leave. Will you walk with me for a while?"

He paused as he calculated the risk to his marriage. Having missed the consult, he concluded there was no additional jeopardy. Aedan shrugged his shoulders with indifference, knowing he could do nothing about the missed appointment. He held tight to the hope that she would forgive him. "Sure, where do you want to go?"

"I want to walk along Michigan Avenue and back to my newsstand. Please join me." Charlie smiled.

"You lead, and I will follow," Aedan said.

Aedan and Charlie walked on the east side of Michigan Avenue, passing one massive tower, after another. He looked worried for his friend.

He's walking much slower; maybe his age is getting to him.

Talked over the Chicago River Bridge.

Charlie stopped at the span's midway point. "I am sorry, I know you're itching to get back. You younger men move faster than us old guys." He laughed. His chortle lost its energy after he viewed Aedan standing inches from the curb, close to the bridge roadway and to the vehicles passing over the span. "Is something wrong? Why are you so close to the road? Are you trying to get hit?"

Aedan looked over the bridge railing, and to the Chicago River flowing underneath. He shivered and turned away. He said nothing.

"Are you afraid of the water?" Charlie said with compassion.

"No, not the water, I love to swim. I set three records on my high school swim team. I want to get off this bridge, okay?" He trembled; his skin took on a clammy, colorless hue.

Charlie glanced at Aedan. "Are you all right?"

Aedan refused to reveal his fear of heights to Charlie. Despite the bridge resting a close distance from the river's surface, the height was enough to cause him to shiver with anxiety. He looked at his friend. "I'm fine — I'm worried about Ciara, Colin, and number two, and I want to get off this bridge." He squirmed and shifted his weight from foot-to-foot, waiting to move off the structure.

"Didn't you agree to stop calling your baby number two?"

Aedan's expression revealed his frustration. "You better tell me where you're learning these snippets to toss at me."

"I know how to listen."

"That's fine, but who's doing the talking?" People around them looked their way. He raised a hand to them, in a calming gesture. He turned back to Charlie. "Who's been talking to you?"

A large city bus came within inches of Aedan's back.

Charlie winced. "Are you thirsty? I have a massive desire for something to drink." He walked toward the span's southern edge.

"Sure, I'll stop. I'm glad we're getting off this bridge, but I still want to know who you've been talking to and why."

Charlie smiled; he ignored him. "The Douglas Hotel is over there." He pointed from their bridge location to the towering structure, east of Michigan Avenue. "They have bars in which we can wet our whistles." He released a deep bass snort from his mouth. "I love that phrase, *wet your whistle*. I can't work the saying into conversations often enough." He laughed with joy.

"Fine, Charlie, let's go wet our whistles." He grinned — a rare gesture for him that day.

"I'm glad you will join me. It is far more enjoyable to have a drink with a friend or loved one." He released a bass snort-laugh. "I am looking forward to downing a few beverages; I've been thirsty since I entered the hospital."

He frowned. "You had nothing to drink at Saint John's?"

"I asked for something to drink, but the accident on the interstate kept the ER flooded with patients. They were too busy to meet my needs. Terrible pain and suffering filled the place. They rolled an unconscious woman, in her thirties, into the ER; they had her neck and head protected with hard braces. A flood of other injured people filled the place."

"Wait," he said, "did you get help? Did anyone at the hospital examine you?" He did not camouflage his surprise.

Charlie walked off the bridge. He ignored Aedan.

"Stop! Did they examine you, or not?" Aedan shouted. He ran to catch up to Charlie as the older man crossed East Wacker Drive heading for the Douglas Hotel. "I will not join you if you don't answer me." He scowled at the older man.

"No, they had me waiting, but everything became hectic with the people from the accident being rushed to the emergency room. I asked several times for a drink, and they planned to get that too, but the accident victims consumed their time. I left." He smiled as he shrugged his shoulders.

"We have to bring you back; better yet, I will call for an ambulance because you shouldn't be walking."

Charlie laughed, which turned into a chortle. "I'm all right. Are we going to get a drink, or not?"

"Sure, I'll call from inside the hotel."

"No, you will not." Charlie smiled. "Don't worry about me because I'm fine. I brought you here to speak with a mutual friend."

"I don't understand." Aedan looked confused.

"You will understand soon enough." Charlie pushed through the entrance doors of the Douglas Hotel.

Aedan followed.

Charlie stopped and looked at him while nodding to several couches arranged in a seating area on the north side of the lobby. "My friend predicted that you would come to see me in the hospital. He asked me to bring you here."

Aedan saw a man sitting on a couch. The man had silvery hair cut to a close-cropped length. Aedan shivered as they approached. The man stood. He held a timeworn black fedora in his right hand. He wore a dark gray three-piece suit, and he stood six-feet-three-inches tall.

"Are you kidding me?" He glared at Michael's powerful face. He turned in a frantic motion to rip into Charlie, but he realized his newsstand friend had left without making a sound.

"Hello, son, perhaps you will chat with me?" Michael said. "Since you now have three-thousand, three-hundred, and one moment left."

Aedan sat in the single cushioned chair installed at the edge of the couch pit. His appearance revealed his exhaustion. He struggled to make sense of his day. Aedan leaped in his chair after a clock on the wall, five feet above him, chimed. He looked at Michael. "Why are you bothering me? Wasn't the time you spent with me in the elevator enough for you? Which reminds me, where did you go earlier?"

"Son, this is not about me."

"I don't care. I'm sick of being followed around town." His anger began to rise. "And, stop calling me, son."

"We are not trying to — "

He raised a hand to interrupt him. "We? Oh wait, you and that stupid Máire woman are together?" he shouted.

"We are not trying to follow you, and we do not want to upset you," Michael said. "We came to bring you critical information. You would help your cause by listening to what we have to say."

"Michael, you don't know me. You have nothing of interest to offer me, and you don't understand who I am and what my needs are. You and Máire have lost your minds." He glared at the older man. "I'm leaving."

"Where will you go?"

"Back to get my car; I have to reunite with my family."

"Please, Aedan, listen to me."

"No, I will not." His expression revealed his anguish.

Idiots and fools fill my day.

His head wounds oozed. His clothes, soaked in sweat and covered with blood, left him looking terrible. People entering the Douglas Hotel avoided him after seeing the mess he presented.

He did not care that he left Michael in the lobby couch pit as he walked outside, his winter jacket draped on his left arm. Aedan hated coats, too binding for him. He looked to the south and back to the north where the Chicago River flowed nearby. The sidewalks remained full of walking traffic; many Christmas shoppers searching for last-minute gifts.

His expression revealed his confusion as he contemplated his next move. His mind wandered through all the impossible chapters in his day; he could not make sense of anything, and his inability to contact Ciara became a constant concern for him.

This is not like her. Where is she, and why doesn't she answer her cell? Is she ignoring me? None of this makes sense.

He shivered as a frigid wind blew across his body. The gusts made loud buffeting noises as the air pounded against and through the steel and glass canyon created by the vertical building walls. In the dark western sky, he looked with growing interest, as low-level storm clouds moved toward the region. He noticed a strange reddish glow dance and echo off low swirling clouds arranged in an extended ridge format. Something about the unusual sight disturbed him.

Why are those clouds glowing red?

He examined the unique formation, but the wind increased again, causing him to turn away from the biting cold.

Lake Michigan must be rough under these high winds.

The large water body laid a short walk to the east. Aedan had seen the lake so many times that his memory held a permanent etching of its nearby Chicago shoreline. He knew the cold gusts would create havoc along the shore — mounds of ice would develop.

Maybe they'll close Lake Shore Drive.

He looked at the lake. For him, at night, the lake offered a creepy, imposing, black ink darkness capable of swallowing a person with no one knowing what happened. Those thoughts raised his fear of enclosed spaces; he shuddered, and with reluctance, he put on his winter coat. Aedan had not moved away from the hotel and did not know what to do next. He shivered in the cold.

Michael approached. "I suppose you do not want to chat."

Aedan turned away from Michael while extracting his cell phone. Dialed Ciara, no answer. Called their home landline telephone number, no response, the call switched to their digital answering machine. He tried reaching four close neighbors, no one picked up. Aedan could not comprehend why no one answered his calls.

"Please, let's take a walk, we will relax and enjoy a short chat. I have important information for you. But you must desire the info; I will not force it on you," Michael said.

"No way old man; I must contact my wife. I don't understand why you keep following me and harassing me." He frowned.

"You're exhausted, and you require relief from this day. I have information for you, but you must trust me." He smiled.

The older man's smiles reminded him of Máire. "Shut up. Why do you people grin all the time? Why are you so happy?"

"Please, you must trust us because we are here to help you. Your future will rely on our guidance. But we must respect your wishes." He smiled.

"Stop talking to me," he shouted. "I must contact my wife, and I couldn't care less about what you want to talk to me about because I must speak with my wife. I'll repeat it for you, I must contact my wife." He turned away.

Michael lost his pleasant smile. "Tell me, Aedan; how have you convinced yourself that your wife wants to speak with you? You did not join her at the doctor consult. You failed Ciara again."

Aedan did not enjoy the response, walked away in a hurry with anger creasing his forehead with such intensity the cold winds could not slow the blood oozing from his wounds. He headed to Michigan Avenue and then on toward the garage.

"Stop," Michael shouted.

He ceased walking and looked back at the older man. "I have had enough dealing with you nutcases today. You're becoming a worse fool and a more troublesome nuisance than Máire. I don't know where you came from, or why you're here, but you must leave me alone. You should get out of here now because I'm tired and I'm growing impatient with you. I'm going home to my wife and son." He raised his voice to counter the wind's buffeting noises. "And you know well enough why I missed the consult."

Michael walked to him. "You missed the consult because you visited your attorney friend, which we both know would shatter Ciara's heart if she learned about that wrongheaded choice." His face held a stern, disapproving glare. "Perhaps your wife learned of the stop you made at Bill's office, during which you sought information about getting a divorce."

He froze in place. "There's no way, how could she know?" His appearance betrayed his anxiety. "And, how do you know about me visiting Bill? Who are you, and why are you injecting yourself into my life?"

"I know things about you; how I receive that information is not relevant. Recall that William Shelton and Ciara were friends in college," Michael said.

He stepped with aggression toward the older man. "I've no way to know how you and Máire have learned so much about me, but you have to remove yourself from my life, and now. My patience is near its end."

"I am not trying to — "

Aedan interrupted him with anger. "Stop talking. Bill is my friend, and he knows I sought his legal opinion, nothing more. He would not betray me by telling you anything, and he knows that he would breach attorney ethics if he did." His voice took on a decisive edge. "That means you're getting your information about me from someone or somewhere else, and I don't like that, at all. You had better stop because my patience with you is running dry." He walked away.

"Stop." Michael glared at him. "How I secure information has no significance in these matters. This is about you and your family, not me. We both understand you should not have pulled that terrible divorce cost stunt with your friend Bill." His face became angry, sour. "Setting aside your irresponsible move, you cannot contact your wife. I have info that you will find helpful if you calm yourself long enough for me to share what I know."

"I don't have any reason to listen to you."

"You have no reason to avoid receiving the information I want to provide. Are you too stubborn to understand I am trying to offer you help?" Michael said.

"This is what you call help?" His voice dripped with disgust. "Leave me alone; you and Máire have brought me nothing but trouble and misery."

"We have offered help."

He glared at him. "Enough. Michael, maybe you're a ghost my mind has produced from seeing the painting in the company lobby all these years. But if you're a real person, you had better stop harassing me." He raised his right hand high to silence Michael. "But no matter your reasons for distressing me, I'm leaving, whether or not you approve."

Michael smiled. "That's how you want to handle this?"

"Yes."

"I must respect your wishes. I will leave you to do as you will. You have three-thousand, two-hundred and twenty-minutes left. I came here to help, and you are ignoring my help again. Perhaps, before your moments evaporate, you will develop the sense to listen to those who are trying to offer you support." In a rapid pace, Michael walked away.

Pain consumed Aedan. *I just want to go home.*

Aedan crossed Michigan Avenue and walked four blocks where he turned right onto E. Washington Street, and then he strode to Wabash. A mixture of ice and snow began to fall. He pulled his jacket tighter around his body; he shivered in the cold wintry night air.

Great, there's nothing better than snow and ice to make my drive home even more difficult. I'll call her before I leave the garage and leave her a message at home and on her cell. She'll understand after I tell her everything that has happened to me.

Aedan grinned, taking comfort from his plan. He walked into the parking garage and entered his sedan. After leaving two detailed recordings for Ciara, he tossed his cell phone onto the passenger seat.

That'll help. Ciara will listen to my messages, and she'll forgive me after I tell her about everything I have gone through today. In an hour, when I'm home, everything will be okay, and we'll have a happy Christmas. I hope.

CHAPTER TEN

BEST LAID PLANS

Aedan intended to take the interstate forty miles to Oak Valley in the northwest suburbs. His hometown brimmed full of residential subdivisions, streams, ponds, ball fields, and forests. Wild animal sightings, such as deer, were a frequent event in the area around their home. The village exhibited a stark difference from the bustling city life he journeyed to every workday and on many Saturday mornings.

Years ago, after buying their house, he forced himself to accept his life away from the city. But he wanted to get back to the action in Chicago's Loop.

The snow and ice continued to plummet at high rates.

He didn't notice the losing effort his sedan's rickety old wiper motor made in its attempt to clear the wintry mixture from his windshield.

Someday I'll get back into the action. Someday.

The winter storm continued unabated as he inched along Wabash Avenue. As he approached Charlie's shuttered newsstand, he noticed that the policed had removed the yellow tape. Despite the darkness, he looked at the physical damage done to his friend's business.

He attempted to grasp the reality the accident had happened earlier that day, for him time felt stretched as if days had gone by since he smashed his head against his kitchen island counter.

I wonder if Michael set Charlie against me — but Charlie wouldn't betray our friendship.

Lost in his thoughts, he did not notice his sedan sliding along the icy mixture covering the road. Reverberating sounds emanated from a Chicago L-Train passing overhead.

He came to the intersection at Wabash and Adams, the location he entered the building every workday morning. He remained at the streetlight for several cycles staring at the building's entrance doors.

The events of this day link, somehow. I don't understand how, but the events of this day connect.

He strained to see the building's higher levels. He could not see the thirty-ninth floor, the Metric & Inch company location, the Chicago elevated tracks overhead blocked the lower floors, and the winter storm prevented him from seeing anything above the fifth floor.

I wonder if James is still working.

Shrieking auto horns sounded from behind, snapping him back to attention. He shoved the manual transmission into first gear and drove through the light, and continued driving on Wabash Avenue, moving with caution across the icy road.

Aedan headed west on Congress Parkway, placing him on a path to the interstate. Music emanated from the sedan's radio. He drummed his fingers against the steering wheel as he crept westward. A smile, unusual for him that day, creased his face.

Why can't I contact her? I'd like to tell her I'm on my way home. She'll forgive me. After she hears my story, she'll forgive me.

With confidence, he sat taller.

She loves me. She'll forgive me. My plan will work. I'll have her back by the end of the day. Then, I will move on to accepting number two into the fold. That'll make her happy. I'll show her how much I have embraced the new baby.

He laughed, it was a pleasant sound, a rare state for him. Happiness often eluded him since he had become fixated on returning to the city. Unknown to him, many people considered him a miserable, unhappy, crabby, and overall unkind person.

As he approached the intersection of West Congress Parkway and S. LaSalle Street, he did not see the fast-moving truck heading toward him. The heavy vehicle glided, out of control through the ice and snow mixture. Other cars in the area swerved to avoid direct contact. The heavy vehicle continued sliding toward Aedan's sedan — nothing could stop the collision.

The truck's front left bumper corner made the first contact, thrusting into the side of his sedan, collapsing the car's two right doors, buckling them into the passenger compartment over two feet. His seat shifted toward the driver's door. Glass flew as the windows broke under stress; shards hit him in the upper forehead. His previous wounds reopened as the glass debris carved new cuts.

The truck pushed the car through the intersection and into a massive street-light pole at the southeast corner. The sedan bounced off the pole, crushing the left rear panels and sending the car into a freakish clockwise rotation away from the pole.

His car settled in the middle of the intersection with all other traffic halted in the four directions possible. Steam and smoke broke free from the engine compartment. The truck came to a sliding stop close to the intersection's southeast sidewalk. The storm continued pounding the area; in seconds, snow blanketed the destroyed sedan.

The truck driver leaped from the cab and ran to Aedan. Frantic and breathing hard, the trucker used his cell phone to dial an emergency number. He shouted into the phone, "Get to Congress Parkway and LaSalle right away, I'm a long-haul driver, and I slammed into a car with my big rig. This is not good. Hurry now." He forced his phone into his jeans pocket. He inched toward the car.

Aedan slumped unconscious in his seat; his head rested on the steering wheel. Blood trickled from his forehead, and from his hands.

The truck driver with caution while stretching his hand right hand through the broken driver's side window. He felt for Aedan's breath and pulse.

A crowd gathered.

"Don't touch him. Wait for the Paramedics," shouted a man.

The truck driver looked at the surrounding people, he shouted, "He has strong breathing and pulse."

"Stay away from him," shouted a woman.

"Don't worry; I used to be a paramedic. I won't move him," the trucker said. He turned back to Aedan.

The winds increased; the snow and ice swirled around them.

A woman, wearing a winter coat, a red knit hat, and green gloves, ran to the truck driver and handed him a large stack of Christmas blankets. They draped the blankets over Aedan, and they covered the windshield and the driver's window, stopping the snow from entering the car.

"Where did you get all the blankets?" the trucker said.

"The ladies at my church make them for people in area hospitals. That's why they're all made from Christmas fabric."

"Tell them the blankets came in handy today."

"I'm glad I had them with me. We already delivered most in time for Christmas giving. I took these before I left church earlier," she said. "I sure hope and pray he'll be all right."

The trucker groaned with worry. "Me too. I'll join you in praying."

Sirens echoed across the area. In the horrific weather, the paramedics, and the Fire Department took longer to reach the scene, in the meantime, the blankets helped keep Aedan warm.

After the emergency crews had arrived, it took them little effort to remove the driver's door, providing them safe access to Aedan.

Battered and bleeding, Aedan woke as the paramedics cut away his safety belts. With cautious moves, the crew removed him from the car. His point-of-view changed from a seated forward position to a horizontal view as they laid him on a rigid board. They moved him onto a gurney where they covered him with several layers of cloth wraps. The snow ice pelted him as they rushed him to the ambulance.

Pain and stress came to him in waves.

I need my family. They don't know what's happened to me.

He looked away with a forlorn expression.

He could not stop shivering as grief overtook him.

I am such a fool.

Aedan was conscious as the paramedics pulled him from the ambulance. For the first time, that day, the bright Christmas lights decorating the streets in the near distance drew his attention.

They wheeled him into the Saint John Hospital ER. He broke into a weak laugh, recalling how earlier in the day he had seen the same sign when he went to see Charlie. He strained his head against the straps to look at a female paramedic. "What day is it? Is it still Wednesday?"

"Yes, Sir, it's seven o'clock on Wednesday night. We'll take good care of you. You're in excellent hands." She smiled with warmth.

He allowed his head to relax.

What a day — I cannot believe this day.

Desperate to contact Ciara, he searched his pockets for his smartphone, he could not find it, nor could Aedan remember where he placed the device. Sweat dripped from his forehead, which combined with the blood already caked on his face. He began to feel the pain, ache, and physical stress, a result of the accident.

He held a distant and helpless glare as he realized that he could not find them. And he knew his stay in the hospital would not be brief, not with the tests, scans, and probes that the emergency room staff would order. His emotional turmoil caused him to shiver as he winced in pain.

My left arm feels wrecked. I bet it's broken.

He waited for medical professionals. His inability to contact Ciara worried him to his soul. As he searched his pockets for his phone, he came upon the pink heart-shaped note that she had left for him in their bathroom that morning. He read it in silence:

> *Aedan, I pray this news will make you happy. I'm pregnant,*
> *and I'm due in the summer. I love you so very much,*
>
> *Ciara*

His expression betrayed his torment. "I'm such a fool," he whispered. "Ciara asked for my happiness. I couldn't even give her that, and I ripped into her like a narcissistic idiot—wish I could take that back," Aedan said while returning the note to his pants pockets. Wracking his mind to remember where he placed his cell phone; he could not recall. Despite the cloth wraps covering him from his foot to his shoulder, he shivered as the emergency room staff pushed him into a cubicle space in the ER, where they began working on him.

He waited for the hospital team to perform tests on him. He could hear the bustle of activity throughout the ER.

I wonder why the place is so crazy. Wait — Charlie mentioned the accident on the interstate.

The ER staff cleaned his wounds and wrapped his left arm in a soft sling. He waited for testing facilities to become available.

While lying in the cubicle, he listened to the staff talking about the horrific multi-vehicle accident on the interstate that morning. He also learned that St. John's received patients from crashes caused by the dangerous winter storm that had descended upon the lakefront region, creating an atmosphere of controlled chaos for the medical staff.

Thirty minutes had crawled by since a female doctor had ordered tests. The possibility of concussion remained high. He drifted toward unconsciousness every few minutes with mental exhaustion and physical pain, which created a harsh struggle for him. The doctor refused to approve pain medication until after they completed testing.

Each time he drifted toward sleep; he banged his left arm on the bed railing to ensure he remained awake. The blows to his arm sent fresh pain waves to his brain. He rolled to his right to reduce the pressure on his left arm. He took calming breaths, banishing the pain.

I wish I had my cell phone; she doesn't understand where I am. I want to go home and hug them. What a fool I am. Why did I leave the house like that?

CHAPTER ELEVEN

AGAINST MEDICAL ADVICE

Aedan watched a female nurse enter his ER cubicle.

"Mr. O'Beirne," the nurse said. "I will take you for an x-ray of your arm. Then, you will receive a CT-scan to make sure there's no severe damage to your head. We see no signs of glass fragments embedded in your skin. We will check further to ensure you're free of all shards."

"When will you release me?" Aedan said.

She looked at him with surprise. "Mr. O'Beirne, do you understand that you've been in a serious automobile accident?"

"I'm fine, and I have pressing matters. When will you release me?"

She sighed. "We must ensure you've received no serious injuries." Her decisive tone ended the conversation. She released the gurney's brakes and pushed him from the cubicle.

"Has anyone seen my cell?"

"Sir, I haven't seen your phone. But you cannot use electronics until we complete your tests. Our priority is to make sure you receive proper care for all injuries you sustained. If there is someone we should call, we will do so." Her demeanor became stern, professional. "Relax, we'll enter the X-ray room in a few minutes."

Aedan did not enjoy the pain in his left arm as the technicians ran the X-rays, and he held a greater dislike for the CT-scan positioning. He remained silent aching to find a way home, and the sooner, the better.

After his return to his emergency room cubicle, he noticed the day was over. It was 01:30am, Thursday morning.

This place is so busy, I'm lucky I received any treatment. What a madhouse. Hospitals — all there ever is in these places is hurry and wait, hurry and wait. I wonder how long I must wait for the test results.

His gruff demeanor had returned with full force.

The test results did not take long; it surprised him when the doctor pushed through the curtain.

"Mr. O'Beirne, you're a lucky man. You have deep bruising on your left arm, but no breaks. We'll place you in a hard sling to help it heal. We also found no evidence of a concussion from the scan, and not from my earlier on-site exam." She grinned.

"Good, please release me."

"No, head trauma remains my concern. We'll keep you here for observation." Her face filled with resolve.

"No way, I have pressing matters, and I want to leave now."

She frowned. "I have a room reserved, Mr. O'Beirne. You will stay at least until the morning." She walked from the cubicle.

He climbed off the gurney and gathered his belongings.

Ignoring the throbbing pain in his left arm, he removed the sling. He extracted a red knit hat from his winter coat pocket, an early Christmas gift from Ciara; she feared he would get too cold walking the downtown streets. Using his right hand — he could not lift his left arm — he inched the hat over his head far enough to hide the bandages; it covered his wounds. Aedan shoved a full bottle of water into an interior coat pocket.

He gathered strength and resolve to complete his next maneuver. Aedan pulled on his winter coat by inserting his left arm; pain raced through him, and he stumbled backward. He took calming breaths while resting on the bed. He increased his pace, hoping the staff did not return. In a display of determination, he stood and slid his right arm through the coat sleeve, pulled the zipper tight, all the way to the neckline, and placed his left hand in the coat's outer pocket, which helped lessen the pain emanating from his bruised arm. After checking his reflection in a well-lit glass-covered wall hanging, he released a nervous laugh.

Satisfied that he did not look like a patient, he walked with boldness into the busy emergency room. He used steel-like calm to weave his way to the exits, adrenalin helped lessen the pain in his left arm. He behaved as if he belonged there, smiling at the hospital staff as he moved around them.

After unsuspecting security personnel had allowed him to leave, he walked through the doors and into the wintry frigid snow and ice-filled air. He departed the hospital without a sling and without pain medications. The staff listed him as a registered patient having left St. John's *Against Medical Advice.*

Aedan walked to Michigan Avenue while shivering in the early morning cold, but his left arm pain kept his focus away from the weather.

He walked along the snow-covered sidewalk. With no people and road traffic, silence cloaked the Loop. Aedan had the walkway to himself. Cold and pain-wracked, while amid thousands tucked inside the buildings all around him, creeping loneliness descended on him.

The strange and unpredicted storm had walloped the city. Road crews struggled to recover from the wintry mess. The sounds of snowplows working in the distance filled his ears as he trudged along the sidewalk. He could not recall the last time he saw the Magnificent Mile in such a subdued and quiet state, sleeping, and waiting for the holiday rush that would begin in a few hours.

It's eerie, yet also peaceful.

He groaned from the pain in his leg as he hobbled through the snow, wondering what Ciara and Colin were doing.

CHAPTER TWELVE

FOLLOW THE HAT

Exhaustion prevailed over Aedan. After hobbling through two blocks of snow-covered Michigan Avenue sidewalks, he stopped to rest at a street-side bench. His left arm throbbed. His head ached.

He cleared the snow from the sidewalk seat. Aedan pulled the bottle of water from inside his coat and took several long sips as he sat on the frozen bench. He shivered in the cold.

Deep loneliness born of a lack of sleep and injuries bore down on Aedan. He could not recall a time throughout their marriage that he and Ciara had not spoken for such an extended period. With no knowledge of where Ciara and Colin were, and knowing they had no way to know where he was, an overwhelming sense of separation and loneliness wrapped around him like a painful blanket.

He pulled his hood tight over his head and wrapped his arms around his body. Aedan clenched his teeth against the pain while drawing his legs

onto the bench and hunching over, his chest contacting his knees —
appearing as a taught human ball. His long down winter coat kept the nasty
weather out; his huddled body produced heat, he began to warm, his
shivering slowed. Snow gathered on his jacket, causing him to blend with
the storm. Sleep fell upon him.

Aedan woke thirty minutes later covered in snow. He shook off the
cold powder; his left arm sent pain throbs to his brain. He peered through
his hood enclosure and looked at a bookstore fifteen feet away. The retailer's
two-story window display remained illuminated with a plethora of books
presented. At the center stood a wooden ladder that tapered from eight feet
wide at the bottom to two feet at the top. On the lowest step were current
hardcover releases in fiction and non-fiction categories, spread across the
board. The ladder contained seven stairs, with each rung up the ladder
containing classic printed works for each century going backward in time.
On the top step was a small-scale model of the first Gutenberg Printing
Press, with a reprinted version of the Gutenberg Bible on display next to the
device. Aedan grinned.

My kids will learn to love printed books. I'll make sure of that.

As he stood, his body pulsated with intense pain.

It didn't take long for my muscles to stiffen.

He grimaced while hobbling south along Michigan Avenue. The
snow continued; he lowered his head as he moved.

He paused at the edge of the Chicago River Bridge. He felt a sense of déjà
vu as if he were reliving portions of his life.

Through the blowing snow, he looked at the river; he shivered as the
water and ice flowed under the edifice. He knew the span's deck rested
fewer than twenty feet from the water's surface, yet he could not escape the
fear he held of opened-aired drops higher than five feet.

The bridge traversed the river for a span not much longer than the length of a football field. The short distance did not matter to him because he had to cross the bridge, at night, in a storm, and through a dangerous layer of ice and snow. He detested all bridges in the Loop, and he loathed the way the Chicago River cut through the guts of the city.

He stepped onto the bridge walkway and began his crossing.

This feels surreal; it seems like minutes ago I crossed the same path with Charlie on our way to the Douglas Hotel.

He took small, controlled steps. As he reached the halfway point, wind gusts shoved him toward the roadway. He stopped his slide. A bright light caught his eye. He looked at the proud Wallace Building standing guard on the northwestern edge of the river. He knew the building well, as he did many edifices in the Loop; years working at Metric & Inch provided knowledge few others received. The building's white glazed terra-cotta outer panels reflected light across the river.

He looked at the higher levels of the famous tower and at the well-known clock installed 425 feet above the ground. At two stories tall, the clock structure had four separate time dials facing in all directions; each dial covered nineteen feet and seven inches in diameter. He looked at the massive clock; it was 02:00am on Thursday morning. Aedan turned away, and with determination, he walked off the bridge and aimed for the Douglas Hotel seeking a warm place to rest. He had no phone; no car and he didn't know what was happening to Ciara and Colin or where they were.

As he reached E. Wacker Drive, a silhouette of a man, a block away, caught his attention. Despite the blowing snow, the man's black hat came into focus, a fedora. Surprise washed over him.

Why is Michael here?

He walked through the deepening snow toward a vintage clock pole on the east side of Michigan Avenue. The pole, one of many in the Loop and aged from years providing the time to downtown crowds, offered no protection from the weather.

He strode to Michael. "What are you doing here?"

"Waiting for you."

"But how could you guess where I'd be?" Aedan frowned.

"After the hospital, it was clear where you would go."

He stared at him. "How do you know these things?"

Michael's always a step ahead of me; I wonder how.

"It does not matter how I gather data," Michael said. "I hope you will now accept the information I have for you."

Exhaustion after an active day stretching to over twenty grueling hours caused Aedan to ignore all the open and obvious questions. Instead, he broke into an uncontrollable shiver resulting from the pain in his left arm, along with the frigid storm swirling around them. He could not stop his trembling.

Snow clung to his red knit hat; tiny icicles hung from the hat's lower edge. His coat zipper rested two layers under the wintry mixture. He looked at the older man with confusion. You don't seem uncomfortable standing out here waiting for me? This is a brutal storm, but you act as if you're out for a stroll down Michigan Avenue."

"I am not troubled by the weather." He smiled. "I have experienced many Chicago winters; this storm does not impact me."

"I'm cold and tired. I need an hour rest before I take a train, the accident destroyed my car." He sighed. "I have to contact Ciara and Colin, but I'm exhausted." He stumbled. He gathered himself and stood more erect. "I planned to go to the Douglas Hotel lobby to take an hour nap if the staff doesn't kick me out."

"No, I have a better plan," Michael said. "Are you able to walk?"

"Yes, but my body has stiffened. How far do we have?"

"We will walk the correct distance. I will help you. The snow will slow us, but I guarantee that you will arrive unharmed at our destination," Michael said.

Resigned to the unstoppable progression of the strangest day of his life, he said, "Fine, Michael, you lead, I will do my best to follow."

Aedan followed Michael across Michigan Avenue. They walked through seven inches of snow covering the walkway. He looked at his feet, disappearing in the snow with each step.

This is nuts. These dress shoes won't last in this mess. I'll end up with frostbite on my toes.

He groaned, revealing his tremendous pain.

I want to go home.

He forced each foot to move in front of the other as he maintained a watchful eye on the older man guiding him.

How does that hat stay on Michael's head? It never budges.

He fixed his attention on the fedora while driving his feet forward.

The storm shrouded the Millennium Park Bean, across the street from them. They strained through a narrow wintry tunnel of snow and ice. He pushed through the raging snowstorm.

I must follow his hat. I'll keep my eyes on his stupid hat.

CHAPTER THIRTEEN

TAKING A TRAIN

Aedan kicked hard to reach the surface, not confident he pushed in the correct direction. Darkness surrounded him. He continued propelling his body upward, sensing he was raising with growing speed.

A sliver of light broke through the darkness.

He kicked harder, seeking the surface. His left arm pain slowed him; he worried the sharks might sense an easy kill as he drove himself to the water's surface. He slowed to make himself less noticeable to the predators he sensed swam in circles around him.

An intense light swath burst through to him; he felt sure he was getting closer. He continued kicking to the surface.

Michael ripped the blankets from Aedan's body and head.

Aedan leaped from the old couch and struggled to break free from his dream-like trance. He fought to understand his situation as exhaustion refused to release its grip. Pain emanated from his left arm. He stifled a scream.

Michael stood ten feet away, waiting for Aedan's mental recovery.

As he improved, he made slow circles observing the beautiful vintage ballroom. His expression betrayed his confusion as he wondered where he was. The room had no bed, no bathroom, no windows, and it contained a single door entry. Long vintage couches, chairs, and tables filled the ornate space. The ceiling stretched about fifteen feet above him, and it held elaborate lighting, which hung close to the plastered surface inside bowl-shaped treatments.

He walked back to the couch, where he sat in a heap. He looked at Michael and laughed; a real, deep, and cleansing laugh of embarrassment and relief. "Wow, I thought for sure those sharks would swallow me whole. The dream seemed so real."

Michael smiled with understanding and warmth. "The mind often produces interesting thoughts and images."

"Yes, Mikey, that's true. How long have I been out?"

He frowned. "My name is Michael. You would do good to remember that. You have been sleeping for ninety minutes."

"No way, it seemed like I was asleep for a week." He regained his composure; he looked around the room. "Where are we?"

"You do not remember?"

"Michael, that's a stupid question; if I remembered, would I ask?"

The older man smiled. "We are in the Prescot Hotel, in a private ballroom on the upper floor, a place few people ever see. We came here through the storm. Do you recall?"

"I remember the storm. How did I get into this room?"

"Do you remember I told you I would help get you to this place?"

"Yes, I remember."

"This is my favorite place in Chicago, and I have easy access to this private room." Michael smiled. "Are you now ready to listen?"

Aedan regained his strength. He had a look of shame after he realized that he had let down his guard. "Thank you for getting me out of the storm; I appreciate your help. I must contact my wife. What time is it?"

Michael sighed. "It is five o'clock on Thursday morning."

"That's good news. I'll take a train and be home for breakfast. I'll put my plan into effect, and I'll set everything straight with Ciara." He beamed with excitement. "She'll forgive me; there's no doubt. She'll forgive me."

"Please, Aedan, earlier you agreed to follow me."

"Stop this, now. I want to go home. What's wrong with you?"

Michael did not smile. "You have twenty-six hundred moments left. What you do with the time that remains is in your hands."

"Whatever, Michael, whatever you say." Aedan frowned as he walked to a vintage washbasin and mirror, where he did his best to clean his face. He straightened his clothes as he prepared to leave for Chicago's Union Station, under one mile from the Prescot Hotel.

I'm going home, no matter what Michael has to say.

His left arm still pulsed with a painful throb. His head remained a mess. He cleaned his wounds — making himself look less threatening. He placed fresh bandages across his forehead.

I hope this time they stay in place; I don't want to scare Colin; it won't help my case with Ciara if he cries.

He looked at Michael. "This will be a wonderful day." As he tied his shoes, he looked up long enough to see several old paintings decorating the walls. One image caught his eye. The picture showed Chicago's old Water Tower, built in 1869; it had remained standing after the Great Chicago Fire. The tower sat on Michigan Avenue within walking distance from Metric & Inch, a prominent location on the Magnificent Mile.

The artist depicted the tower standing alone; with evidence of the fire all around, in the distance, swirling red clouds filled the sky. The fire had destroyed over 2,000 city acres. Chicago lost seventy-three miles of roads, 120 miles of sidewalks, and 17,000 buildings. About one-third of the city's property value vanished.

The Water Tower was castle-like and stood at the forefront of the artwork, with its Joliet limestone gleaming against the background. It stood 154 feet tall and a historic landmark. It symbolized the city's recovery from the fire.

"Why is this painting here?"

"It reflects and records an important piece of history," Michael said.

"But, I don't get it, what's the tower have to do with the Prescot Hotel?"

"The original hotel fell to the flames of the Great Chicago Fire. There have been several iterations of the hotel over the decades. I had this canvas moved here to provide a sense of the fire's destruction. Take note that many earlier paintings of pre-fire structures and buildings exist throughout this ballroom. They all fell victim to the Great Fire."

"Why is any of that important?" Aedan looked curious.

"The disaster resulted in significant fire department changes for the city, with Chicago developing one of the strongest fire fighting forces in the nation, no small historical event. It is prudent to keep major events of the past fresh in our minds, we can learn from them." He smiled.

"Okay, I understand." He stared again at the painting; something troubled him, but he could not bring it to the surface, he let it go. "I'm getting out of here. I'll take the 05:39am train out of Union Station."

"Wait, I have something for you." He handed Aedan a small metal card about the size of a credit card. "You might need this."

"What is it?"

"Something you might need."

He frowned. "You're a strange one, Michael." He took the card. Without looking at it, he shoved it into his wallet. He left the ballroom and later walked through the Prescot Hotel exit doors. Aedan took Adams Street and moved with a slight left-leg-favoring limp, his body's reaction to the damage it received during the automobile accident. He stuffed his left hand into his coat pocket, relieving the pain.

I left home almost a full day ago; Ciara must be so mad at me. I will straighten out everything when I get there.

The air temperature had risen. Aedan saw little evidence of the snowstorm that had gripped the Loop, though water streams offered proof that the storm was not a dream.

He walked along Adams Street. The city had returned to life, with people, taxis, and vehicles moving about; though, with the holiday approaching, the Loop had less business traffic than usual. He increased his pace. The pain came to him in waves.

Twenty minutes to get to the train station. I'll soon be on my way home.

He pushed himself to S. Canal Street, where he would take a left turn to cross the final leg to the station. Aedan rushed through each city block with resolve; he ignored the Chicago River Bridge crossing.

I will do this; my plan will work.

Chicago Union Station lay west from the Chicago River. The station's most iconic structure, which was constructed in 1925, rested between W. Adams Street and W. Jackson Boulevard. Bedford limestone covered its exterior, which also offered massive old Corinthian columns for passengers to walk through.

Those entering the old structure often had a sense of having leaped back in time after they viewed the Great Hall. The building offered a visual throwback to the time trains ruled over all forms of travel. The massive hall's atrium stretched to 110 feet high, with a large barrel-shaped skylight. Brass and lavish decorations filled the building, with long age-old wooden high-backed benches placed throughout.

As he stopped between two towering columns outside the building, he noticed that the walk from the Prescot Hotel had not lessened his physical pain. His breathing deepened.

Aedan pushed through a set of old doors along S. Canal Street and walked down the steps of the Great Hall — he had no time to waste as he headed for the passageway connecting the old station to the new, where he moved on to the tracks and the trains.

Aedan looked at a digital wall clock, he had four minutes to spare. He found his departure track. Several additional trains rolled to a stop at the station. After entering the first coach, he dropped onto a bench seat and smiled. He planned to take a nap on the way out to his stop until a nagging voice interrupted his victorious demeanor.

"Good morning, Aedan," Máire said. She sat across the aisle.

He sighed with frustration.

CHAPTER FOURTEEN

A TRAIN STOP

Aedan's demeanor and expression displayed his contempt for her.

Máire pulled the bench in front of him to the opposite position, creating a two-seat arrangement in which double passenger seats faced each other. She smiled. "It is early for an outbound train. We have this car alone. Perhaps, now, you will speak with me?"

"I will not stop you from talking, lady."

She smiled. "You have experienced much. What have you learned?"

He stared at her in disbelief as the train lurched forward and away from Union Station. "Lady, many of my troubles began with you yesterday morning, so I'm not feeling all warm and fuzzy about allowing you back into my life. I'd rather you leave me alone." His voice became a cruel snarl. He looked through the window as the train inched away from Union Station. Darkness covered the inner rails, created by the massive infrastructure above. He squinted at the daylight breaking through at the end of the covered regions. He felt amazed that he was on his way home.

"Aedan, what have you learned?"

He glared at her with anger. "Listen to me, lady."

She interrupted. "My name is Máire." She smiled.

"I don't care what your name is. Your voice makes my skin crawl; at least Michael does not grate on my nerves as you do."

She smiled. "What have you learned?"

He sighed as he stood and began pacing the aisle while looking through the coach windows. "I've have learned that you're willing to push me, no matter how much resistance I offer, and I've learned that I'm sick of seeing you, and I've learned I want to go home. I plan to set things right with my wife. Other than that, I'd have much more appreciation for you if you left me alone. I don't want you here." He glared at her. "Did you hear me? I don't want you here."

"Mr. O'Beirne, we must follow your wishes." She smiled. "I have come here to offer help. You continue to refuse my attempts. I will follow your request and leave you now." She stood, returned the seat to its original position, and walked from the passenger car.

He flopped into his seat — filled with relief. He grinned as he realized the conversation had ended.

Maybe they're starting to learn to leave me alone.

He rested his head against the seatback. The train's melodic swaying calmed his nerves. In seconds, sleep fell upon him.

The train slowed as it approached another stop, causing him to wake. He looked through the large window to make sure he had not missed his station. Aedan beamed with joy and satisfaction; he had escaped the Loop and was on his way home. His confidence soared.

Ciara knows I love her, she'll forgive me, and she never needs to learn about my meeting with Bill. My plan is coming together.

He looked through the window.

The train slowed further and inched its way to the station. Familiar buildings came into his view; he had seen them for years. An aging four-story red-bricked office building lay across the street, north of the train station. To the left sat a hardware store, owned by a local family. To the right was a classic old bakery. During spring and fall months he liked to stop at the station for donuts and other baked goods. He loved the bakery's sugar twists, and cinnamon rolls, a high-calorie weakness dating back to his childhood, his mother cranked out baked treats he loved.

In the near distance, at the base of a slight hill and set well back from the roadway, stood twenty aging red-bricked shops, which formed an open courtyard. It was the place where townspeople gathered for seasonal events, including Christmas, Fourth of July, and all the rest. A tall Christmas tree stood at the center, various decorations hung across the courtyard, with decorative wreaths dangling from wires throughout the square. The location had all the trappings of small-town USA. He detested the look, he preferred the concrete, steel, and glass canyons found in the Loop. He scanned the area looking for Michael and Máire.

At least those nutcases aren't around.

As he looked at the area around the station, he noticed that the morning light revealed an ice layer covered the roads. The dangerous roads left him feeling relieved he was taking a train.

Close to the holiday traffic remained light with a scant two vehicles moving across the area. A road ran along each side of the tracks. Another street ran from the north to the south; it curved around the courtyard where it straightened and ran underneath the tracks.

He saw an auto one mile away moving south toward the station. The vehicle slid on the ice; the car had little hope of stopping on the declining icy road. Aedan shivered as he replayed the West Congress Parkway accident in his mind. His left arm sent him sharp pain throbs as a reminder of the damage he experienced.

He stood and glared through the window, his nerves on edge as the car continued to move toward the tracks. The vehicle did not lose speed as it glided over the slippery road, about two blocks away and out of control. To his right, he viewed a minivan with a woman driving, a car seat with a young boy sat in the middle of the second row. He stared at the scene; each second seemed to last for minutes. The female driver did not see the sliding car coming toward her. He realized they were on the same path; they would collide.

The conductor made the station call.

"No," he shouted as he pounded on the train window. "No more accidents, enough." He did not think any further, and he did not hesitate; he left the passenger coach and ran to the double-door train exit. The doors opened as he arrived. Without hesitation, he leaped through the opening and away from the train. Aedan slipped and fell on to the icy sidewalk, his left arm and leg taking the brunt. He screamed while fighting away the pain — he stood and began running.

Aedan used a sliding motion with his dress shoes to move along the icy surface to the road's center. He pulled off his coat and waved it back-and-forth over his head, ignoring his left arm pain, and he jumped up-and-down to get the driver's attention. He motioned for the woman to turn from the oncoming sliding car; they were two seconds from making contact. "Turn away, turn away, turn away," he screamed. He continued to flail his arms.

The woman saw him. She looked at the car moving to her right, she turned the minivan to her left, causing her vehicle to slide toward the underpass. She entered the icy decline, placing it on the same path, but ahead of the sliding auto.

The minivan had a slight lead on the car; it glided toward the road's lowest point, below the tracks. The auto continued moving along the declining icy surface about twenty feet behind her. He ran to the road's underpass, he slipped and fell on the ice, again slamming his left arm and his left leg; pain raced through his body. He remained in the street waiting for the horrific crashing sound. None came.

He climbed to his feet and slid to the underpass opening. He observed ice covering the road's surface to at least a quarter-inch thick beyond the underpass's edge; however, below the tracks, the street's surface remained free of ice. The minivan and car had found dry pavement on which to stop. Both vehicles sat near the bottom of the station underpass — no collision had occurred. He jumped up-and-down in excitement, understanding that he had helped to avert a nasty situation for those drivers. Aedan's leg and arm sent him pain waves each time he landed — he did not care since pain followed him everywhere.

He hobbled to the woman. "Are you okay?"

"Yes, thank you so much." Her face gripped in confusion, gratitude, and relief. She looked back at her five-year-old son playing as if nothing had happened. "Who are you? How did you do this?"

"I'm nobody, and I was sitting alone on the train, and saw the accident developing. I have a wife and a son. My boy is about the same age as your son; it freaked me out to see you and your child heading for a collision. It seemed too familiar. I had to do something. I'm sorry if I scared you. If you need help, you must make the call yourself, I lost my cell phone." He did not wait for her to respond; he walked from the scene and began limping back to the roadway.

As he came to the crest of the underpass hill, he ambled to the side of the road, which contained an uneven and less slippery surface. His pants had a tear in the left seam, and he had several left leg scrape wounds. He laughed; a deep cleansing sound, which revealed his relief and joy at being able to help them.

He looked at the empty train station. Several people waited for an inbound train. No one remained waiting on the outbound side; the train had left. He did not care; he would find a way home without the train.

His stomach churned with hunger. He looked at the courtyard, where Michael stood next to the towering Christmas tree. He crossed the vacant icy street. Aedan cupped his hands around his mouth to focus his voice. He shouted, "Hey, Michael, I'm starved and thirsty. I'm getting donuts and coffee. Join me or not, it's up to you." He laughed as he shook his head in disbelief.

They sure don't give up.

He walked into the bakery.

Aedan loved Strothmann's Bakery, which exuded the pleasant smell of donuts, cinnamon, cookies, brewed coffee, and all manners of baked goods. The enticing aromas wafted across the bakery's front interior space where early morning customers gathered. Because of the coming holiday, Aedan and Michael were the business's sole on-site customers though in the rear workers prepared last-minute treats ordered by their party patrons.

Aedan viewed two long counters, one on the left, and the second against the back wall displayed the day's product for sale. There were few baked goods for sale because the owners expected fewer walk-in customers with Christmas approaching.

The establishment took its name from Elmer and Betty Strothmann. The bakery was approaching its ninetieth year in business, operated by the grandchildren of its founders. Elmer Strothmann and Betty Humbold were born two houses apart in northern Germany in 1905; their parents emigrated from Germany. They moved to Chicago in April 1914, before the outbreak of World War I. They came from an extensive line of bakers, with Betty being the creative force and foundation behind the great success they enjoyed.

Aedan recalled that the young German friends remained together through the tumultuous war years following their move to the USA. In 1922, at age seventeen, Elmer and Betty married in St. Michael's Catholic Church in the area later known as Old Town. Years later, they moved to an incorporated suburb northwest of the city where they opened the bakery. The young Strothmann couple had fallen into a strategic choice; commuter rail services had a steady growth rate through most of their lives. The new train lines spurred development in communities stretching from Chicago to the city of Elgin in the far northwest suburbs. Train lines connected towns across the region, and they created access to jobs up-and-down the line, including in the Loop where Aedan worked.

The early railroad, from the mid-1800s on had no rail connections to Chicago, but in 1872 it built a line running from Wisconsin to Chicago, ending at Clinton and Carroll Streets. Later the line stopped at the first Union Station, which was built in 1881. In 1925, Union Station moved to the well-known structure of modern usage.

After the *Great Chicago Fire*, a need for bricks to help rebuild the city arose. The northern line ran through the village where two brick companies began their businesses. The single rail line helped haul the materials to Chicago during the time of great need for raw building supplies. At peak production, the plant manufactured 300,000 bricks a day. That activity resulted in the rail lines of modern Chicago suburbia.

Aedan viewed a large painting depicting the couple outside St. Michael's Church on their wedding day. The framed canvas adorned the back wall behind the long product counter. He stared at the painting; he had a gnawing sense of déjà vu as he looked at the swirling cloud formation in the background with a reddish glow at the center. "Why does this look so familiar?"

"Perhaps because it is of the same era as the painting you viewed in the Prescot Hotel," Michael said. He smiled.

"No, that has nothing to do with why it seems so familiar."

"Perhaps it is because St. Michael Church survived the Great Chicago Fire. They built the structure in 1869. In 1871, it received considerable damage to the fire's destructive flames."

He looked at Michael. "That is a significant connection. I didn't know the Church existed before the fire, but, that's not it either." He stared at the reddish cloud formation.

Those clouds trouble me. But why?

He finished his donuts while Michael waited with patience.

"Will you now let me share pertinent information with you?"

"No, that will not happen," Aedan said.

"May I ask why?"

"Michael, I have warmed-up to you over these many hours; I do not consider you as frustrating as Máire, but I am still sick of dealing with people I don't know. I have never required help to find my way in life, and I will not start now." He sipped his coffee. "I have a plan, and it's working well, which means I don't need your help. I'm on my way home."

"It is not a matter of finding your own way; it is a matter of accepting information that will assist you in making critical choices. Your time is lessening. You now have twenty-four-hundred moments left. A wise man receives timely information; it is a fool who plots to strive through life alone," Michael said.

Aedan glared through the window and across the tracks to the other side. He broke into a joyful smile as an idea entered his mind. "Well, perhaps you're right; perhaps I'm a fool. But a fool or not, I'll make my way through this on my own." He stood as he looked at Michael. "Will you do me one courtesy?"

"What is it?"

"Leave me alone and let me handle my life and this situation on my own. I think well when I'm not harassed, and I need you and Máire to leave me alone to make whatever choices I have in front of me. Will you do that?"

"Yes, we must respect your desires and requests. I hope you find the proper path, yet that rests in your hands," Michael said. "We hope you make the correct choices. We will not trouble you further." He stood and walked to the exit door.

"Stop," he shouted. "Do you mean what you say, or will I find you around the next bend?"

Michael smiled. "Son, I do not lie or speak falsehoods of any kind, ever. You have requested us to leave; we must respect your request." He placed his fedora on his head, and he pushed through the door and walked into the street.

Aedan filled with surprise when he saw Máire walking toward Michael at the road's center. The mysterious pair moved untroubled across the icy street. They were soon well out of sight.

He shivered despite the bakery's warm interior.

I hope I didn't make a mistake by sending them away.

Aedan remained sitting in a chair, taking time to drink another cup of coffee. He looked across the tracks and sighed.

The place won't open until eight or nine. I must wait.

Aedan beamed with excitement while looking at the shops along the street on the south side of the tracks.

Aedan left the bakery and walked over the tracks at the passenger sidewalk. He crossed the street. He entered the cell phone carrier's retail location and advanced to the sales counter, where he approached a female technician. "I have your service, but I lost my phone and need to get a new one right away, and I want the same contract. I'll also need you to download my contacts because they were on my lost device."

"Sir, I can't offer you the same cell number. We have a problem with our carry forward assignment system. It will return to full operation by eleven o'clock this morning," she said. "You could come back then."

He frowned. "I need it sooner. Is it possible to receive a new cell number, and can you download my contacts to the new device?"

"Yes, I can do that," she said.

"I'm in a hurry."

"No problem, Sir."

"Thank you," Aedan said.

Twenty minutes later, he left the store with a new cell. He walked toward a new car dealership. He grinned. His demeanor had improved since receiving his new phone.

Aedan limped along while dialing Ciara's cell, no answer.

He called their home landline, no response, the call switched to their answering machine.

He dialed numbers for all their neighbors; there were no replies as various voice mail systems picked up.

He called his in-laws, no one picked up. His call switched to their digital answering machine.

He repeated all calls several times, leaving messages after each. Confusion and concern consumed him.

He arrived at the upscale suburban auto dealership.

Ciara hated my mega-beater. This will show her I've changed.

Aedan pushed through the entrance doors leading into the dealership and walked to a brown metallic X5 SUV placed in a prominent position on the showroom floor. After glancing at the sticker, he looked inside to make sure it contained three rows. Aedan grinned as he thought about the surprised look Ciara would have after seeing his new purchase.

A woman from sales approached. She looked tired as if she had not yet consumed her morning coffee and did not want to deal with customers on the day before Christmas Eve. She did her best to reflect a joyful demeanor though she acted as if she would rather be any place, but there. "Good morning, Sir, Merry Christmas to you." She offered a weak smile as she looked away, not expecting anything significant to happen.

"I'll take this SUV, but this transaction must be quick because I've no time to waste. If you give me ten percent off the sticker price; I'll have the funds for the purchase price transferred to the dealership within thirty minutes. Let me know the final number as soon as possible, so I experience no delays waiting around. I expect to leave with the new vehicle within an hour, and I want a full-sized spare and a full-sized tire iron placed in the storage area." Aedan grinned when he saw her surprised expression.

Cash buyers were rare; her attitude changed in an instant. She thanked him, and in a flash, she left him to go work on his purchase. As she walked away, Aedan laughed when he heard her whisper, "Merry Christmas to me."

Cash purchases sure help cut out a lot of nonsense.

The staff had welcomed him to their dealership family as they hurried to complete the deal. Aedan wandered around looking at the other cars while waiting for the transaction to close. He pulled his cell phone from his pocket and dialed Ciara's cell number, no answer.

The salesperson approached. "Sir, the documents are ready to sign."

"That's good news," he said.

This is getting out of hand. Where could Ciara be? Why would she ignore me like this? This is not like her.

After maneuvering the SUV to the roadway, Aedan turned left and punched the accelerator, increasing its speed in a flash. He was excited and could not wait to show Ciara his new vehicle. A grin filled his expression as he tapped on the steering wheel to the beat of the music coming from the high-end sound system.

An image of Ciara and Colin entered his mind. He lost his smile as he pulled the pink heart-shaped note from his pants pocket. He read it in silence. Sadness and worry caused him to lose his upbeat mood.

Where are they, and why won't she answer my calls.

He pressed hard on the accelerator pedal.

CHAPTER FIFTEEN

HOME WITHOUT ITS HEART

Aedan pulled the SUV onto his home's street. Snow blanketed the road's surface. He shook his head in disgust.

This town never clears the streets well.

He slowed the vehicle as he drove toward his residence at 11135 Washington Street. Victorian-style houses lined the block, with each one set well back from the roadway. The one-hundred-year-old neighborhood had a mature appearance, with massive oak trees off the curbs creating a green canopy stretching from side-to-side, allowing a smattering of sunlight through. Anticipation had him sweating as he pulled into his driveway. The SUV carved a path through the seven inches of snow remaining on the drive. He felt as if time had stretched since he last saw his home, which gave him a sense of surreal foreboding.

He viewed the unattached garage at the far end of the driveway, set back about fifteen feet from the main house. Both manual garage doors were open; no cars were there. He parked in the middle of the driveway. He walked to the garage through the snow.

It's empty. No car. I doubt they're home. What's going on with them?

Turning toward the driveway, he looked at the new vehicle thirty feet away. Disappointment and pain covered his face.

There goes that surprise. I so much hoped I'd find Ciara and Colin home. Where are they?

He walked to the home's rear door. His energy level had dropped since finding the garage empty.

I hate how I left them Wednesday morning — wish I could take that back, and I didn't tell them I love them. I've never left home like that.

He walked into the kitchen through the rear door, reversing his steps from the previous morning. He looked around the room. His sad expression revealed his fear and loneliness. It gave him a creepy feeling to see his own kitchen after the many struggles he endured to get home, now it was empty, and it felt as if the heart had gone out of the place.

He examined the room, searching for clues to where they had gone. The stool Colin used for breakfast remained positioned next to the island, with cereal spread on the floor below. He smiled as he recalled Colin dropping food onto the floor.

The kid cracks me up — man, I miss him.

The cookies, which had fallen on him, remained scattered on the floor, including the baking sheet that burned his back. His dried blood still covered sections of the ceramic tile. He exhaled with fear. The room looked terrible; Ciara had left the floor a mess.

Something happened. Ciara would not leave the house like this.

His concern changed to a growing fear as he continued assessing the kitchen landscape. A small bowl sat on the counter which contained the pieces of the angel ornament he had stepped on and crushed. He searched for a sign of where Ciara was and why she had left in such a hurry. Nothing in the house had changed since Wednesday morning, not the slightest clue where they had gone. He hoped he could find evidence somewhere else in the house.

I can't let her see the place in such a terrible state.

He hobbled to the cookies and to the baking sheet, he snatched them from the floor. The cookies landed in the trash, and he threw the baking sheet into the sink. He swept the cereal from the floor, he tossed it into the wastebasket. After taking a spray bottle and paper towels from under the sink, he kneeled on the tile and scrubbed the floor. He stepped back and surveyed the room.

Well, at least now it's cleaner.

Aedan took the back stairway to the second floor, where he searched for clues. He found blood on the bathroom floor, proof of the injury he suffered to his left foot. Aedan did not want her to come home to his bloody mess. Aedan grabbed a towel from the rack and cleaned the blood from the floor; he tossed it into a hamper.

He found his used clothes still lying on the bedroom floor, yet there was nothing to help him locate his family. Everything looked as if he had left two minutes ago.

He ambled down the front stairs to the living room where he stopped at the last step and stared at the decorated Christmas tree stretching from floor-to-ceiling close to his living room window. The tree lights remained on; they illuminated the room with an unnerving festive atmosphere. Tree ornaments, both old and new, filled the branches. His anxiety rose.

She wouldn't leave the Christmas lights on. Perhaps I should call the cops.

He sat in a chair. He frowned at seeing a stack of gifts Ciara had already placed under the tree. So close to Christmas everything appeared as it should, except Ciara and Colin were missing and didn't know what to do next. He sighed.

Should I call the cops? I haven't talked to her for more than a day.

He pounded his right hand against the arm of the chair. Aedan did not know his next move and worry filled his mind while recalling Michael speaking to him about fewer moments. He could not see how less time could have anything to do with his family's disappearance. Aedan pounded again-and-again trying to search his mind for clues.

An almost inaudible sound came from their home office in the hallway, across from the bathroom. Aedan hobbled to the noise and found a television with its power on, installed on the left wall, its volume set to a low level. He approached the desk and searched through the papers piled on the work surface. "There's nothing, nothing anywhere," he shouted. His voice cracked under the strain of increased worry.

He looked at the television. A midday news broadcast filled the screen. With interest, he raised the volume so he could hear the transmission. The female anchorperson began the program by updating the viewers about the multi-car accident on the interstate close to the Loop Wednesday morning. The crash involved over one-hundred cars, and terrible fires had broken out, with at least ten vehicles suffering complete destruction. Emergency personnel rushed one-hundred people to area hospitals. Video film clips showed the Loop filled with emergency vehicles moving through the towering office buildings and towers. Sirens blared for as long as two hours. Loop traffic had come to a near standstill as emergency crews drove back-and-forth through the streets.

Saint John's — they took most of those people to Saint John Hospital. I let nothing in; I remained oblivious to it all.

Stunned, he listened to the news anchor describe how crews freed several people from their cars, including women and children. It took hours to clear the highway of vehicles, in time for the freak winter storm, which had descended upon the lakefront and Loop areas later that night.

He learned the accident occurred at 08:35am on Wednesday morning. He strained to understand everything he had experienced. His mind strained to search for some clue.

I remained stuck with Michael when the accident happened. That's why I didn't hear all the sirens. The elevator insulated me from the world for two hours; the entire time ambulances were busy rushing people to area hospitals.

He wracked his mind for relevant events from the previous day. He tried to determine what he was missing. Stress lines creased his sweaty forehead. He looked around the room, his confusion and worry increased.

I remember, he couldn't get a drink at the hospital — the place was flooded with patients from the accident. Charlie left the ER before he received help.

Aedan drummed his right hand against the edge of the desk. He tried to connect Charlie to Ciara's and Colin's disappearance, yet he could think of no link since his family remained forty miles away in the suburbs when his friend was in the hospital.

Aedan turned off the television and looked at a large stack of papers, he shoved it from the desk in an outburst of frustration. The papers scattered across the small room. "Where are they?" Aedan shouted. "What am I missing?"

He wandered back to the living room. Exhausted, he sat in a chair.

Who can I call, where should I go, what can I do to find them?

Using his cell phone, dialed Ciara, no answer.

Dialed his in-laws, no response at their home phone number.

His expression revealed his sense of hopelessness.

He began walking in a circular path from the living room, through the dining room, into the kitchen, down the hallway and back to the living room. He continued walking the path over-and-over trying to calm his nerves while thinking through his options. After pausing in the living room, he looked at the tree and did not have the heart to turn the lights off.

Anguish consumed him.

I made Colin worry about Christmas. Man, that was a terrible thing for me to do to the kid.

He collapsed into a living room chair, physical and mental exhaustion had taken its toll.

Where are you, Ciara? How am I going to find you?

CHAPTER SIXTEEN

DOOR BREAKING

Aedan detested sitting in the empty house. Everything he saw reminded him of his missing family.

I must do something.

He walked to the front door and through to the outside.

I'll figure this out. I'm missing something important.

Aedan trudged through the snow on his sidewalk and driveway, heading to his neighbor's home. Rang the doorbell, no answer. Rang a second time and a third. He pounded on the door. "Come on, Frank, your car is in the driveway," he shouted.

The door opened a crack. "What do you want?" Frank said.

"I need your help."

Frank began to shut the door.

Aedan shoved his left leg into the opening, blocking the doorway.

"Why should I help you? You came close to crushing my foot with your car yesterday. Remove your leg, or I'll break it." He glared at him.

Aedan softened his expression. "I'm sorry about that, you didn't deserve that treatment, but right now I need your help."

Frank looked at him with shock. "You're saying you're sorry for something? Man, this must be the first apology I have ever heard from you." He laughed. "You look a mess. What's happened to you?" He released the door, allowing Aedan free access.

"I can't find Ciara and Colin and haven't heard from her since I left yesterday morning, not a word. I need someone to help me work this through, and I'm sorry for behaving like such a jerk yesterday. She told me she's pregnant again, and I had a meltdown. I acted like an idiot. Have you or Cindy seen them?"

"I haven't seen them," he said. "Come in." He turned to the stairway behind him. "Cindy, have you seen Ciara or Colin?"

Cindy Ausio, Frank's thin and tall wife, came to the top of the stairs. "No, why, should I have?

"When did you last see her?" Frank said.

Cindy said, "I saw her leave, with Colin, yesterday around seven in the morning. I recall she didn't close the garage doors."

Aedan sat on the last stairway step, thinking.

"Did you find a letter or anything at home?" Frank said.

"No, nothing, nothing anywhere."

"Did you have a bad fight?" Cindy walked down the steps.

"I left in a crummy manner yesterday. I wasn't supportive of the new baby coming, but it wasn't a terrible fight, at least I didn't think so."

"Could she be with her parents," Frank said

"I've called them several times, there's no answer."

"Perhaps she's at her parent's house, but ignoring you," Frank said.

"Why would she do that? It's almost Christmas; this is a horrible time for her to stop talking to me."

Cindy on a step. "Sometimes you *can* be a real jerk."

"Yeah, I know," he said with resignation. "But that's not new."

"Listen to me," Cindy said. "Ciara's pregnancy is new to her too. I doubt she wanted to deal with you behaving like a jerk. Her patience might have worn thin. She might be mad enough to make you squirm for a while. Women want to feel supported when they're pregnant."

His demeanor improved. "You're right. I'll drive over to Ciara's parents; they'll be there." He stood. "Cindy, Frank, thank you. I'm sure you're correct." He walked from their home.

He entered his vehicle and sped away from his home.

She'll be there — she used to visit her mom after we married, every time I made her angry.

He drummed his right hand against the steering wheel to keep the beat with the music.

Ciara's parents lived on St. Gregory Court, three miles from their home. He pulled into their long driveway, leading to a substantial house set back about one hundred feet from the road, in an exclusive subdivision. A professional service had already cleared the snow from the driveway.

He walked to the front door, inside a wrap-around porch about ten feet deep. Rang the doorbell, no answer. Rang again, nothing.

I am tired of all these roadblocks.

He pounded on the door. "Ciara," he shouted. No response.

She'd ignore me if she's still angry.

He tried the door and found it locked.

I've had enough of this.

Aedan slammed his right fist into the jam, then hobbled to the SUV and to its rear storage space. He extracted the full-sized tire iron. It had a flat blade on one end and a hefty bolt socket on the other side.

He returned to the front door and used the tire iron to pry the lock open; it failed. Aedan thrust the flat end into a crack in the doorjamb. He pushed against the bolt end while driving his legs. His left leg and arm sent his mind waves of pain as he pushed harder. Soon, the door burst open as the frame shattered under stress.

He ran back to the SUV and tossed the tire iron into the rear, returned to the house while ignoring the growing pain in his left leg and walked into the quiet home. He groaned after a wall-mounted security panel light flashed – the system had sent a silent alarm to the police.

I'm up to my ears in it now.

He turned on the interior lights as he moved through the home. He walked along the central hallway leading to the kitchen and to the back of the house. "Ciara," he shouted. No one responded.

He hobbled to the basement door, called her name, no answer.

Sirens filled the air. Aedan increased the pace of his search.

After climbing the stairs to the second floor, he called her name as he entered each bedroom, nothing. He limped down the rear stairway and into a large media room built for watching movies and entertaining.

"Ciara," he shouted. No answer. He sighed as he sat in a stadium-style chair, waiting for the police.

Where are they? I am out of ideas — where are they?

Four police officers approached the house, ready to extract their weapons if required. Two officers walked to the front door. After seeing evidence of forced entry, they pulled their firearms. The other cops moved to the rear, to help cover attempts to escape.

"I'm in here," shouted Aedan.

The officers, using due caution, entered the media room with their weapons drawn.

Aedan sat in a rear seat. The overhead lights were on.

"Sir put your hands on the chair in front of you," barked the lead officer.

He obeyed. "I'm a family member."

"I'm Officer Jackson," the lead cop said. "My partner is Officer Hunter. Why is your forehead covered in blood?"

"It's been a rough day. I have taken several blows to my head."

Hunter walked to Aedan. He conducted a careful search of him, ensuring that he carried no weapons. He pulled his hands behind his back, cuffed him.

"Why must you do that?" Aedan winced with pain.

"Sir, you broke into this home," Jackson said.

"Yes — I'm a family member." His left arm sent him sharp pain waves; the result of the position caused by the cuffs.

"Sir, this is not your home. Correct?" Jackson said.

"Correct, it belongs to my wife's parents."

Hunter yanked him from his seat. "We need to see identification."

"Are you kidding me?" His anger and frustration rose. Pain caused him to shiver — he forced it away. "I'm looking for — "

Jackson interrupted. "Stop, Sir, we will listen to your story, but do not resist, or we'll make a formal arrest. Is that clear?"

"Yes," he said. "Please, remove the cuffs so I can get my ID."

Hunter grabbed Aedan, spun him around, and unlocked the handcuffs. "We cuff people for our protection. We have no way of knowing if a person is dangerous or not." He smiled with warmth.

Aedan retrieved his wallet. He handed his driver's license to Officer Jackson. "I live three miles from here, on Washington Street, four blocks east of Oak Creek. I *am* family. This house belongs to my in-laws."

"You live close to Oak Creek?" Hunter said with interest.

"A mile or so from the creek. Why?"

"No reason. I loved the place when I was a kid. Sometimes, I take my seven-year-old nephew there. Little Caiden likes to catch fish, and he loves the forest surrounding the creek. He's made the place his home away from home. I don't give him grief about it; the boy lost his mom last year. His dad, my younger brother, Jaydan, is raising him. I love my brother, but he's making a mess of the kid, it's a shame." He grinned.

Jackson glared at Hunter. "Noah, stop socializing with him, we have work to do." He entered Aedan's data into his pad, and then he pressed send. "We'll have a background check on him in a few minutes."

"Can I sit down? It hurts to stand."

Hunter motioned for him to sit. "Why did you break in?"

"I'm worried about my wife and son. I haven't seen them or heard from them since yesterday morning. It's the Christmas season; my wife would not disappear like this," Aedan said.

Hunter frowned. "You avoided my question. Why did you break in?"

"I thought she and my son might be here. Sometimes, when my wife gets mad at me, she comes here to her parents."

"How often does that happen?" Jackson said.

"Hey, rarely, I love my wife," Aedan's anger soared.

The two officers, who were covering the outside rear of the home, walked into the room.

Jackson looked at the cops. "Search the rest of the house, top to bottom. Make sure no one else is in the building."

"I already did that." Aedan frowned. "Will you help me, or not?"

Jackson ignored him. "Mr. O'Beirne, your background check came back. You have a spotless record. However, we still must do our jobs, which means we must search the house because you broke in. You might as well relax because this will not end until we have done our jobs."

"Did you have a fight with your wife?" Hunter said.

"Yes, she told me she's pregnant again, and I didn't react well, at all."

The officers broke into knowing smiles.

"When I left our home around seven yesterday morning, there was nothing wrong with Ciara and Colin. I've called her cell and our home, no one answers" — he beamed with sudden excitement — "but wait, I can prove I made those calls."

"How?" Hunter said.

"The answering machine; we have to find their answering machine." He walked to the kitchen, where he searched for the house telephone. Finding it on the counter, with a digital message recorder, he looked at the officers. "This proves what I'm saying."

"How?" Jackson said.

"I called my wife's parents here at their house. They never answered; my calls switched to their machine every time." His face became brighter. "The machine has recordings of me saying I'm looking for Ciara and Colin. There must be at least five messages from me. I had hoped her parents knew where they were." He pressed play. They listened to the first message.

"Stop, we've heard enough," Jackson said.

Aedan stopped the recording. He looked at them.

"Mr. O'Beirne, all that proves is that you called your in-laws, nothing more than that. So, where are your in-laws? We have to talk to them about this situation," Jackson said.

Aedan looked confused. "I wish I knew. That's part of the mystery. It's as if my family and her parents disappeared. I can't figure out where they are."

Hunter approached. "They're in London. They left their itinerary and contact information on the counter." He raised the paper to them. "They had a ten o'clock flight yesterday morning."

"Do you not like your wife's parents?" Jackson said.

"Why do you ask that?"

"Because you didn't know they traveled to Europe. It seems you're not aware of things happening in your own family." Jackson frowned.

Aedan's expression revealed his anger. "What in the world's wrong with you? I don't monitor what they're doing. They're grown people, and they can do whatever they want. I'm sure my wife mentioned it to me, but that stuff doesn't take hold in my mind. I'm not good at scheduling and people stuff."

Jackson grinned. "I hear you, Mr. O'Beirne. I wait for my wife to tell me what's on the schedule for any day; the rest rushes through my mind." He laughed.

Aedan looked at them. "I don't have the cell numbers for her parents, or else I would have known about their trip yesterday when I first tried calling them. I don't remember Ciara telling me her parents were taking a vacation, but I'm sure she did, and I didn't commit it to memory."

"Mr. O'Beirne, I think we're done, for now. We have enough to create a report for your missing wife and son; we'll get that moving after we return to the station. In the meantime, you need to contact and include everyone you and your wife know to help find her and your son. You're free to go, but we can't allow you to remain in this home," Jackson said.

"I understand, and I will do as you suggest." His shoulders slumped with sadness. "I'm no closer to finding my family."

"The difference is, Mr. O'Beirne, we're joining you in your hunt for them, and we're good at our jobs," Jackson said. "We'll contact your in-laws and question them. We will call you if we learn anything."

"Thank you, officers." He left the house.

Now, what do I do? Ciara, where are you?

CHAPTER SEVENTEEN

BUSINESS DISTRICT

Aedan stopped at the end of the driveway and hobbled through the snow into the open garage. He turned on the light by pulling a hanging string leading to an old single bulb receptacle, walked to the first overhead door, yanked it to the ground and latched it in place.

As he approached the second door, a white card on the concrete floor drew his attention. He walked to it and snatched it from the oily surface. It was Doctor Miller's business card, with the appointment time.

Ciara keeps everything organized. She runs this place and our family so well — I could never do the things she does.

He yanked the second door to the ground, latched it in place, returned to the house and to the living room, where he spent the next two hours calling everyone in their lives, friends, and extended family members, trying to build a network. No one had seen Ciara.

Blood drops from his head wounds, mixed with sweat, dripped into his eyes. He stumbled into the kitchen, removed the mixture with a towel.

Hunger and thirst consumed him. He grabbed a beer and a hotdog from the refrigerator. He microwaved the hot dog and bun while he looked at Doctor Miller's business card posted on the fridge. The appointment time on the last line read: *3:00pm, Wednesday, December 22*. He ambled to the calendar hanging on the wall next to the pantry — the appointment was recorded there too.

He took long swigs from the beer as he stared at the business card. Nothing stood out to him. He felt sure he was missing something — it gnawed at him as he stared at the business card.

He returned to the chair in the living room where he ate the hotdog and downed the beer. The clock completed its hour chime cycle, and then an eerie silence fell. He tried to remember what Michael said about moments; he strived to recall the last number the older man cited.

We were in the bakery; that's the last time he told me how many moments I have left. I must remember.

He strained to recall while tapping his right index finger on his thigh.

What significance could the number hold? It seemed like a countdown. What does it mean? It seems there is a certain amount of time until something happens, but how does it apply to Ciara or Colin? What does it all mean?

He sat back in mental weariness. He continued sifting through his memory for the number.

I sense the number is significant. Where's Michael?

He frowned.

At the bakery, I told them to get out of my life. I'm such a stubborn fool. I can't remember the number.

Aedan groaned in frustration, and then he sighed with resignation.

While staring at the business card, wondering, again, what information evaded his grasp, exhaustion rushed over him — sleep came upon him like an unstoppable wave. He still held the doctor's business card.

The grandfather clock's second hand woke him, as it moved one ticking second after another. He fought to break free from the vice-grip sleep held on him. Through blurry eyes, he looked closer.

Oh no, it's three in the morning.

He came to a seated position.

I can't believe what a fool I am — sleeping as if I haven't a care in the world. How could I do that?

His body had stiffened in his sleep; it sent rippling waves of intense pain to his mind. He doubled over while clutching his arm. The doctor's business card jettisoned from his right hand; it fluttered before his eyes and then it floated to the carpeted floor. He snatched it and twirled it in his right hand.

What am I missing with this business card; it keeps gnawing at me every time I look at it. It's something obvious.

Just then, his excitement rose as he continued staring at the card. He left the living room and walked through the rear door, headed for the X5.

Aedan turned onto Maple Street, part of the town's business district. Old red-bricked three-story buildings lined the street for three blocks. The snow covering the sidewalks and the parking lots added to the classic winter setting.

Kids in Oak Valley sure got their wish for a white Christmas.

He found the building at the corner of Maple and Oak Street. He turned right onto Oak Street and guided the SUV to the parking lot behind the doctor's building. The lot was empty, he drove around the business district. He found no other vehicles. He continued searching.

It's creepy here — like a ghost town.

He returned to the parking lot behind Dr. Miller's office, where he parked and left the vehicle and strode to the building's rear, where all patients accessed the medical offices, on the first floor. He pulled on the doors.

They're locked — no surprise, it's early on Christmas Eve.

While looking inside the dark building, he pounded on the thick glass, no response — repeated his assault, nothing. Ciara was not there. He hoped to see her car or some other clue, but there was nothing, not a single person or car in sight.

Aedan walked to the Maple Street entrance, tried the door, it opened.

They forgot to check these locks.

He strode into the lobby, and then he hobbled along the hallway leading to Dr. Miller's offices in the rear. He pulled on the locked door leading to her medical practice. In growing despair, he pounded on the glass. "Ciara, Ciara," he shouted. He heard the wailing of sirens approaching.

A single squad approached the building, sirens, and lights pulsing.

Aedan cleared the snow from a street-side bench outside the building's Maple Street entrance — he sat and waited as the squad stopped at the center of the intersection.

Officer Noah Hunter opened the cruiser's door and walked to him. "O'Beirne, haven't you seen enough of us?"

A second patrol car stopped along the Oak Street side. Officer Jackson exited the vehicle and walked to Aedan. "Are you trying to get arrested?"

"No, this is our pediatrician's office building." He frowned. "I'm looking for my family. I was hoping I'd find them here."

"O'Beirne, we told you we are on the case," Hunter said.

"I understand, but my wife and son are missing. What would you do if your wife and son were missing? Would you sit around waiting, or would you look in places they might be? I can't sit in my empty house doing nothing. I have to find them." His expression revealed his resolve.

"This not a home, and it's not a hospital. Why would you think you'd find them here?" Hunter said.

He shrugged his shoulders. "I'm going to places they might have been. What other options do I have? I will not wait at home."

Jackson frowned. "How did you get into the building?"

"The door was unlocked," he pointed.

"Noah, watch him," Jackson said. He walked to the door and examined the entry. Jackson searched the hallway looking for damage. Nothing was out of place, he returned to the Maple Street side and to Aedan. "This time you haven't destroyed property. But if we catch you breaking into another building, we will arrest you with formal charges."

"I understand." His shoulders slumped.

"Get out of here, O'Beirne. Do nothing like this again," Hunter said.

He walked to the SUV, shivering in the cold. Once inside the vehicle, with pent-up frustration, he pounded the steering wheel.

Where can they be?

Aedan's lonely and dark drive along snow-filled Trevor Street brightened when he approached Dug's Dog Fortress, a favorite stop for many Oak Valley residents.

The classic food stand, founded by Douglas Cooke, a man from an English family, became an instant success after its establishment in 1933. In continuous operation since its inception, and managed by Cooke family members, the stand remained in its original location at the corner of Trevor and Wilson streets.

Aedan grinned as he looked at the eatery's towering illuminated vertical bun with a hotdog inside, it had a smile at the top of the hotdog, and a king's crown sat atop. The unique figure stood at the center of the structure's roof. A human-looking arm and hand extended from the figure's side; the hand clutched a pointed spear in an upright King-like pose. Castle-styled parapets circled the outer wall. The distinctive character contained glowing neon lights installed along its edges, making it visible in the dark from miles away.

Dug's is the one place in this town I love; best hot dogs ever.

He left the neon lights behind as he moved to a darker section of the village which contained fewer homes and businesses. The darkness increased when he approached the murky and ominous Oak Valley Forest on his left.

Oak Creek flows through those trees, it always floods in the spring, wreaking havoc on Trevor Street.

He scowled as he investigated the darkness of the forest.

I wonder why Hunter's nephew loves the place; it's creepy.

Aedan swerved around a deer on the road. He turned right on President's Drive and headed to his home on Washington Street.

The kitchen phone rang as he entered — he gritted his teeth through his left leg pain. After limping to the device as the soreness on his left side increased, he extracted the handset. "Hello?"

"Aedan?"

"Yes, this is Aedan," he said. "Who is this?"

"Hey, buddy; this is Frank from next door, sorry for calling so early in the morning. We couldn't sleep. We're worried about Ciara and Colin. Did you find them or hear anything?"

"No. I'm sorry, nothing yet. The police haven't called, and I'm no closer to a solution. I'm still working it through, I'll call you if I find them or if I hear anything." He returned the handset to the base.

The telephone's recorder light flashed; a digital number revealed there were fifteen new messages. Aedan looked at the machine with a stunned expression knowing that after searching everywhere in the house, he never thought about the traditional landline phone.

Aedan snatched the handset and pushed the caller ID search. He scanned backward through the calls viewing the incoming numbers looking for anything that could help. He continued moving through the messages until he stopped at one that grabbed his immediate attention.

It's Doctor Miller's cell number from Wednesday. What the — He looked at the card to check the number.

That's her cell number.

While staring at the card, his expression betrayed his surprise. He saw, for the first time, that Doctor Miller had two offices. One in Oak Valley, and the second in downtown Chicago at 3960 N. Franklin Street, Suite 890, 20th floor.

Ciara had a three o'clock appointment out here. I never thought she'd be anywhere but, Oak Valley. What a fool I am.

In frustration, he kicked a lower cabinet door panel. The wood broke under the assault. He did not notice the pain stemming from his left leg.

He pressed play on the recorder.

"*This is Dr. Miller calling for Ciara O'Beirne…,*" the recording stopped with an abrupt click.

She picked up in the middle of the call. What's the rest of the message? Why did the doctor call?

While looking at the business card, he paced back and forth until the pain caused him to sit at the kitchen island counter. He leaned on his right arm to relieve the pain from his left side; the effort did not help as waves of pain emanated from his left arm and leg. He ignored the pain, a valuable learned trait he had developed since leaving home Wednesday morning.

The doctor must have changed the appointment to the downtown site.

His mind filled with visions of the interstate accident close to the Loop. He continued pacing.

It makes sense, it's the holiday season, and the doctor had appointments available downtown. Ciara drove to the Loop for an early consult, and she had to hurry. She took Colin with her. She must have been there around the same time the power went out in the elevator. If that's correct, then they were only a few miles away from me when I was in the elevator.

He did not want to accept the obvious; he extracted it from his mind with great mental pain and distress.

Ciara was in the accident on the interstate. That's why I haven't heard from her, and that's why I haven't been able to contact her. It explains everything except where they are now.

Filled with fear, he stopped pacing.

But why didn't the medical professionals contact me?

He forced himself to focus. He recalled the news broadcast had provided details about the accident.

Perhaps they're in a hospital. If Ciara and her belongings perished in a car fire, and if she and Colin are unconscious, or worse, the hospital might not identify them in time. Oh, man, if that's true, it's not good, at all.

He fell into a shiver as his mind filled with images of Ciara and their little boy Colin. His breathing labored, and blood-filled sweat covered his forehead. He shook his head back-and-forth as if to cast off the alarm saturating his mind. His jaw set in a tight clench.

I won't let myself think the worse; they need me to find them, and the sooner, the better. Ciara and Colin will be okay.

He snatched the telephone handset. The operator connected him to Saint John Hospital.

A Service Representative answered. "May I help you," she said.

"Yes, I'm looking for a patient by the name of Ciara O'Beirne."

She searched. "Sir, we do not have anyone registered under that name."

"Try Colin O'Beirne."

"I'm sorry, Sir, we do not have anyone registered under that last name."

"Does the hospital have an area set aside for unidentified patients?"

"Yes, Sir."

The woman sounded familiar to him as if he had heard her voice before. His tone became firm, severe. "My name is Aedan O'Beirne. I am trying to find my wife and son. Is it possible they were in an accident on the interstate on Wednesday? Is it conceivable they are in your hospital, but not identified?"

"Sir, I do not see — "

Aedan interrupted her. "If their belongings perished in an accident, and if they are unconscious, isn't it possible they're in the hospital and not yet identified?"

"Yes, Sir, that is possible."

Her voice haunted him, it was so familiar, he could not determine why. "Where would the hospital place those patients?"

"On the third floor, room nine-hundred and sixty, unless they require intensive care," she said. "But, Sir, that's a secured location. You cannot enter that space."

Confusion consumed him while listening to her. Her voice rang through his mind; he searched for where he heard it before.

"Is there anything else you need, Sir?"

"No, thank you." He hung up the telephone. He ignored thoughts about her voice. As he turned from the phone, he came to a sudden halt; he grinned.

I remember now. Twenty-four-hundred moments, that's what Michael told me at the bakery. What does it mean?

Aedan opened a drawer and extracted a calculator. He divided twenty-four hundred by sixty minutes per hour.

There were forty hours left when we were in the bakery at eight yesterday morning.

He grimaced as he carried the time forward.

"Midnight tonight," he said aloud. "That's the start of Christmas Day. What happens then, and what will it mean for Ciara and Colin?"

CHAPTER EIGHTEEN

BOUND FOR 3960

Aedan paced the kitchen floor. He stopped at the counter where he grabbed a pen and paper. He jotted down the various numbers he could recall: 3540; 3301; 2600, and 2400. Now that he understood the numbers represented time he had left; it was easy for him to notice Michael and Máire had provided the information in a countdown format.

They tried over-and-over to tell me. I am such a stubborn fool.

His left leg throbbed. He returned to pacing to help bring blood flow back to his sore muscles. Realizing that there were 1200 moments left, he set himself to creating a plan.

Since the hospital keeps unidentified patients on the third floor, Ciara and Colin must be there. That's where I'll find them; there's no doubt — and it all ties together with a hospital location of thirty-nine-sixty. That was the exact number of moments I had when this nightmare started Wednesday morning.

He walked to the island counter where he sat in a chair. He fiddled with the ornament pieces in the bowl.

But I still don't understand what happens at midnight; perhaps nothing happens — maybe the point is for me to get down to the hospital before midnight, so we will have a happy Christmas. My priority is to get to them. Michael and Máire were trying to tell me they're at Saint John Hospital.

Aedan walked to the front closet where he extracted a stored red Santa gift bag on a high shelf. Hobbled up the stairs and to his bedroom closet where he filled the Santa bag with Colin's wrapped gifts from him and Ciara.

After returning to the Christmas tree, he extracted a wrapped box marked for Ciara from him. He grinned as he placed the gift in the bag.

I don't understand why she loves film photography, but I'm sure she'll like this Pantec K10 35mm film camera. Stupid thing's thirty years old, and it cost too much, but she'll love it.

He sealed the Santa bag tight, locking the gifts inside. He could not wait to see Ciara's reaction when he told her of his plan to build a darkroom in their basement. His hope for a happy Christmas soared.

After turning off the Christmas tree lights, he walked to the front porch, pulled the timer and plugs for the outdoor lights — and paused at the front entrance as an eight-by-ten framed black-and-white photograph hanging on the wall caught his attention. It was a shot Ciara had taken of him and Colin sitting together on their front wooden porch drinking lemonade. The photo helped him understand her love for film.

It looks alive and warm. Ciara's right — film is a lost art.

Aedan frowned at the realization he was wasting time. He walked to the kitchen telephone and dialed a number. "Frank?"

"Yeah, buddy, any news?"

"I might be close to finding Ciara and Colin are. Do me a favor, call the Oak Valley Police and let them know I will contact them within a couple hours, or they can reach me on my cell."

"I'll do that, buddy, but why not tell me now?"

"It's too complicated, and I have to leave right now because Ciara and Colin need me." He hung up the telephone, grabbed a bottle of water and his cell phone from the charger, picked up the Santa bag, and headed out the rear door.

After placing the bag in the vehicle's rear storage area, he pulled away from his home.

The interstate had little traffic. Aedan hoped another freak storm would not fall upon the area, blocking his progress to the Loop.

They might lie stuck in hospital beds unconscious right now.

Christmas music played from the stereo. He hummed along with the tunes while rushing to the Loop.

He came to Ohio Street, his favorite exit into the downtown area. The roads remained empty as he took Michigan Avenue to Erie Street, where he turned right and entered the St. John Hospital parking garage.

He walked to the hospital's entrance carrying the Santa bag filled with gifts. His expression revealed his internal joy at the prospect of reuniting with his family while hoping they had not suffered critical injuries. He prepared his mind for whatever he might find waiting for him in room thirty-nine-sixty.

He pushed through the entrance doors.

Here I come, Ciara, Colin, almost there, two floors away.

As Aedan approached the front desk and noticed the elevator bank stood in the distance — he headed for the units.

"Sir, may I help you," a security guard at the desk said.

Aedan kept walking to the elevators with the Santa bag slung over his right shoulder.

I will not stop three floors below them.

"Sir, please do not enter an elevator," the guard said.

He looked at the guard. "I'm bringing Christmas gifts to my family."

"Stop Sir, we will help you," the guard shouted as he stood.

He ignored the man. He entered an open elevator. Once inside the unit, he pressed the button for the third floor.

He walked from the elevator and followed the signs on the opposite wall, which stated room nine-sixty lay to his right. Aedan struggled to remain calm. He walked toward room nine-sixty. The door on the right opened, the security guard burst through and ran toward Aedan, tackling him to the floor. The Santa bag slammed into his left side and arm. He screamed in pain. "What's wrong with you? Stop treating me as if I were a criminal."

"You're behaving like a criminal. You came up here carrying a large bag, you refused to halt, and now you wonder why I stopped you. Your Santa bag might contain a bomb," the guard said.

"I don't have a bomb. I have Christmas gifts for my family."

"No matter what you say, we don't know you, and our job is to keep the patients in this hospital safe," the guard said. "Do I need to restrain you?"

Aedan calculated the chances of his making it to the room before the guard could stop him. "I'll cooperate. Where will we go?"

"To the lower level, where we'll determine what to do with you. I've no idea what you were thinking with this stunt."

He dropped the Santa bag. He ran toward the room.

I'll make it there—I will make it.

He could not move with any speed. His left leg refused to cooperate; his muscles began cramping. He was moving in a lurching motion; he could not help but take the weight off his injured leg.

"Are you serious?" shouted the guard. He took off in pursuit.

He made it to the room's doorway, which he noticed remained unsecured. As he looked around the room, nerves in his lower back sent waves of pain and surprise to his mind with the violent tackling thrust from the leaping guard.

While falling to the floor, he continued to look inside the room. He observed two empty beds ready for new patients. "They're not in there," he shouted. "They're not in there. Where are they?"

He shrieked in pain as he struck the floor. He rolled over and grabbed the guard; all thoughts of holding back his anger had vanished from him. He flipped the guard onto his back and held him down by the shoulders. The guard looked stunned by the display of overpowering strength. "They should be in there. Where did you put my family? Tell me now, where are my wife and son?"

"I don't understand," the guard said. Fear creased his face.

"I called the hospital earlier this morning; the operator told me the hospital cares for unidentified patients on the third floor in room nine-sixty. But that room is empty. Where are they?"

The guard appeared shocked. "Sir, the hospital never releases patient information over the phone to strangers."

He grabbed the guard's shoulders and shook him. "But you did, that is what the operator told me a couple hours ago. She said unidentified patients go to the third floor in room nine-sixty. It all added up to a combined number of thirty-nine sixty." He looked frantic and on edge. "And the woman on the phone, she reminded me of someone." He looked away. He wracked his mind for an answer. "Wait, she sounded like Máire; her voice irritated me for a reason." Confusion and raw frustration flowed through his mind, as he maintained a firm grip on the man, determined not to let go.

A police officer approached. He had his weapon aimed at Aedan. "Sir let him go, and back away, now."

Aedan looked at the officer and released the guard.

He crawled along the tiled floor to a section of wall closest to room nine sixty, sat against the wall in a confused heap, and looked at the guard and then at the officer. "Where is she? Where is my boy, my poor little man, Colin?" He looked at them. "Where are they? I want my family back. Where are they?" His voice betrayed his deepening sense of desperation and brokenness.

They looked at him; their faces filled with sympathy for the broken man on the floor searching for his family.

A look of torment filled Aedan's eyes. He pulled the pink heart-shaped note from his pants pocket. After reading it, he looked at the officer. "Where are they?"

CHAPTER NINETEEN

SUSPICIONS TURN

The officer pulled Aedan from the floor. He yanked him to the elevator.

"Am I under arrest?"

"If the hospital presses charges, yes. If not, I will let them take care of this matter on their own," the officer said.

Aedan shuddered.

I doubt they'll give me a break; I've had to fight for everything. Why should this be different?

He waited in a cold basement office.

The Santa bag rested on the floor. He had remained there for three hours, waiting to meet with the hospital's Director of Security.

I hope I will find them somewhere else on the hospital campus. But I will need the Director's help.

A woman, forty years old with brown hair, walked into the office. "Hello, Mr. O'Beirne, my name is Sheridan Clarksmore. I'm head of security at the Saint John Hospital campus. We've run a background check on you, and we've researched your story, and there is no record of a telephone call coming from your home. We can't guess who you spoke with you earlier today, but I assure you the hospital never releases personal patient information to strangers, not over the telephone, and not in person."

He frowned. "I called the hospital earlier this morning looking for my wife and son. The person answering the phone told me the facility moves unidentified patients to room nine-sixty on the third floor. I didn't invent the call. It happened." His anger soared.

"Mr. O'Beirne, please, I didn't mean to upset you."

He glared at her. "I've been sitting here for hours waiting for someone to help me. Will you at least look for my wife and son?" His voice level had risen to an ear-hurting pitch. "We're talking about my wife and my five-year-old son. What would you do if it were your loved ones missing for over two days?"

She contemplated his situation. "I suppose I would be as upset and as agitated as you are."

"Thank you for admitting that. I love my family, and I want to find them. That is not so tough to understand."

"Mr. O'Beirne, the problem is this: we do not have any unidentified patients in our hospital. We cannot help you find your family because they're not here. You received this information earlier, yet you press for something else."

"They must be here. I've explained the scenario." He pleaded.

"Yes, I have read the entire account," Sheridan said. "Your friend Charlie came here after an accident at his newsstand. Later you received injuries in a car crash, and you left this hospital against medical advice. Now, you think your wife drove to the Loop for an appointment with Doctor

Millar at her downtown office, and you believe that she and your son were in the interstate accident on her way to the doctor's office." Her expression revealed her compassion. "We called her doctor. They have no record of an appointment for her at the downtown Franklin Street office though Ciara's three o'clock consult in the suburban location remained set and went unattended. The police have no record of your wife or your son, from the accident. They have no record of her car being in the crash though they said several cars were burned beyond recognition."

He grimaced. Through emotional pain, he forced himself to ask the obvious question. "Did the crews at the crash site find any burned human remains inside the destroyed cars?"

She took his hands. "No, all burned autos were empty. If your wife and son were in the accident, the people on site didn't find them. I'm sorry, but they're not in this hospital."

"Could they be in any other hospital?"

"It's not likely because we called the one other hospital that received patients from the interstate accident. They don't have any patients listed under your family name," she said.

"Do they have any unidentified patients?"

"We did not ask," she said.

"What's the hospital?"

"The Great Lakes Medical Center on West Congress Parkway."

"Am I free to go?"

Sheridan looked downcast. "No, you're not free to leave. The police want to speak to you."

"Speak to me about what?" Aedan shouted.

"That is not my business, Mr. O'Beirne. A detective is waiting to talk to you." She stood and looked at him. "I hope you find your family."

Aedan waited for the police. His expression revealed his hopeless and defeated mood, though, after learning about a second hospital, he wanted to hear from the cops.

A tall, dark-skinned, stocky man entered the room. He walked to Aedan and extended his right hand in greeting. "Hello, Mr. O'Beirne. I am Detective Gerald Bellson. Are you comfortable? Would you like a cup of coffee?" His deep bass voice echoed off the walls.

He did not respond.

"Mr. O'Beirne, I'm here to help."

"Am I under arrest?"

"No, and you do not have to speak with me, but I would advise you to cooperate with us because we're trying to help," Bellson said.

"Detective, I'm sure you know my situation. I don't understand what you want from me." His voice had taken on a sharp and impatient tone.

"Mr. O'Beirne, when was the last time you were with your family?"

Aedan stood. "Is that all you have? If so, I'm leaving."

"You're best served by cooperating with us, Mr. O'Beirne. Please take a seat and have patience."

"Have I broken any laws?" He did not sit down.

"The hospital refused to press charges," Bellson said.

"So why are you here?"

"To ask you questions about your case."

"My wife and son are missing, and I'm trying to find them. You have all the information. You either help me find them, or I will do it on my own." He walked away from the detective.

"Mr. O'Beirne," Bellson called. "We are seeking additional information to help find your family. We expect cooperation from you."

"Detective, you're stopping me from finding my wife and son." He sighed. "I'm leaving because I have to continue looking for them." He wanted to tell the detective that he had to find them by midnight. But, opening that path would lead to a demand for an explanation, and he had none to give because he did not understand what would happen at that precise moment. If he tried to explain, Bellson would conclude he was nuts or a fool or both.

The detective looked at him. "Mr. O'Beirne, I am asking you, again, to take a seat and cooperate. Your reluctance to answer questions about your missing loved ones is not helping your situation. You filled out a missing person report. You also promised to contact your local police, which you have not done." His deep voice rumbled across the room.

"Why do they care if I call them?"

"Because they have a job to do — you filed a report."

"If they needed to speak with me, they could have called my cell. I had my neighbor tell them that."

"They tried your cell, there was no answer," Bellson said.

Aedan frowned. He was on the verge of telling the detective he purchased a new cell phone yet chose not to say a word. Offering nothing to the detective provided him a chance to look for his family without constant harassment by the authorities. He looked at Bellson. "I'm sure I had my cell turned off. Batteries do not last forever." He hated to lie, yet he did not want them to slow his search for Ciara and Colin.

"I'm sure you understand why that would upset them."

"I understand. But why are you speaking with the Oak Valley Police?"

"It is a professional courtesy to our friends in the suburbs. We let them know where you are." They asked us to question you," Bellson said.

"Do I have to answer your questions?"

"No, but I cannot understand why you will not help us find your family. You become angry if we do not jump at the chance to assist you in the manner you desire. But now you want to ignore me when I'm trying to help. Do you want our aid, or not?" Bellson said.

Aedan considered the detective's plea, knowing he would ask nothing more than routine questions. He glared at Bellson in exasperation. "You have five minutes, after that, I'm getting out of here."

Aedan dumped the Santa bag into the vehicle's rear storage area and pulled away from the garage, headed to Michigan Avenue.

His expression filled with a disconnected stare as he drove to West Congress Parkway, feeling as if he did not belong there anymore. Those sites, including the Bean, Millennium Park, and the Art Institute, caused a surreal feeling to come upon him.

Aedan took Wabash Avenue and slowed when he approached his work building. He ignored the structure as he pressed on the accelerator, launching the X5 through the intersection and turned right on West Congress Parkway. While approaching S. LaSalle Street, he fell into an intense shiver while recalling the horrible crash from two nights ago.

I don't understand how I survived that accident.

His watch alarm chimed. It was noon on Friday, Christmas Eve — seven hundred and twenty moments left to find them. He pushed on without having a sense of what would happen at midnight.

Aedan stepped on the gas pedal and continued to the interstate while drumming his right hand against the steering wheel, keeping beat to the music playing through the stereo. He strained to improve his attitude, convinced his family needed him to find them, no matter the difficulty. He entered the interstate and headed for the Great Lakes Medical Center.

Aedan pulled into the parking garage on Harrison Street; the road ran through the middle of the Great Lakes Medical Center. Four Chicago Police cars rested along the hospital's northern curb hugging the street.

He entered the center. He walked to the welcome desk.

"May I help you, Sir?" the man said.

"I'm trying to locate my family," Aedan said. "They might have been in the multi-vehicle accident this past Wednesday morning on the interstate, and I want to see if they're here."

"What are their names?"

"Ciara and Colin O'Beirne."

"May I have your name and identification, please?"

"I'm Aedan O'Beirne, Ciara's husband, and Colin's father." He showed him his license. "Please, help me; I'm desperate to find my family."

A somber look came over the attendant. "I'm sorry, Sir, we have no patients with that last name."

"I want to speak with a supervisor or someone higher than you."

"Yes, Sir, I will contact the Director," the attendant said.

"Thank you," Aedan said.

A young woman with short black hair, medium olive-colored skin, and a broad smile approached Aedan as he sat in a chair in a small waiting area about twenty feet from the welcome desk. She sat across from him. "Mr. O'Beirne, my name is Jennifer Hernandez; I am the Director of Registrations. How may I help you?" She smiled.

Aedan had grown tired of seeing people smile. He glared at Jennifer. "I'm trying to find my wife and son. Can you help me, or not?"

"There are no patients with those names registered in our hospital."

He saw several Chicago Police officers walking toward the waiting area, where they stopped about five feet away. He looked at Jennifer. "Do you have any unidentified patients brought here from the multi-car interstate accident this past Wednesday?"

Detective Bellson approached. "Mr. O'Beirne, what a surprise you came here." He rolled his eyes. "Are you going to attack someone here too?"

Jennifer's face filled with concern.

"Stop that nonsense, detective. I didn't attack anyone at Saint John's. I asked the guard the same questions I am asking this lovely person." He smiled. He figured he would try the fake grinning robot routine, it seemed to work for everyone he encountered over the last two days. "Are the squads outside waiting for me?"

"Yes, after what you did at Saint John Hospital, it was obvious you would come here. We take every precaution," Bellson said.

"Precaution against what?" His anger soared.

"You already attacked a guard at Saint John's," Bellson said. "You're lucky the hospital did not press charges. It's obvious you've had a rough time; you're a mess. How would it look if I did not protect this hospital from a person who appears on edge?"

Aedan became sad. In a low and exhausted voice, he said, "I'm trying to find my wife and son. I wish you'd help me, rather than suspecting me of criminal intent." He glared at Bellson.

Jennifer stood, her face filled with concern and discomfort. "Mr. O'Beirne, perhaps I should leave this to the authorities."

"No, please, Ms. Hernandez, answer my question." His voice took on a pleading tone. "I'm trying to find my wife and my young son; it would be nice to have someone help me. I'm desperate and running out of options."

She took her seat. "We had patients brought here from the interstate accident — the hospital discharged them."

"Hey, O'Beirne, what an interesting concept, those patients left after a doctor released them," Bellson said.

"Shut up, detective." Aedan glared at him. "I left the hospital because I wanted to find my family and I couldn't afford to let more time pass. A truck rammed into my car on West Congress Parkway, which put me in the hospital. The accident caused me damage, yet finding my wife and son is more important than my injuries. They *are* missing. I walked out of the hospital because I love my family and need to find them, there is no crime in that." His voice level rose.

"Leaving the hospital is not a crime, but it makes you look suspicious."

"Wow, you sure are fishing. Stop this, detective; I want to find my family. Please, let Ms. Hernandez finish."

"Mr. O'Beirne, we have two unidentified patients, but we cannot let you have access to them," Ms. Hernandez said. "If you have pictures of your wife and son, we will compare the photos to the two patients. Then, we will let you know if they are your loved ones. We cannot let you join us. How would that be?" Her expression showed the sympathy she had gained while listening to his exchange with the detective.

"That is better than nothing." He pulled photographs from his wallet. "The first one is Ciara, my wife; she's standing at the entrance to the Brooklyn Bridge." He grinned as he viewed the picture. "She's loves taking 35mm photos, but that was a painful day for me, I refused to walk the bridge with her."

"Why?" Ms. Hernandez said.

"I have a nasty fear of heights, and I couldn't make myself walk the bridge with Ciara. Trust me, I wanted to do, but it was impossible with my fears. I froze like a piece of iron, but I should've overcome my fears, and I should have walked the bridge with her." His voice held a deep sadness.

"Tell us about the other photo," Ms. Hernandez said.

"The second picture is of Colin, our five-year-old boy. He's about three years old in that picture, and he's standing on a seat watching a baseball game with us. Look at his huge smile; he takes after Ciara, not me." He beamed with pride. "Man, I love him so much." His breathing became quick and shallow. "I want to find my family. I want to find my wife and son." His voice faded as pain consumed him. "It's almost

Christmas, I want to find my loved ones and go home with them. Is that so hard to understand?" His expression betrayed his pain.

The detective's face softened. "Thank you for sharing information about your family. We will come back here to let you know what we find."

Aedan watched them walk toward an elevator.

I sure hope they're here; otherwise, I'm out of ideas.

He sat back in the chair; a pain-wracked groan escaped his mouth.

Aedan jumped to his feet when he saw Hernandez and Bellson approaching. He scrambled to meet them halfway. "Where have you been? Is it my family?"

Jennifer's demeanor had softened. She looked at him with compassion. "I'm sorry, but the two unidentified patients are not your loved ones."

"We're sorry, Mr. O'Beirne," Bellson said.

His shoulders slumped. "I hate to ask — "

His pain ran too deep; Aedan could not speak the question. He shook his head and refused to allow himself negative thoughts, remained convinced that if he had no hope of finding them, Michael and Máire would not have tried to help him.

She looked at him, understanding his torment. "I checked. The hospital has no patients fitting their description, not alive or deceased."

Aedan stumbled. His ashen appearance revealed his agony. "I'm out of ideas. I have no next step."

"Maybe you should go home and let us do our job."

"No," Aedan said. "I'm sure she came downtown. I have to go back to the Loop, thank you for your help."

Minutes later, he entered the interstate, heading for East Congress Parkway and the Loop. He was quiet as he searched his mind, hoping to create a plan to find Michael and Máire. He understood that his time had dropped to about five hundred and thirty minutes left until midnight and that he needed help from his mysterious friends. Aedan's fatigue and emotional turmoil had reached its peak as he sped to the Loop.

CHAPTER TWENTY

DIFFICULT IDEAS

Aedan grew tired of viewing the area around Metric & Inch. Everyday sights depressed him while knowing his personal life had fallen into such painful disarray. He could not think of anything other than Ciara and Colin. And, there he was passing through typical sites and locations with no idea how to find them, and with no ability to create a plan. He was at an impasse — could conceive of no path through the nightmare.

He drove past Chicago's Art Institute.

I wonder if I'll ever feel the same about working downtown. So much has happened — regular routines seem impossible.

The familiar buildings and sites took on the role of enemies in his mind as if the Loop itself stood in his way.

Aedan parked in his usual location in the garage, close to Charlie's newsstand, though he could not shake the notion something had transported him into a strange new world where nothing made sense, and answers to his problems seemed out of reach.

He left the garage and walked to Wabash, crossed the street and strode to Charlie's newsstand. To his surprise, his old friend continued to work hard on the stand to restore his business to full capacity. "Charlie why are you here, it's Christmas Eve?"

"Hey, Mr. O'Beirne, it is nice seeing you. What brings you here?" His voice reverberated off the walls.

"That, my friend is a long story."

"I have time," Charlie said.

"How are you? Any more problems with dizziness or fainting?"

Charlie laughed. "I didn't have a problem. I was fine."

"No, that's not true, you blacked out."

"No, I stumbled, and everyone thought I fainted," Charlie said. "Recall, Michael asked me to go to the hospital. He was trying to speak with you. I always do as Michael requests," Charlie said. "He asked me to direct you to the Douglas Hotel — you do not recall?"

"It's been a rough time for me. It's hard for me to remember everything that has happened. What's going on? How could Michael predict that a car would ruin your newsstand and why would he ask you to go to the hospital if you didn't need help?" Aedan scowled at him.

"Do not look at me for an answer. I have known Michael for years, and he has his ways of doing things. I don't understand why he went to so much trouble to speak with you. But, I can tell you he coached me on how to get you to the hotel — and his plan worked."

"I don't understand any of this," Aedan said with confusion. "Where is Michael? I need to talk to him; he's a man with answers."

"Mr. O'Beirne, I could not tell you where he is — Michael comes and goes as he pleases. What is going on with you? Why are you downtown? You should be with your family, it's almost Christmas." His voice sounded lower than usual; it had a bass quality.

Aedan frowned. "I can't be with my family because they're missing. They've been missing since Wednesday morning. That's why I'm in the Loop, and that's why I need to find Michael. I'm hoping he will provide me a clue about where my wife and son are."

"Why? What happened to them?" Charlie said.

"The background story is too long to tell. I plan to seek a friend's opinion." He grinned. "Will you do me a favor? If you see Michael, tell him I'm looking for him. I'm running out of time, and I need to locate my family soon, within the next seven hours. Or else I'm not sure — "

Charlie interrupted. "Not sure about what?"

"I'm not sure what will happen if I don't find them by midnight."

"What does that mean?" Charlie looked worried.

"That is a question I need to ask Michael."

He looked at him with concern. "Mr. O'Beirne, are you all right?"

"Don't worry about me. Please, tell Michael I'm looking for him and that I need to speak to him soon."

"I will, Mr. O'Beirne."

As he walked away, he looked back at Charlie. "Call me Aedan; we have known each other too long for such formality between us."

He walked across the street and toward Eddie's Pub. Aedan frowned as he thought about Máire following him to the pub Wednesday morning though Aedan understood that he would experience great relief in seeing either of his two mysterious friends.

Aedan pushed through the front door of the pub. The empty bar revealed the season, with customers choosing to remain home for the

Christmas holiday. Festive music filled the empty bar, and a classic black-and-white Christmas movie played on the televisions.

There was no sign of Máire.

He sat on a barstool. He looked for someone to place an order.

"Hey, Wyoming, what are you doing here on Christmas Eve?" boomed Edward *Eddie* Sherman, Aedan's best friend from childhood, and the owner of the pub. He walked from the kitchen area and moved behind the bar to face Aedan. "You look terrible. What happened?"

"I came here because I'm tired, hungry, and thirsty," Aedan said.

"Man, you've never looked this bad. What happened?"

"I can't find Ciara and Colin. I need help."

Eddie laughed. It was a loud booming sound. "Hey, that's your dream problem, no more worries about having kids."

He glared at him with intense eyes.

Eddie stepped back. His face filled with surprise. "Wow, sorry pal, I thought you were pulling a joke. What's going on?"

"Do you remember a couple days ago I was in here having lunch?"

"You were acting like a fool," Eddie said.

"I *was* a fool. Not anymore."

"Tell me what's going on." Eddie's face had changed to one of worry, his usual happy smile gone.

"I haven't seen Ciara or Colin since I left for work Wednesday morning — I've tried everything to find them, including working with the police. I'm out of ideas. And, to make it worse, I have to find them before midnight." He strained to hold his raw emotional pain in check. "I figured I'd stop here, connect with my best friend, get something to drink and eat, and maybe that will help me create a plan."

"What do you mean you have to find them before midnight?"

"Something happens then; I'm not sure what. But it seems like it's a dangerous or scary event. I have experienced a constant countdown for over two days. I cannot figure out where they are." He looked at his friend with pain-filled eyes. "All my talk about hating kids and hating our marriage, I was blowing off steam. I love my family, and I want them back." His head slumped.

"I'm sorry pal, there's more to this than I realized. What's with the midnight piece? You know that that's the start of Christmas?"

Aedan glared at him.

"Okay, okay, I was just making sure you did not forget that fact."

"Eddie; be serious about this. I need help. I need ideas because I have no clue where to find them. They could be anywhere, and they could be in horrible condition, or worse." His voice held a pleading tone.

"Okay, let's do this: I have Christmas food in the kitchen, turkey, stuffing, the works, and I'll add beer to the mix to loosen up your brain. Tell me everything while we eat, and we'll do it as fast as possible. I hope we can create ideas to help you find them." He locked the front door and turned on the closed sign.

"Thanks, buddy, I appreciate your help," Aedan said as they headed toward the kitchen.

He breathed a sigh of food contentment as he stared at the food remnants covering the long wooden kitchen counter.

"You sure know how to create a feast," Aedan said.

Eddie laughed. "Why do you think my pub still does so well? It's the food that makes them come back for more."

"Well, any ideas? Any suggestions?"

"Yes, contact the pediatrician and ask her what she knows."

"The police called the doctor's office. They have no record of Ciara arriving there for an early appointment on Wednesday. The Oak Valley office still had her listed for a three o'clock consultation that afternoon. They don't have a record of her making that appointment either. None of this is like Ciara. If she wanted out of our marriage, she wouldn't make me worry like this. It isn't like her." His voice cracked under stress.

"But your home is not downtown, so why are you still in the Loop? Isn't it possible that Ciara and Colin are out in the burbs?"

"No."

Eddie sighed; his concern for the three O'Beirne's had grown many levels as his friend's account unfolded. "Why are you in the Loop and not at home? They might return. Maybe she took a trip out of town. If she did that, then she'll be returning soon."

Aedan became hopeful. "That's not a terrible idea."

"Where's your favorite place to go on vacation?"

"There are several places."

"No, what is the one destination you and Ciara love the most?"

"It can't be that."

"Why not?"

"Because traveling to Ireland is not a short trip." He frowned. "And she would not do something so cruel."

Eddie smirked. "Maybe she needed to get away from you."

"No. No way — she wouldn't take Colin away from home with Christmas coming," he said. "They're downtown somewhere; I can feel it in my bones… and something happens at midnight."

"Okay, so where does that leave you?"

"I'm not sure, but if I need help, can I call on you?"

"Anytime, pal. Call whenever you need me."

"Thank you for everything." Aedan walked from the pub.

CHAPTER TWENTY-ONE

DOTS NOT CONNECTED

Aedan walked to the entrance to the building at Wabash and Adams where Metric & Inch lived on the thirty-ninth floor. As a director, he had building entrance keys with twenty-four-hour access. He strode toward the elevators. The building's lobby lights were off, creating darkness he never experienced going to work each day. It was easy to see Christmas was coming, with the lobby vacant and silent, like an empty cave.

He paused before entering the left elevator, recalling his time spent with Michael, and hoping his older friend would join him in the ride to the thirty-ninth floor. He walked into the unit, and within seconds, it had gained rapid speed. Soon it slowed as it approached the thirty-ninth floor.

Well, that sure didn't work — Michael still won't show himself.

The unit's doors opened; the hallway leading to Metric & Inch held one overhead lamp for off-hour illumination. A spotlight shined on the Michael Williamson painting. He stopped at the canvas. He shook his head in confusion as he stared at the all too familiar image. His rational mind told him it could not be his Michael, but his emotional side forced him to study the image.

How could it be him?

In the piece, the Trenton Tower stood along Michigan Avenue, a glowing red cloud ridge hovered in the background.

What is it with the red glow? Does it mean something? How will it help me find Ciara and Colin?

He turned away in frustration. He unlocked the entrance door and pushed through.

A single emergency overhead lamp cast light upon the welcome desk, along with the waiting area. Aedan walked toward his office. He stopped at the door. He read the office nameplate:

60. AEDAN O'BEIRNE – DIRECTOR OF ACCOUNTING

Aedan paused as he stared at the nameplate, had never noticed his office, and floor numbers created a combined location of thirty-nine sixty. He frowned wondering why the number haunted him — he could not fathom how it would help him find his family.

After walking into his office, Aedan looked at his family pictures sitting on the wood credenza behind his desk. He sat in a pain-filled heap in his chair. He looked at the photos. "Where are you?" he said in a whisper. He looked at his digital desk clock, it was 07:30pm. He had two-hundred and seventy moments until Christmas Day.

Noises from the hallway caused him to turn to the doorway.

James Williamson walked into the office. "What are you doing here?"

"I could ask you the same question, Sir."

"Enough of the *Sir* routine." James sighed.

"I'm here to gather my thoughts."

"Why? What happened to you? You look terrible."

"I've had a rough time," Aedan said.

"Why aren't you with your family so close to Christmas?"

"They're missing. I'm trying to figure it out."

James crossed his arms. "What? What do you mean? Your family's missing on Christmas Eve?"

"That's why I came back here. I want to gather my thoughts and work through the events of the last couple of days to figure out where they are." He leaned back in his chair.

James looked confused. "You lost me. I need more information."

He cleared his thoughts. "I've not seen my family since I left home Wednesday morning. Ciara doesn't answer my calls, our friends and neighbors have not heard from her, and she didn't make the doctor's consult." He glared at his boss. "I'd appreciate it if you'd leave me alone. I have until midnight to find them."

James scowled. "I am working on an important contract that must go out tonight, or else I would be home with my wife. Join me in my office and tell me more about what is going on with your family."

"Please, Sir, leave. I have to work this through," he shouted. "I have little time to find them."

"It's your problem, not mine." James left the office.

Aedan's expression revealed his frustration with his boss.

Why can't he see that I'm knee-deep in this search?

Aedan worked on a long grease board installed in his office, creating drawings of boxes, with descriptions, and arrows, detailing the various events and data points that entered his life over the many previous hours. He tried, in vain, to find a connection between those points with his missing family. "I don't get it. There's something that I'm missing." He tossed the black marker across the room. "I can't connect the dots." He pulled the pink heart-shaped note from his pocket. He read it in silence. "Where are they?" His loud voice echoed down the long hallway.

James came into the office in a hurry. "Aedan stop doing this alone, work with the authorities."

"No, they are conducting their own search. The cops would only get in my way because Bellson sees me as a suspect. I've gone through a lot with him." He glared at James.

James looked at the grease board. "What is that?"

"I'm plotting the events that have happened since I left home Wednesday morning. I'm hoping to discover a clue." He frowned. "So far, it hasn't helped." He released a deep sigh.

James pointed to the board. "Who is the *Michael* you have highlighted? Why is the name written so many times?"

"You would not believe me if I told you."

James cleared his throat. "Still, I want to hear about that name."

He chewed on his lower lip while trying to remain calm. "Can't you see I'm working out this problem? Leave me alone and go back to work," he shouted, too loud. "I wouldn't have come here if I thought you'd be here to bother me, I'm not working as an employee of this firm, it's a personal problem. Go back to work and let me have time to work this through."

"You're still working for this firm, and while it's obvious that you're under stress, it is unwise to order me to do anything. You're working on a personal matter, but you're in the firm's office space, and you are using company office equipment. I suggest you remain calm. You look a mess; go get cleaned up. I expect you in my office in five minutes." In a display of authority, James focused his eyes.

Aedan sat back in the chair. He grinned; it was not pleasant. "You can expect anything you want, but I have to work this out, and I don't much care, what you expect me to do."

"This is an order: five minutes from now be in my office."

"I'll do what I have to do to find my family." Aedan glared at his boss.

"I too will do what I must," James said. He left the room.

"Whatever," Aedan said. "I don't care what you do."

After erasing the board and gathering his things, Aedan walked to James' office; he carried a large box. He entered the room and sat in front of his boss. "Mr. Williamson, I'm leaving. It's clear you have no desire to help me; instead, you want to chastise me for what you see as my personal failings." His expression was mature and resolved.

"What is in the box?"

"My belongings — pictures, books, and such."

James raised an eyebrow. "Why do you have those items?"

"Mr. Williamson, I'm in a personal crisis. After speaking with you, I've learned that it's true we discover who our friends are when we experience challenging times. You have shown me that the lives of the people working for you do not matter; you think only of yourself and of this firm. My life is a mess, and you can see my clothes and body are a wreck. Yet, instead of offering me help, you became upset with me. I will not continue working for a person who treats me as you did."

"I became upset because you would not inform me of your situation," James said. "Earlier tonight I received a call from Detective Gerald Bellson. His account of this matter differs from the one you're telling."

He frowned. "You heard from Bellson, and you didn't bother to tell me about him when you came into my office troubling me. What's wrong with you?"

"I wanted to hear your side of things first."

Aedan exhaled. "But you acted like you didn't care, and now I learn you already had skewed information from Bellson. I've known you and worked for you for a long time, and this is the trust I get from you?"

"I wanted you to offer a detailed explanation, so I could compare it with the detective's account." His appearance was cold, expressionless.

"Why you arrogant — who do you think you are? I don't owe you an explanation about my private life, as long as it doesn't affect my job." His frustration increased. "I've had enough of you, and of this firm."

"Are you resigning?"

Aedan looked beyond James to a framed photograph. It was a copy of the original in the entrance hallway, which hung to the right of the Michael Williamson painting. In the picture, Michael stood behind his desk in the firm's old location. In the image's background, a framed photo of snow-peaked mountains drew his attention. An emblazoned phrase read:

66 HOURS – THE IMPOSSIBLE HAPPENS

A cloud ridge floated above the mountains with a reddish section at the center of the image. Aedan took a deep breath as he tried to discern the reason for the glowing clouds. He sensed they were vital to finding his family, yet he could not determine their significance.

James grew impatient. "Are you resigning?"

He ignored him as he continued staring at the photo. His head began to ache under the intense scrutiny he gave the image. He dug deep into his mind to unlock the reason the red clouds troubled him. He sensed they were important, and that they would help him locate his family. With fatigue bearing down on him, he gave up his study of the image.

"What are you looking at?" James said. "That' a photo of Michael Williamson, my grandfather, and founder of this firm."

"Yes, *he* was a great man. I wish he were here right now. Do you recall the name on my grease board that grabbed your attention?"

"Yes, you wrote the name, Michael," James said.

He looked at the photo and back at James. "Yes, Michael *is* the correct name. Think about that name." He walked away carrying his box. He looked back at his boss. "We will finish this conversation later."

He walked along the hallway, stopping at the large painting of Michael Williamson. He looked to the right and at the photo with the mountains and the phrase: 66 HOURS – THE IMPOSSIBLE HAPPENS emblazoned at the center. The red glow illuminated the center portion of the cloud ridge.

Aedan sighed and walked to the elevator in silence.

CHAPTER TWENTY-TWO

YOU MIGHT NEED THIS

Aedan dumped the box into the X5's rear storage area. He entered the vehicle. Exhaustion caused him to shiver. After turning on the radio, he scanned the dial and stopped on a local radio station playing a Christmas song. The song's melody and lyrics brought his pain into sharp focus.

I don't understand what's going on with them. Where's my family?

He looked at a classic manger scene in a bookstore window across from the parking garage. The sight sparked an idea; Aedan grinned as he put the SUV in gear and pulled away.

He parked in a public garage close to N. Clark Street, left the vehicle and hobbled fast to the Catholic Church. As he approached the structure, he looked at the massive statue of Jesus hanging on a cross, installed in a gothic archway above three large bronze entrance doors. It had become his church of choice whenever he attended Mass on weekdays during Holy Days of Obligation, a primary source of spiritual comfort and refuge for him in the Loop.

The Church remained open for Christmas Eve Mass. He pushed through the middle door; most pews brimmed full of people. He found an empty location on the right side, where he kneeled in prayer. Those around him, seeing his physical appearance, appeared concerned for him.

An older woman, who looked like Máire, approached him. "Is there something I can help you with?" she whispered. She smiled, the same smile Máire and Michael displayed.

"No, thank you. I'm here to pray," Aedan whispered.

The older woman smiled and walked away.

He lifted his head and prayed, *Lord, I'm sorry for being mean to my family; I love them and miss them so much. Please, point me in the correct direction, and I will do the rest. No matter what it takes.*

He looked at the front of the Church and to the left of a large framed image of *Divine Mercy*, where a tall Christmas tree stood. The star on the treetop seemed on fire; it gave off a red glow which shined on the vaulted ceiling creating a cloud-like image along a ridge. An inspired thought came to him as he grinned and lifted his head and prayed, *thank you, Lord* — he left the pew, kneeled, did the sign of the cross and walked from the church.

I must verify this, and I know the perfect place to go.

He jogged away from the church. With renewed energy, he ignored the pain in his left leg as he headed to E. Washington Street. He ignored the damage to his body — he operated on adrenalin.

He turned right on Washington and ran across the street to Daley Plaza, where Chicago's outdoor Christmas tree stood. The sixty-foot tree shone like a beacon with thousands of lights and several hundred ornaments. It was a favorite holiday stop for Chicagoans and tourists alike. He never paid attention to it despite working nearby.

He sat on a concrete planter and gazed at the massive star on top of the tree;, it cast a red glow on the buildings to his right. The tree swayed back-and-forth in the wind, causing the red light to undulate, it appeared as a cloud ridge floating close to the building, with a reddish hue at its center. He was getting closer to a solution. The image fluctuated; the red glow increased. His eyes drifted to the tree base where a sign read:

CHICAGO OFFERS ITS APPRECIATION TO THE PRESCOT HOTEL FOR ITS GENEROUS CHRISTMAS SEASON GIFT

"There's the answer," he shouted. Several people looked at him.

I can't believe I didn't think of the Prescot.

He grinned, as he prayed, *thank you, Lord.*

It was 08:00pm, four hours until Christmas as he ran from the plaza, cutting through the downtown sidewalks, weaving a path around the holiday throngs, while ignoring the pain his body sent in waves to his brain. While gulping enormous breaths, he turned left and continued to the Prescot Hotel entrance doors. As he brought himself to calm, he walked into the hotel's Grand Lobby trying to appear as if he belonged there though his clothes and overall appearance worked against that tactic.

Aedan sat in a chair and gazed around the impressive room,, yet he could recall nothing from the time Michael dragged him there during the fierce winter storm. He glanced at the ceiling which contained beautiful candelabras, gold inlays, and Greek frescoes.

Why haven't I visited this hotel before? It's gorgeous.

While scanning the vast space, he attempted to create a plan to move beyond hotel security and up to the private ballroom on the top floor where Michael had brought him to get out of the storm. His confidence soared believing he would find them there, somewhere.

Michael loves this place; he must be here.

The lobby bustled with people walking back-and-forth. Holiday decorations adorned the room, with a thirty-foot-tall Christmas tree standing close to the classic staircase which extended to the second floor. Two large ceramic angels, resting on concrete pedestals, were standing watch over the lobby.

A hotel employee walked to him. "Hello, Sir. My name is Shirley. May I help you with something?"

"No, I'm relaxing and taking in this fantastic view." He grinned.

"Are you staying in this hotel?"

"Oh yes, I'm a guest; though, I need to find my family. I'm hoping they'll be coming through the doors any minute. They walked to Daley Plaza to view the Christmas tree." Aedan loathed lying though he could not accept further delays since his time was running short. He hoped the hotel staff would leave him alone.

"Please, let us know if there is anything we can do for you. Enjoy your time in the hotel."

"I will, Shirley, thank you."

He noticed security personnel maintained a close watch on him. The reasons were obvious. He was a mess and stood out among the well-dressed people filling the space.

I bet they think I came into the lobby to get warm.

The elevators lay in the distance, across the Grand Lobby. He walked toward them, but a security guard intercepted him.

"Sir, may I help you?" the guard said.

"No, I don't need help."

"Where are you going?" the guard said.

He glared at the guard. "Why are you troubling me?"

"Sir, we would like you to speak to the hotel manager."

"Why?"

"To verify your status as a registered guest of this hotel."

"Is this how you treat guests?" he shouted. Various hotel patrons stopped to listen to the exchange. He smirked, hoping the commotion would cause the guard to leave him.

"Sir remain calm; we want to verify your status as a guest. There is no need to trouble the others." The guard squirmed.

With deliberate anger, Aedan said, "Maybe the others should learn how you treat your guests."

A tall, thin, graying man, sixty-five years old and dressed in an expensive suit, walked to Aedan. "Sir, my name is Jonathan Sheffield. I am the manager of this hotel. Will you please accompany me to my office?"

"Why? What have I done?"

Jonathan, a man with a business-like countenance, left no doubt he wanted the crowd to disperse. He glared at them. "Please, go about your business. This man requires our help." He turned back to Aedan and moved close. He whispered, "I do not believe you're a hotel guest, and I do not want to embarrass you further. Follow me to my office."

The people milling around dispersed.

He followed Jonathan to the second-floor balcony. They moved on to an office in the south corner, an ample, but dull space.

"Please, take a seat," Jonathan said. "What is your full name?"

"Aedan O'Beirne."

Jonathan typed the name into the computer.

"Where did you get the framed photo behind the desk?"

The manager ignored him.

In the picture, Michael Williamson stood in the Prescot Hotel's Grand Lobby with his left hand extended to a woman in her thirties. He was offering the woman a metal card, identical to the one he gave to Aedan Thursday morning after the snow and ice storm hit the area.

"Where did you get the framed photo behind the desk?

"Why?"

"Let's just say I'm curious," Aedan said.

Jonathan's eyebrows shot up. He glared at him. "That photo has been here for a long time; I am not sure how long. The man in the picture is Michael Williamson. He was a prime Prescot Hotel benefactor, and he was on the board for at least ten years. There are several framed photos of him throughout the hotel." He viewed his computer monitor. He looked at Aedan. "As I expected, I did several searches using different terms, and you're not listed as a guest in this hotel, we will escort from this establishment straightaway."

"That will not happen, Jonathan. Instead, you'll be escorting me to the top floor of this hotel, where I will enter the private ballroom." He grinned as he viewed the photograph.

Michael sure is clever. I've no idea how he knew I would need the card, but he's been ahead of me this entire journey.

"Mr. O'Beirne, I'd prefer the straightforward way without calling the authorities. If, however, you resist removal, I'll have no choice but to call the police to have you arrested and taken from the hotel. Do I make myself clear?" Jonathan took on a severe appearance.

Aedan stood; he grinned and laughed.

"Do you think being arrested is funny?"

"Not at all." He extracted his wallet from his rear pocket. He pulled the metal card from an inside sleeve. For the first time, he viewed the strange metallic piece. On the front, carved in full block letters, he saw: P B A. On the rear etched along the lower edge was the serial number: MM120025.

I thought nothing about this card when I received it from Michael. I forgot I had it until now. Michael always helps me.

"What do you have there?" Jonathan said. His eyebrows rose.

"What is the name of the private upper ballroom?"

"It doesn't have a name. It's known as Private Ballroom A." He frowned. "Mr. O'Beirne, the police, will arrest you if you refuse to cooperate."

Aedan looked into Jonathan's eyes. "You have such little trust. I'm a guest of this hotel." He handed the card to the manage, grinned while waiting for a response, not knowing how the card would get him to the private ballroom yet knowing it would.

Michael told me I might need the card. Remarkable.

He waited for the manager's response.

Jonathan looked stunned. "Where did you get this?"

"From a kind and influential friend." He grinned as he looked at his watch; it was 08:30pm, two-hundred, and ten minutes until midnight.

Aedan sat back in his chair. He grinned.

Jonathan twirled the metal card in his right hand. "I've seen only one of these cards in the twenty years that I have managed this hotel." He frowned as he walked to an eight-foot-tall by six-foot-wide safe, built into the wall at an angle in the left corner as seen from Aedan's viewpoint. After unlocking the safe, he pulled out an old manila envelope, with worn edges, returned to the desk, where he extracted a thin booklet.

"What is that?"

"It is a written protocol for approving the card you presented to me." He handed the card back to Aedan. "I have several questions to ask. This is an authentication process to validate the card and the person holding it, that is you, Mr. O'Beirne."

Aedan squirmed in his chair. He hoped he could answer the questions.

"State the three letters engraved on the front of the card?"

"P, B, and A."

"What is the serial number on the lower rear edge?"

"M, M, 1, 2, 0, 0, 2, and 5," Aedan said.

"Please, give me the card." Jonathan took the piece, and after flipping through several pages in the booklet, he verified the numbers against the protocol expectations. He looked at Aedan. "What was the first name of the person who gave you the card?"

"Michael."

"Would you describe the man as middle-aged, or older?"

"Older."

"Did the man remind you of someone when you met him?"

"Yes."

"Is your life in order, or in disarray?"

He grinned. "My life is in disarray."

"After meeting him, did you experience a stressful incident?"

"Yes."

"Has an unknown woman enter your life?"

"Yes."

"What is her name?" Jonathan said.

"Máire."

"Has a recent important moment drawn your attention?"

"Yes."

"What is that time?" Jonathan said,

"Midnight tonight."

Jonathan looked doubtful. "The protocol recognizes that its holder might deduce the answers; however, there is no means to guess the response to this final question, and it holds the key to confirming you as a valid cardholder," Jonathan said. "What are the four numbers in the authenticating sequence?"

Aedan grinned with relief. He thought about the last two days of his life, and he came to an instant conclusion there could only be one answer. "Three, Nine, Six, Zero."

The hotel manager appeared stunned.

I sure took him off guard — he wanted to kick me out of the hotel. He thought I was a vagrant.

Jonathan fidgeted as he accepted the reality of the situation. "Mr. O'Beirne, under protocol rules, you must provide the correct answer to every question. One wrong response would cause rejection of the person presenting the card, and then the card must return to the hotel's possession. Therefore, since you have provided correct answers to all questions, the hotel accepts you as a valid cardholder, and you're now an honored guest of this hotel. I will escort you to Private Ballroom A whenever you are ready."

"Thank you." Aedan grinned. "Let's go now. I'm in a hurry."

It's about time.

CHAPTER TWENTY-THREE

PATH DISCOVERED

Aedan stood inside the elevator as it sped to the highest floor. Soon, the unit slowed and came to a stop. The single door opened to a hallway. He could not remember much after having left Michael in the ballroom.

"Mr. O'Beirne, I'm not allowed on this floor," Jonathan said. "It's a strict rule in the protocol; people who are not holders of the card, cannot access this level unless there is an emergency. I hope you enjoy your stay." He handed the metal card to Aedan. "This belongs to you, make sure you keep it safe; those cards are rare."

Aedan stepped away from the unit as the door closed. The elevator was at the end of a hallway that was twelve feet wide, ten feet tall, and one hundred and twenty-five feet long. At the far end, a single door opened into the private ballroom Michael had taken him to during the snow and ice storm.

Paintings and enlarged photographs, in doubled stacked frames, lined each side of the long corridor. The images hung in two rows on each wall, twenty-five per row. One foot separated the higher rows from, the lower. Each frame was forty-eight-six inches tall, and thirty-six inches wide and constructed of solid oak wood stained a dark brownish hue with small white angels carved in each corner of every frame. The angels appeared to float away from the frame.

The elaborate treatment given to the ballroom entrance space astonished Aedan. He glanced down the hallway and made a rapid count, noted there were one-hundred painted canvases containing images of various men and women adorning the walls and wondered what they might represent.

With intense focus, he viewed the individuals captured in the paintings and photographs. The people represented many professions, with each person seen working in their chosen occupation, career, or vocation. Accountants were working with spreadsheets, lawyers reviewing contracts, carpenters measuring boards and pounding nails, doctors examining patients, surgeons performing operations, electricians installing new power circuits, plumbers installing new pipes, teachers writing on age-old chalkboards, professors speaking in auditoriums filled with students, secretaries using typewriters and answering old rotary-style telephones, scientists delving into new theories, and there were professions in the images he could not decipher.

What is the purpose of this place? Who are they?

He walked in a left-leg-favoring gait along the wall viewing everything. He came to the corridor's end and to the final frames along the right wall, several inches from the ballroom entrance door. His expression revealed his surprise as he viewed the second-to-last picture. It was an enlarged photograph of Charlie, his friend, and owner of the newsstand.

Why is this picture here?

He saw the frame below Charlie's was blank. No space remained for additional images.

Why is there only one empty frame left? What is this place?

He looked at the entrance. On each side hung a large framed image; each was seventy-two inches tall, by forty inches wide. On the left wall hung a framed picture of Michael, while on the right hung a portrait of Máire. The image of Michael showed him working in his office at the original Metric & Inch location, his black fedora sat at the edge of the desk. The portrait of Máire showed her wearing a nineteenth-century nurse's uniform and hat; it appeared like a Catholic nun's habit. She stood by a sign, which read:

MÁIRE'S HOSPITAL FOR THE POOR

He could not make sense of the hallway. In frustration, he pushed through the door. He smiled with joy, his body relaxed, and relief washed over him as his eyes settled on Michael and Máire sitting in vintage chairs across the room. "It's about time." He looked at his watch; it was 08:50pm. He had one-hundred and ninety moments left.

Michael smiled and went to Aedan. He grasped the younger man by the shoulders. "I had confidence that you would find your way back here. But you wasted too much time, son."

Aedan looked at Michael and then at Máire. "What happens at midnight? I can't fathom what might happen."

Máire walked to him. "We cannot tell you more. You hold much more information than you realize. Consider everything." She smiled.

"No, please, tell me now." Her smile no longer irked him as it did during previous encounters. Two days ago, he had disliked them both.

"Máire is correct; you have all the information you need. It is at this moment, you must clear your mind of clutter and put the pieces together. Think about everything you have gone through. Try to draw from the various messages we imparted to you, along with the information you have gained on your own."

"Think, also, of the numbers and different images you have seen, such as strong and noticeable colors," she said.

"You mean like red?"

"Yes. Red is easy to notice," she said.

Michael and Máire looked at each other. They smiled.

Aedan filled with frustration. "Why can't you tell me?"

"We can direct and guide you, nothing more," Michael said.

"Why haven't you guided me when I needed you the most?"

"We have, you did not see us. Your pivotal moment came when you entered the Church," Máire said.

"Why?"

"Because you reached a point where you sought help. It is in moments of trials we discover clarity. During those instants, we cast aside our egos, and we throw away our stubbornness and pride, and then in true humility we welcome help," Michael said. "That led you back to us."

"You are close, and time is short," Máire said. "Inspect the paintings in this room. Recall the other photos, images, and sights you have witnessed. Stretch your mind to the proper conclusion using that information. Remember how I pushed you to look further at the people walking around the Bean. If you do that now, you will find success., but you have little time."

Aedan stared at them. "Who *are* you?"

"We help," Michael said.

"Help with what?"

"We help people on edge. People who will fall hard if they have no one to guide them away from the abyss," Máire said. "Everything we have done had a purpose. You are where you belong now."

Aedan moved with swift purpose across the room, taking in each painting and attempting to tie them back to the events of the previous sixty-three hours. He stopped. He turned to them with a resolved stare. "The Douglas Hotel," he said. "I should have figured it out long before this."

"What does the Douglas Hotel have to do with your family?"

"Oh man, I should have put this together a long time ago."

"Put what together?" she said.

"The weather turned harsh after I left the Douglas Hotel. I recall shivering in the frigid wind buffeting against the buildings coming from the horrible winter storm that struck the Loop area."

"So?" Michael said.

"I remember thinking about how large water bodies are creepy at night. After that, I looked to the west and saw storm clouds moving toward the Loop. A strange reddish glow danced along a swirling cloud ridge." His appearance became hopeful. "I've seen glowing clouds in many images over the last couple days. In various photos, in pictures inside James' office, in paintings here in this ballroom and in the bakery, in a framed picture in the hotel manager's office, in a cloud-like red glow shining on the vaulted ceiling in the church I prayed in, and I saw a similar image created by the star on the Daley Plaza Christmas Tree. I now realize that an event on the ground produced a red glow northwest from the Douglas Hotel."

Filled with excitement, he extracted his smartphone and searched the internet for breaking news stories. He found a relevant headline:

FIRE ON ASHER AVENUE
OFFICE BUILDING DESTROYED

His mysterious friends watched, smiles crossing their faces, as he worked through the news. Aedan looked at them. "Thank God, it's not the doctor's building, but it must be in the area, all signs point there. Everything has pulled me toward that location. I have no other option, and time is running short."

He activated his smartphone's navigation application and typed in the address; the Douglas Hotel rested southeast from the doctor's office. He grinned. "That's the correct location. Her office is in building thirty-nine sixty — that has to be the place."

His friends smiled.

"Thank you for everything. I have to go retrieve my family."

Michael went to him and put his hand on his left shoulder. "Son, you must prepare your mind for what lies ahead."

He nodded in agreement. "I'm ready and don't care what happens to me. I want to get Ciara and Colin back."

Michael and Máire smiled.

"Please, listen to Michael," she said. "Prepare your mind for what lies ahead, or you will never complete your task in time to help them."

He grinned with warmth. "What matters to me is finding them before it's too late. I will put them first, no matter the difficulties. I love them and will do whatever it takes."

He ran from the room and jogged to the elevator; pain did not enter his mind. He pushed the unit's button.

Minutes later, the hotel's manager, Jonathan, with a look of surprise, watched Aedan running down the classic staircase and then through the Grand Lobby on his way to the exit doors.

He burst into the frosty night air. He ran to the parking garage to retrieve his vehicle. "I will get to you…hold on, please hold on."

CHAPTER TWENTY-FOUR

MEDICAL COMPLEX

Aedan stopped at the Chicago River; the drawbridge was open. While waiting, he pulled out the pink heart-shaped note.

"Come on, lower the stupid bridge; the doctor's office is blocks away. I could run there faster than this," he shouted.

Aedan turned on the radio, scanned through the stations trying to avoid the Christmas songs playing throughout the dial, stopped the scan at a classical music station playing the emotional piece, Adagio for Strings. The soul-wrenching music caused his pain to come into sharp focus; his mind and heart yearned to find his family. The climatic chords from Adagio produced a shudder in him as his mind flooded with images of Ciara and Colin as they laughed and played in their backyard.

I want them back. I love them so much.

His expression exposed his barren and remorseful soul.

The bridge lowered. Aedan crossed in a reckless rush.

Aedan dropped his speed as the address numbers increased toward 3960. The Medical Center tower rested in a plaza to his left. It sat between N. Franklin on the east, W. Grant on the south and Lincoln Street on the north. Aedan looked at the new complex and noticed the tower remained untouched by tragedy or fire. He was, again, relieved to conclude the reported blaze must have taken place in a building close by. Without the destructive fire, he would not have seen the red glow in the clouds, and he might not have come to the doctor's office in search of his family. He had to move fast to find his family — time was running short.

He looked west along W. Grant, saw a tall parking garage on the western side of Asher Avenue, scanned the area looking for a location to park. Metered parking existed along N. Franklin Street. He found an empty spot. After parking, he placed Doctor Miller's business card on the passenger seat. He put the keys in the glove box; the vehicle's security system would sense their presence inside the car, preventing the doors from locking.

In the darkness, light reflected off the tower's thick tinted glass panels installed on its outer surface, stretching to thirty-five stories high or four-hundred and fifty feet. The tower consumed ninety percent of the north-south city block.

Aedan scanned the front of the building and the main entrance on the Franklin Street side. A security guard was talking on a phone while sitting behind a desk about thirty feet inside the building, at its center.

He pulled his cell from his pocket; he dialed a number. "Eddie?"

"Hey, Wyoming, I can't believe it, you called me." He laughed.

"Are you still willing to help me find Ciara and Colin?"

"What a stupid question. I said I would help. What do you need?"

"The only place they can be is in the doctor's office or somewhere in the building. It's a long story, but do you remember the reddish glowing clouds west from the hotel?"

"Yeah, I remember. What about it?"

"Those clouds pointed me to the doctor's building. It took me two days to put those pieces together; I'm a stubborn and dense fool."

"Hey, I could've told you that." Eddie's laugh rushed through the phone.

"Anyway, I did a search and found out there was a fire on Asher Avenue, somewhere close to the doctor's building. I added it up, and I realized everything points to the North Franklin address."

"So, what do you need from me?" Eddie said.

"Do you remember the time at college?"

"Oh man, that was a tense situation," Eddie said.

"I need you to do the reverse here," Aedan said.

"I understand — that won't be easy." Eddie laughed. That's when I started calling you, Wyoming. We got out of there by the skin of our … well, you recall." His laugh boomed.

"Don't remind me — they almost arrested us," Aedan said.

"You saved me big time. We thought we were a bunch of cowboys going to school there. But, hey, the nickname Wyoming stuck after that," Eddie said. He laughed. "Tell me you don't have yourself in anything that intense."

"No, at least not yet, and I'm hoping not to get there. I'm sitting in my car close to the doctor's building. I might need your help if things progress as I think they will."

"You're in it deep. I understand. Where do I go?" Eddie said.

"Hover around the area close to thirty-nine-sixty North Franklin. I will search for them; they should be in the building somewhere. Stay close and wait for my call, like in college."

"Okay, I'll do that. But how can they still be in the building?"

"Everything points to Ciara and Colin being at this location. I figure they're somewhere on the twentieth floor. Maybe something bad happened to them, and they're waiting for someone to find them. Time is short, I have to hurry."

"Okay, but it's thin; not much to go on. Ciara is young, and she's healthy. What could have happened to her, and what are the odds no-one in the building would have seen her?" Eddie's voice had taken on a serious tone. "Colin would have cried and screamed if his mom were in trouble. I'm not buying it; it's too thin. And if you're wrong, think of the multiple charges the cops will bring against us." His hearty laugh had vanished.

"I agree, but everything points to this address; I can feel it in my gut that I'm in the correct location. But if I can't find my family, it won't matter what happens after that." Aedan's voice shook with anxiety.

"Hey, dump those thoughts, you'll find them."

"I'll understand if you don't want to help. You'll be taking a huge risk."

"Hey, we're talking about Ciara and Colin. I'd do anything to help them. You'll find them, I'm sure of it. Don't worry about me; I'm not without connections — this won't be a problem. Do you have any idea how many cops and lawyers visit my pub? Most of them are my friends." He released a weak laugh, no booming waves burst forth. "But, Wyoming, be careful."

"Thank you, pal. Be in the area as soon as you can. One way or another I'll get inside the building; my time is running short." He pushed the end button. He left the vehicle and ran across the road.

It was 9:20pm on Friday, Christmas Eve. Aedan had one-hundred and sixty moments to find them.

CHAPTER TWENTY-FIVE

SHATTERING ENTRY

Aedan walked to the tower. He strode toward a large concrete sign installed at the plaza's center that read:

MEDICAL CENTER COMPLEX
3960 NORTH FRANKLIN STREET

"It's about time. This is the place." He approached the tower's main entrance, which included three revolving doors and a single glass door to the left. He checked the doors and found them locked. The security guard remained sitting at the welcome desk in the stark white lobby. He pounded on the locked single glass door.

The college-age male guard approached the door. "The center is closed, it's empty," he shouted.

"Still, I need to search the building for my wife and son," he yelled; his voice reached the guard through the thick glass.

"Sir, the building is empty. Try again on Monday."

"No, I must get in tonight."

The guard scowled. "Sir, please leave, or I will call the police."

"Can I speak to your supervisor?"

"No, my supervisor is not here," the guard said. He grimaced, knowing that was information he should not share with a stranger trying to get into the building.

"They left you here alone?"

"Leave now, or I will call the police." His face filled with concern.

"I didn't mean to disturb you. I apologize." Aedan grinned and walked away, using intentional calm strides to help make the guard feel at ease.

After returning to his vehicle, he extracted the tire iron from the rear storage area and strode back to the building's front door, where he used the iron to bash in the lower half of the door's glass panel. At first, the hardened glass would not break, yet it began to weaken with each pounding from the tire iron's bolt end.

The guard ran to the door. "Are you nuts?" he shouted. He ran back to the desk where he pressed several buttons notifying the Chicago Police of an emergency. He picked up the telephone and dialed a number.

Aedan continued pounding the tire iron into a two-inch round location on the door glass about one foot from the ground; soon, he had created a slight crack in the formidable material. He turned the tire iron around to the flat blade side. He forced the blade into the cracked glass. The tool became wedged inside the fissure and extended away from it for one and a half feet.

He paused, knowing his next move would cause enormous pain in his left leg. In a decisive act, he leaped into the air well above the tire iron. He pulled his legs together into a tight clench; his feet and his full weight came crashing down upon the tool. The bottom half of the glass pane shattered. He leaped into the air a second time; the lower portion of the panel broke away in a cloud of glass. His actions created a three-foot-wide hole. He crawled through the opening. He ran to the security desk at a frightening pace.

The young guard looked terrified after viewing Aedan's violent entry; he took several steps backward to create distance between himself and the tire iron.

"Did you call the police?"

"Yes, it's standard procedure," the guard said.

He glared at him.

"The complex doesn't hold any money," the guard said.

"I'm not here to rob the place. Where's your gun?"

"They don't let us carry guns; we're to call the police when trouble happens. This place will crawl with Chicago cops and firemen soon. I'm not sure what you think you can do with them surrounding you."

Aedan moved close to the guard; he raised the tire iron into a daunting position. "Hand me your radio and your cell phone."

"Why?"

"I don't want you telling the police where we are. Hand the radio and cell to me."

The guard gave him the devices. Aedan placed them on the desk where he crushed them under a swinging tire iron assault. He pulled his wallet from his back pocket. He extracted two one-hundred-dollar bills and handed them to the guard. "Use this to replace the cell phone."

The guard looked stunned. "You're not here to steal anything, are you?"

"No, I told you I am here to find my wife and son." He grabbed the smashed cell phone and radio — he stuffed them inside a hooded trashcan. He looked outside. "I can still gain enough time on the cops, and you'll come me, which will provide me another time advantage. If you don't want me to cave in your head, you better come with me with no struggle," he shouted. "We'll take the stairs, that way they won't know what floor we're on. Grab two flashlights in case they turn off the power to the building. Move."

The guard ran to the desk and extracted the flashlights.

"Where are the elevators and the stairwells? How many are there?"

"They're in the cross hallway," the guard said. He pointed. "There are four elevators, two on each side of the main concourse that runs to the rear. There are two stairwells, one on each half of the building, north, and south."

"Let's go, I have no time to lose," Aedan said.

The lobby contained a central corridor dividing the space, which extended to the rear of the building where the second set of exit doors lay. A hallway, positioned at the mid-center, ran north to south. In that passage, stood the elevators, the stairwells, and the main floor restrooms, with interior meeting rooms facing the eastern and western outer walls.

Aedan followed the guard to the cross hallway; he paused and looked at the rear, wondering why the building had duplicate doors on the back end. He turned to the guard. "Go to each elevator and push the same floor numbers on the panels, five, fifteen, thirty, thirty-one, and thirty-five. Do it now." He raised the tire iron in a threatening pose. "Consider what I did to the entrance door; don't make me do the same to you, move now."

"Why do you want to do that with the elevators?".

"I don't want the cops on me, I need to gain a few minutes on them. Sending the elevators to the top while having them stop at different floors will provide time for me to locate my wife and my son before it's too late." Aedan glared at him.

The guard looked doubtful, but he said nothing.

"What? What are you not saying?" He lifted the tire iron.

"I'm the guard; they can't see me helping you. Please, I need this job, it's helping me get through school, and I'm almost done," he said.

"I don't think they'll let you keep your job after this event."

The guard looked shocked. "Why? I didn't have any way to stop you. It's unfair if that happens."

He looked at him. "How many years do you have left?"

"One semester."

"If you help me, I will pay for the full semester." Aedan looked hopeful.

The guard grinned. He looked excited. "How can I trust you?"

"It's a chance you must take."

"You promised to pay my last semester if I help?" the guard said.

"Yes, but we have to hurry; the cops will be here soon."

The guard grinned. "They won't be a problem. If I cut the power to the elevators, it will take them at least thirty minutes to override the commands and turn them back on."

"Can you do that? How?"

"Yes, I can turn the power off in segments, including the circuits controlling the elevators. They don't give us weapons, but they train us on the building's systems in case of emergencies."

Aedan looked at him with surprise. "How much time?"

"One minute." The guard walked back to the security desk. He tapped the computer display. He logged in and drilled down to systems control. A blaring sound emanated from the cross hallway as he turned the power off to the elevator shafts.

"Are those alarms expected?"

"Yes." He pressed a button; the sirens stopped. "I cut the power to the elevators, which includes lights in the stairwells, they are on the same circuits. They'll use the stairs to chase you until they get the power restored."

"Can't the cops reverse what you did?"

"Yes, but it will take some effort. By the time the cops figure it out, you will have had time to search for your family." He grinned. "The emergency floodlights in the stairwells are not operating; a sensor system failed last night. Building maintenance scheduled the repair for Monday. We will have to use the flashlights."

Aedan looked at him. "Thank you for helping me."

"Make sure you keep the promise you made." He grinned. "And you better not tell them I volunteered for this."

"I won't say a word about you helping me." He scowled as flashing lights filled his eyes. "Squad cars are pulling up. Hurry." He pointed at the vehicles entering the plaza.

They ran to the stairwell positioned in the southern half of the center hallway or the left side when viewed from the Franklin Street doors. They opened the door and began running up the stairs. The guard's excess weight slowed him.

When they reached the second floor, the guard stopped and took in deep breaths. "Where are we going?"

"To suite eight ninety on the twentieth floor."

"What? Eighteen more flights. I'll never make it."

"What's your name?"

"Jacob Shultz."

"Don't worry about it, Jacob; you'll make it, keep moving." He allowed the guard to go ahead of him. "I will follow you, keep moving." He climbed just below Jacob. They churned through the steps leading to the third floor. "Keep moving — don't slow down."

"I won't slow down," Jacob said. "But I don't get this. You seem like a reasonable person. You didn't bring a weapon. Instead, you brought a tire iron to what will soon be a gunfight; the cops will not hesitate to use their firearms if you pose a threat. And, you had no way of knowing that I don't carry a weapon. You might have been walking into a superior force situation, and yet you did it, anyway." He took long deep breaths. "Why?"

"Jacob, I guessed there'd be no guns, nothing more involved than that."

"But why?"

"Because this is a medical office center, not a bank or any other high-value location. I didn't think I'd face weapons."

"You misunderstand me. Why are you taking such an enormous risk?"

He sighed. "I'm looking for my wife and my son. I wasn't joking before, and I'm not joking now."

Jacob interrupted him. "No, that is not what I mean. Why didn't you get the cops to help you search for them on twenty? Why are you risking arrest and why aren't you getting help?"

"The cops, including Detective Bellson, consider me their primary suspect. My story didn't matter to them; they won't help me. I have to find my family myself." He groaned. "Move, move fast. I will let you go once we get to the twentieth floor, after that you can go back down the stairs. The cops will climb these same steps. So, you can tell them I over-powered you and forced you to help me."

"The cops will think I'm part of this." His face filled with fear.

"No, they'll question you and let you go."

Aedan glanced at his watch; it was 09:50pm. He had one-hundred and thirty minutes to find them. He looked at the twentieth floor through a small open space between half-floor stair sections. "I'll be there in moments Ciara. Hang in there, Colin, I'm on my way."

He stopped between floors. He pulled out his cell phone, dialed a number, and placed the phone in speaker mode. "Eddie?" He returned to climbing the stairs as he spoke with his friend.

"Hey, Wyoming, are you in the building?"

"Yes, I had to hack my way in using my tire iron."

Jacob listened to the call.

"Okay, now what?"

"I will go to the doctor's suite and search for them there. Are you in the area?"

"Yes, but I've done no good acting in a long time, and I'm not looking forward to it tonight." Eddie's hearty laugh rushed through the cell, causing Jacob to laugh. "It's almost Christmas, and I'd rather be home, but we're talking about Ciara and Colin, so tell me what to do."

"I'm sending you a text with my vehicle type and location, and there's a starter seed on the passenger seat, you'll understand. I left the door unlocked. If you see the cops searching cars along Franklin, you're to act right away."

"I'll do that, but I still think this is too thin," Eddie said.

"Yeah, I hear you, pal. But, what am I supposed to do, watch the time click by and do nothing to find them?"

"No, you must do this; I hope you find them and that they're okay."

Jacob listened to the exchange as he continued climbing.

"Hey, pal, after I find them, I'll tell Ciara how you helped and talk her into naming the baby after you if it's a boy." He pushed the end button, pulled his wallet from his back pocket, extracted two photos, one of Ciara, and the second of Colin. While continuing to climb, he handed the pictures to Jacob. "This is my family. You should see the people I'm looking for … they're the reason I'm risking so much."

"I understand and don't blame you for the way you've acted. I'd go nuts too if I couldn't find my family."

Aedan shined his light on the stairs. "Keep moving."

"They'll be sending teams up these stairs after us," Jacob said.

"It's all a matter of timing. I'm trying to get to twenty and search the floor before the cops reach us."

"What happens if we do not find your family?"

He groaned with anger. "There's no *we* in this situation. I'm releasing you when we reach twenty."

"No, don't dump me," Jacob said. "I want to help you find your family. Besides, I have to make sure you keep your promise." He laughed.

"Jacob, I don't want to put you in danger. I will keep my promise, even if they arrest me. I see no reason to place you at risk."

The night guard took deep breaths as they continued laboring up the stairs. "I am sticking with you. I want to see this through, and I want to see you reunited with your family," he said. "You ignored my question. What happens if we do not find them?"

"Don't say that Jacob, don't think it. They're in this tower, there is no other place." His breathing quickened with worry. "If we don't find them, it won't care what happens to me. They'll be on twenty — they'll be there."

They better be there.

CHAPTER TWENTY-SIX

STREET LEVEL

Detective Gerald Bellson exited an unmarked car. He walked to the tower.

Chicago Police cars filled the area surrounding 3960 N. Franklin Street; their rooftop flashers intermingled with the street level Christmas displays. The multi-colored lights seemed to dance upon the tower's glass, creating a festive, yet surreal spectacle. A fire truck approached, with an ambulance behind. Sirens echoed in waves, as onlookers from apartments and condominiums began to flood onto the sidewalks and streets. Police worked to construct barriers using wooden horse-styled barricades to hold back the growing crowds.

Bellson walked to a group of police officers thirty feet outside the building's front doors. He approached the officer in charge. "Get me up to date, now."

Officer Genswolt glowered at Bellson. "Who are you?"

Bellson sighed as he showed the officer his badge. "I will take the lead in this situation. I've been watching the suspect for two days."

"We're not sure who the suspect is," Genswolt said.

I'm always stuck working with these morons, thought Bellson. "His name is Aedan O'Beirne. He's married with a five-year-old son. He came here to find his family, or at least I'm sure that is what he told the building guard. So far, he hasn't carried weapons, but his state of mind might've changed. What's the status?" Bellson said.

"We've pushed back citizens to a safe distance with officers at each street location but can't locate the security guard and assume the suspect is holding him."

"Place officers in the taller buildings around us. They might spot movement in the tower. Make sure they have excellent marksmanship in case O'Beirne becomes violent. I don't trust this guy," Bellson said. "I wonder what that fool thinks he will accomplish here."

"What's O'Beirne's deal?"

"He claims not to have seen his family since early Wednesday morning. We have attempted to contact every significant person in his life. We have little to go on, and we've made O'Beirne our prime suspect. Though, there is something about the guy's story that rings true," Bellson said. His voice faded.

"Rings true?"

"He's a mess, and he has slept little. We've monitored him as he moved throughout the Loop and back out to the burbs where he lives. He's behaving like a frantic husband and father, as any sane person would if their family went missing," Bellson said. "Either way, we must find him and get him under wraps, so he does no more damage."

"We're working on it," Genswolt said. "Have you tracked his cell?"

"We've tried, but there are no recent calls made using his number. He might have lost his cell in a nasty accident two days ago. The Oak Valley Police are working on it. They think they can get information from calls he made to his in-law's home. We also have a telephone company creating records for us. We should have information soon," Bellson said.

"Oak Valley?"

Bellson became impatient. "That's where he lives."

"Maybe he has a new cell," Genswolt said.

"That's possible, but so far we can't find any records. If O'Beirne has a new cell, we should be able to gain the number soon. Until then, we'll do this the old-fashioned way, through direct contact," Bellson said.

"I understand."

"Do you have anyone inside?" Bellson said.

"Yes, two officers. They reported O'Beirne cut the power to the elevator shafts. I have a man working on those systems."

"How did he manage that?" Bellson said.

"It's probable that he forced the night guard to help him."

"That's smart. O'Beirne's trying to gain time," Bellson said.

"It worked … we will have to use the stairs to pursue him."

"Yeah, but we'll show him he can't escape the net we will place around him," Bellson said with a laugh. "How many stairwells?"

"Two, there is one to the south and the other to the north, both in the tower's cross hallway."

"Gather ten armored officers in a hurry," Bellson said.

"What's your plan?"

"Get passkeys for the building's locks," Bellson said.

"We've already done that; there were universal cards at the security station, and we found steel keys. O'Beirne didn't cover that angle."

"Good, send two four-person teams into the stairwells, one group to the south, the other to the north. They are to stop at each floor," Bellson said. "Two officers from each team will enter each level and meet in the middle to make sure O'Beirne does not pass them. The two remaining officers in each team will stay in the stairwell to ensure there is no escape route. Have them check everywhere. If they don't find and capture O'Beirne, they are to go to the next floor and repeat those steps on each level. My team will cover the lobby in case he tries that route. It won't take long before we have him trapped."

"What if he's carrying a weapon?"

"Make sure each person is wearing armor; they are to report back to us after they complete each floor. I don't think O'Beirne has a weapon, but make sure no one takes a bullet for that idiot."

"The team will assemble straight away," Genswolt said.

"This guy makes me sick," Bellson said. "It is time to end this."

The detective entered the tower. He stopped to make a detailed examination of the door Aedan ruined to get into the tower. "Old-fashioned brute-force at work there," he whispered. He walked to the welcome desk, which also served as the security station. He looked at Genswolt following close behind. "Can you access the security video recordings for the front door?"

"Yes, this is a new building; it has the latest security technology."

"Play it back for me," Bellson ordered.

Genswolt activated the forty-inch-wide LED flat panel embedded in the countertop. He played the digital video from a point before when Aedan approached the building's entrance door for the first time. "You can see on his first attempt he was trying to convince the guard to let him in. But the guard denied him entry, and then O'Beirne left."

The detective looked at the front doors as a large contingent of officers entered the building wearing protective armor and holding weapons. They walked toward the stairwells. He looked at Genswolt as the video continued to play. "Take notice," Bellson said, "that there are seventy-four seconds between the time O'Beirne left the door and his return with a tire iron. His vehicle must be close, find it. He used to own an old red sedan; he wrecked it a couple days ago in a crash on Congress Parkway. Look for new cars in the area around the Medical Center and check their VIN numbers. He might have purchased a new car, and it doesn't show on the DMV records yet."

"He could have taken a cab or a rental car."

Bellson looked impressed. "Valid point, but we already did those searches. We found no car rentals under his name. I doubt he used a taxi because he got to the suburbs and back with no one spotting him. We are continuing to search through mass transit security recordings and logs. He might have taken a train, but I am inclined to think he has a vehicle because he left the scene to get a tire iron. When your field officers locate his car, tell them to go over it with a laser focus."

"I will do that — " Genswolt said.

The detective interrupted. "O'Beirne used a tire iron, not a gun. He's unarmed; unless he took the guard's weapon. He hasn't used weapons in the various locations we've tracked him."

"The guards in this complex don't carry guns."

"Then, there is every chance he doesn't have a weapon," Bellson said. What have you learned about the guard?"

"Our stat sheet tells us he's a twenty-three-year-old man named Jacob Shultz, a college student."

"What about cameras? Can we get a look at them climbing the tower?" Bellson said. He looked hopeful.

"The tower owner ran out of funds and could not install security cameras. We don't know if the suspect is working with the guard."

Bellson's frustration rose. He glared at Genswolt. "How much longer before your man restores the power?"

Genswolt looked at an officer sitting at the computer panel, ten feet away at the end of the bowl-shaped security desk. "Hey, Ghost, how long will it be until you get into the system?"

The pale, short, and plump officer looked at Genswolt. In a high nasal-sounding voice, he said, "This takes … takes time. Whoever did … did … this changed the passwords. I need at least a half-hour, maybe … maybe an hour."

"Okay, keep at it," Genswolt said. "And get there sooner."

Bellson looked at him. He whispered, "Ghost?"

"Look at the guy," Genswolt said. He chuckled. "But don't underestimate the guy, he's the best there is, you would not believe the systems Ghost has cracked."

"Okay, I hope he gets in soon."

"He will," Genswolt said. "But go chase O'Beirne down and arrest him. Why are we wasting time searching the floors?"

"I'm giving O'Beirne a chance to look for his family," Bellson said. "He'll be far more compliant if we let him think he did his search. We'll play along while we tighten the noose. He's a brilliant man, and he's manufactured a robust search path, and somehow, he has ignored significant pain from many injuries he received over the last two days. This tells me he doesn't care about his own welfare, and that makes him a volatile and dangerous person. I assume he took the guard hostage, which means we need to tread with caution because he's a man on the edge. I don't want this situation to have a bad ending. We will use caution and inch our way toward him. We will surround him and close off all paths, and then we will take him into custody once he comes to his senses. I want this to end tonight."

An officer entered the building and walked to Bellson. "Sir, I'm Officer Robert Wilson. We've found the vehicle. It's a brand-new SUV parked across the street and owned by a certain Aedan O'Beirne. He purchased it yesterday morning. I found a business card for a particular *Doctor Miller* on the passenger seat; her offices are in this building, the twentieth floor, suite eight-ninety." He handed the business card to the detective.

"Nice work, Wilson," Genswolt said.

"Thank you, Sir." Wilson walked away.

"Great, that's just what I expected to hear." Bellson grinned. "This situation will end soon." He looked at Genswolt. "When your teams reach the twentieth floor, tell them to wait for me there. We'll get that fool. Maybe we can close this case in time for me to enjoy a holiday beer before I go home. I must hurry; my kids are in bed, waiting for Santa."

CHAPTER TWENTY-SEVEN

SUITES A PLENTY

Aedan continued climbing to the twentieth floor; he and Jacob carried flashlights.

He noticed Jacob's breathing had worsened; despite his youth, he struggled to move his 270lbs body up the stairs.

"We have to stop," Jacob said. He took deep breaths. He looked at Aedan, his clothes stuck to his body, soaked in sweat. "I'm bigger than you, give me a break."

"We can't stop, we're almost there, and the cops will close in on us soon. We have one floor left." He looked at Jacob with worry and compassion, concerned he was pushing him too hard.

Jacob sighed. He began climbing.

"No, stop, I'll tell you what, stay here and wait for them. I would release you soon; I will do it now." He grinned as he looked at Jacob. "Thank you for being so cooperative and for your help. When this is over, I'll keep my promise."

Jacob glared at him. "Stop — don't go without me, I told you I want to help you look for them. I didn't crawl up this stairwell for nothing." He continued climbing the steps. "You can be a real piece of work. Did you know that?"

"Ciara tells me that almost every day." He laughed.

"It had to be 418 steps from the lobby; my typical bad luck," complained Jacob. "It must be nice to be skinny."

Aedan laughed. "How do you know how many steps it is to the twentieth floor?"

"They train us in a bunch of facts about the tower, so we can impress potential occupants. Sometimes visitors ask questions about the building because it's still new." He laughed. "Stupid stuff, right?"

"They told you how many steps there are to reach the 20th floor?"

"No, its basic math. This building has thirty-six floors. There are seven hundred and seventy steps to the top of the tower which equates to twenty-two steps per level. There are nineteen levels between the lobby and the twentieth floor. Multiply nineteen by twenty-two. It's not a complicated problem."

"And you're majoring in European Lit?"

"Yes. It's a family tradition and a long story."

"We're here," Aedan said. He pointed to the door leading into the twentieth floor.

Just then, cell phone ringtones split the silence. Again-and-again, the sounds echoed off the stairwell walls. Aedan looked at the caller ID number. "The Chicago Police have found my cell number, how clever of them." He canceled the call.

Ringtones split the silence.

"Take the call," Jacob said. "Either that or turn it off."

"I don't want to talk to Bellson right now."

The cell phone rang.

He accepted the call while in speaker mode. "What do you want?"

"O'Beirne, you might as well give up, you have no escape route. We have teams moving toward you," Bellson said.

"Detective, you know why I'm here. If I don't find my family, I will not care what happens to me," Aedan said. He pressed the end button. He turned the power off.

"Why did you answer the call if you planned to hang-up?"

"I wanted to see if we still had time," Aedan said.

"Do we?"

"Yes."

"How do you know?" Jacob said.

"If the cops were close, Bellson would not have called me; instead, they would have moved in and arrested us. I'm guessing they are checking every floor and moving to cut-off all paths to escape."

"You got all that from a thirty-second call?"

"Yes," Aedan said as he pushed through the door and walked onto the twentieth floor, where darkness combined with the rays from their flashlights created eerie shadows across the long hallway. He looked at Jacob. "We have to move fast. Give me the key." Aedan turned to the exit door and placed the key in the lock and slammed it with his right palm, breaking it away at its insertion point, let the door close. "There, that will slow them down if they try to access this floor before we're done searching. Quick, give me another master key." He ran to the north exit door and repeated the maneuver, breaking the key off at its lock insertion point, ran back to the guard.

The stairwell exits rested on the western half of the hall. Doors leading to the floor's suites ran along each side of the north-south corridor. There were two elevator banks, one at the southern end running along the east wall next to a glass double-door entry into larger suites. The second lay at the northern end, also next to a glass double-door entry into larger office suites. The stairwell building exits sat three feet from each.

"Now, where?" Jacob said.

"We have to find eight-ninety — it's Doctor Miller's office."

"The suite numbers start at one-hundred at the south end, and they go up from there heading north," Jacob said. "That's the standard layout for every floor, except on the tenth, fifteenth, and thirty-fifth floors; single medical firms use all space on those levels with different configurations."

The ten-foot-wide hallway held sparse wall coverings; it ran along the building's centerline from north to south. The multi-office spaces at the north end contained eleven thousand square feet of space, much larger than any other office on the floor. Along the hallway sat four single wood doors, two on each side. Bathrooms sat on each side of the south suites. Aedan shined his flashlight at the south glass double entry, the printing on the door read:

SUITES 100-190 MEDICAL TESTING CORPORATION

He moved the light to the eight doors spanning the rest of the hallway going to the north. Doctor offices and medical services occupied suites 200 through 700 extending to the opposite end closest to the northern double-entry suites. They rushed to the north suites, the sign on the glass read:

SUITES 800-890; MILLER MEDICAL GROUP
OBSTETRICS & PEDIATRIC CARE
DOCTOR STEPHANIE MILLER
DOCTOR KATHERINE JONES
DOCTOR DAVID SAMUEL

"It's about time," he said with joy and relief. "I've made it to the doctor's office. Now we have to find them."

"But where do we start? This place is quiet as a mouse, no one here," Jacob said. "Are you sure about this?"

Aedan looked at him with anger. "No, I'm not sure about anything this week. I've no idea where else they could be. I'll start in the bathrooms at the south end." He looked at the guard. "You're a good man, Jacob. Thank you for helping. Unlock every office. I will check the 100-190 suites and the restrooms. Go to the smaller offices one-by-one. Make it quick, okay?"

"Yes."

"We'll meet at Dr. Miller's suites. Please move, and fast, we have almost no time before the police get to this floor."

Convinced they had to be somewhere on that level, Aedan ran to the restrooms to begin his search. Midnight was fast approaching, he moved with a swift purpose as he entered the men's bathroom.

Aedan ran from the women's restroom after having found it empty. The same results had occurred in suites 100-190 suites.

He moved to Dr. Miller's office suites. He pushed through the double glass doors, which opened to a curved shaped registration desk setback about thirty feet from the entrance. To each side of the desk, stretching for forty feet in a rectangular space lay a waiting room lined with cushioned chairs. The room had four flat screens mounted in many locations, it had various toys for kids to play with, and it had magazine racks that held about one-hundred different periodicals. The right wall ended in-line with the welcome desk, and it contained a door allowing access to the patient rooms. He jumped at sounds coming from the entrance door.

Jacob walked into the waiting room. "Did you find anything?"

"No, but if this isn't the place, I will never find them in time."

"Don't give up," Jacob said. "This suite has about eleven thousand square feet."

"Is that normal?" Aedan said.

"No, the average office size in this tower is far smaller."

"How do you know that?" Aedan said.

"I have told you before; we night guards learn a lot on the job."

"I'm sure that's true. We have to move fast; the cops must be close."

"But if they know you would go to these offices, why wouldn't they come here first and arrest you right away?"

Aedan sighed with impatience. "They don't want us to double back or hide somewhere else in the building, and they don't know if I'm armed and hostile, and holding you as a hostage. They will do a slow and careful sweep of the entire building to make sure they have me contained before they move in to arrest me. I'm in a rush to find my family; the police are not in a similar hurry; they can take their time to make sure I don't get away." He glared at Jacob. "I'm also guessing Bellson is giving me time to do my search; he likely figures I won't be as hostile if he offers me enough time to examine this floor. No matter the truth, it all plays into my need to find my family."

"It seems you're in a battle against Bellson," Jacob said.

"No, he just thinks he's a step ahead of me, but I know Belson could charge up here to arrest me anytime he wants. My story has impacted him, so he needs to create a plan to cover himself." He smiled.

"Do you think he believes you?"

"I don't care." He looked at Jacob. He turned and leaped over the registration desk. Shining the flashlight, he searched the area. There were two workstations with chairs at the curved counter, one to the left side, and the other on the right. Both work locations faced outward toward the waiting room and each had a flat panel computer embedded in the workstation surface. Photographs of various people lined the cork boards tucked under the curved counter, well out of the view of incoming patients. He paused at the right-side station while looking at stuffed animals perched on two shelves. On the higher shelf was a gray nine-inch-tall elephant wearing a black decorative t-shirt with a nameplate, which read: **ORANGE**. The lower one contained a yellow six-inch-tall stuffed and puffed bird wearing a wrestling t-shirt with a nameplate, which read: **FLUFFY**. Two separate five-inch by seven-inch framed photographs sat on the counter. Each photo depicted a young boy holding their respective stuffed animals with broad smiles covering their faces. Next to those pictures lay a larger frame containing an image of a family. The photo showed a middle-aged father and mother, surrounded by three young women, one teenage man, and the two young boys from the smaller frames. The two boys from the separate images stood at the forefront, they were holding their respective stuffed animals.

That's all I need to see. A picture of kids with their parents.

Jacob pounded on the patient entrance door. "Hey, did you forget about me? Let me in?"

Aedan left the registration area. He opened the door for Jacob. "Sorry. Come on, hurry, we have to find them."

They stopped at a large room filled with patient files, desks, cabinets, computers, and other equipment they did not understand. Aedan motioned to Jacob to enter the room. "Check it out, in case." He turned to the hallway. "Ciara, Colin," he shouted. Aedan walked along the corridor, stopping at a small lunchroom, entered the room, which contained a refrigerator, a sink, a toaster, a microwave, various small cabinets, four small round tables with chairs, and a storage room at the rear. He rushed to the storage closet, opened the door; it contained nothing but supplies and brooms. He ran back to the hallway, where he met Jacob. "Anything?"

"Nothing."

"I'm sick of this," he shouted. "I need a clue or at least a break in this search." His forehead creased with anxiety.

"What do you want to do now?"

"You go to the east wall of the building, and I'll go to the west wall. Check every patient room, every closet, every doctor office, and every cabinet large enough to hold a woman or a young boy. Work back to this location. Scream if you find anything. Go now, the cops must be close."

"Ciara, Colin," Aedan shouted.

Aedan came out of the last patient room. His expression betrayed his feeling of hopelessness — he had no ideas left. He looked to the east; Jacob walked toward him along the long hallway. The young guard's walking body slump told Aedan all he needed to know, his search to find Ciara and Colin would end with him arrested by the Chicago Police. Aedan's heart ached with the realization that he would sit in jail when his family endured whatever will happen to them at midnight. He wandered to the western outer wall with Jacob following.

A large window, eight-feet-wide by seven-feet-tall, rested at the hallway's end on each side of the building, east and west. Aedan sat on the floor three inches below the window, let his head drop to his bent knees in a sign of pain and defeat. He pounded the carpeted floor, over-and-over again. "Ciara, Colin, where are you? What happened to you? I can't find you." He pounded again-and-again-and-again.

Jacob looked at him. He frowned. "It won't be long now. I looked at the plaza, and there are an awful lot of cops out there; they must have a bunch heading our way. I think they spotted my flashlight when I looked through the eastern hall window, and there were silhouettes of several cops with rifles on the building rooftop across the street. I refused to take chances and moved away from the window and turned off my flashlight. They are getting serious out there."

Aedan looked at him. "I knew they would. For all they know, I'm a nutcase ready to get violent," he said. "Will you sit here with me, please?" He pounded his head against the window as they waited for the police.

"I'm sorry, Mr. O'Beirne, you worked like crazy to find them," Jacob said. He sat close to Aedan, on the floor under the window. "This is a horrible time for you."

He looked at him. "Thank you. You're a good soul."

Jacob smiled. "While we wait, tell me about your family. I'd like to know them better. We've been searching for people I've never met, and I know nothing about. So, while we sit here waiting for Chicago's finest, maybe you could help me get to know them better."

Aedan pulled the pink heart-shaped note from his pants pocket. He handed it to Jacob. "She left this for me in our bedroom on Wednesday morning. I freaked out after I read it — my reaction caused a terrible fight. Ciara didn't deserve any of that. The fight was the last thing we did together, and I feel so miserable about how I treated her and Colin." He returned the note to his pants pocket. "She's everything to me, but I don't tell her. I've often mistreated her by trying to put my garbage on her as if my problems are her fault." He released a pain-wracked sigh. "She's so brilliant and beautiful; she was a lawyer and worked for a law firm for two years. We agreed to have kids and Ciara remained at home during their younger years, which worked out well for us. Yet, now, with them missing, our house feels like a tomb without her there making it a warm home filled with love.

"Ciara does it all without a whimper for her personal needs, and she's one of those people who work hard all day without whining or complaining. For her, it's all an act of love for us while expecting nothing in return." His watery eyes revealed his torment. "I can see her smile. She fills my world to the brim with love and kindness, and I don't think she knows how much I love her. It feels as if we've known each other forever. She's my best friend, my soul mate, and the air I breathe, and she loves Colin and me so much. I'm an utter fool because I haven't seen what I have with them.

"Now I want to find her, so I can tell her all of that and much, much more. But the odds of finding her and Colin are becoming slim. I have such little time now, and soon they will arrest me, which will consume more time. It all feels so hopeless."

"You cannot release hope," Jacob said.

Aedan looked at him with bloodshot eyes. "I don't know if I'll ever see them again."

CHAPTER TWENTY-EIGHT

CHARRED DISCOVERY

Aedan continued pounding his head against the window glass. He had lost his energy and hope.

"You have faith, right?" Jacob said.

"Yes, but I'm not sure where God is in all of this. Why isn't God helping me find them? I don't understand."

"Maybe God is trying to help you, in His way?"

He stared at Jacob with surprise. "How old are you? You approach this as if you're fifty years old — maybe older."

Jacob became solemn. "I'm old enough to recognize it when I a person who has a harsh challenge they are grappling with. I can recognize heart-wrenching human pain. Don't give up, have faith because what seems impossible is possible. In our human weaknesses and fears, we often refuse to take a leap of faith and trust."

Aedan looked astonished by the young man's response. "Wow, where did the European Lit student go?"

"I'm still here." Jacob laughed. "Tell me about Colin? You spoke with love about Ciara, but you have said little about your son. I'd like to hear more about him."

"Oh man, Jake — "

He exclaimed. "My name is Jacob, not Jake."

"Okay, Jacob, I understand, you like your name."

"No. It's not a matter of liking my name; it's about accuracy. Many names have a significant meaning. My name is Jacob; please use my name, without alteration." He placed his right hand on Aedan's left shoulder. "Please, respect my wishes."

A slight electric jolt raced through Aedan's left shoulder; he pulled away from Jacob's hand. An image of Máire in Millennium Park entered his mind. "What did you do?" he shouted, with anger.

Jacob smiled.

Aedan had grown a dislike of robotic smiles, and the night guard was flashing too many of those.

"Please, Mr. O'Beirne, tell me about Colin."

He looked at the night guard. "Oh, Jacob, I hope you get to meet Colin. He's a terrific kid, smart, funny, structured, and yet creative too. He's five years old, thinks I'm a superhero, and yet Colin's a pure reflection of his mother," he said with anxiety. "The boy will be something special in this life, unique. I love him so much it makes my heart pound with pain, wondering what's happened to him. I'd do anything to help him and his mother." His head slumped to his knees.

He looked at Jacob. "I want to see him again, and I want to hold him and Ciara. I've been such an idiot … blessed beyond measure, and I couldn't see it through my desire for ball games and bars and city nightlife." He swung his arms over his head in frustration and emotional pain. His arms contacted the window glass, which vibrated against his hands.

"Aedan?" He held a warm, almost gentle, expression. "Are you ready to trust?"

"Yes." He looked at Jacob, as he pounded on the glass, relaxed, his facial color returned to normal from an intense emotional red hue. Aedan pulled his arms away from the window, and lowered them to his side, took deep breaths. "Thank you, there is much more to you than I thought."

"You mean there is more to me than a chubby, irresponsible, punk college kid you thought I was?" He chuckled.

"Yes, that sums it up." He laughed. He smacked Jacob on the back.

"I'm glad you'll trust. Because since you're now far more relaxed, I was wondering if you've seen the painting hanging on the wall to your right? It's one of my favorites." Jacob pointed.

Aedan stood, and using a flashlight, he examined the image. The picture displayed a view of downtown Chicago from somewhere on Lake Michigan. He noticed that the piece came from the time when the forty-story Trenton Tower soared above everything else standing along Michigan Avenue. Beyond that structure, a cloud ridge with a reddish area appeared to reflect or echo something from below. He looked at Jacob. "What is this doing here?"

"It's a painting donated by a friend of the Medical Center. Dr. Miller loved the old-fashioned feel of the piece. I have to say; I agree with her."

Aedan peered through the western window. He saw another structure in the near-total darkness, seventy-five feet from the main tower. "What is that building?" His voice filled with surprise.

"That's building number one," Jacob said.

Aedan looked shocked.

"You didn't know there are two buildings?"

"Jacob, how could I have known? Tell me about it; tell me now." His excitement rose while he chastised himself for not having driven along Asher Avenue before he entered the new tower. He felt like a fool, making one mistake after another throughout his search for his family. Yet, he had not seen the narrow dark tower, even when he had looked west to the parking garage. A surge of nausea raced through him, knowing he might have placed his family in jeopardy.

"That's the first medical building, constructed in 1945. It has twenty-one stories while this tower has thirty-six. That edifice is square, one-hundred and twenty feet on each side, while this building is rectangular, two-hundred feet wide by one hundred and fifty feet deep. The architect moved to Chicago from New York. He liked the Empire State Building so much he used the same Indiana Limestone panels at this site, to cover the exterior. If you shine your flashlight, you will see the grayish facade," Jacob said.

"Is it used anymore?" He aimed the light at the building. The beams illuminated the surface.

"Fifty doctors used it until Wednesday morning."

He looked stunned. "What happened?"

"A massive gas explosion from somewhere in the middle of the building wrecked the structure. The concussion slammed the ten highest floors the hardest, with the explosion bursting through the roof. You can see the yellow police tape surrounding the base of the building. It took hours for the Fire Department to put out the blaze. No one died, but the emergency crews took one-hundred people to local hospitals. They said there would have been far more injuries if this were not a holiday week. They shut down this new tower because the fire was so close. We reopened yesterday afternoon."

"What's the address for that building?"

"The same as this tower, **3960** North Franklin Street, number one. It was the original building at this address, and it's scheduled for complete demolition next year, so the developers can construct another tower in its place to complete the Medical Center campus," Jacob said.

Aedan frowned. He looked, again, with anguish, at the painting on the wall. He recalled standing outside the Douglas Hotel, where he had suspected, even then, that the red clouds were significant.

"Where were you this week not know about the fire? It was all over the news. I assumed you knew what to the old building. I would have told you in the lobby if I knew your full story. It's been a freaky time between the bad accident on the highway, the rough snowstorm in the Loop, and the fire that destroyed the building, what a week this has been. And the fire took all day to put out because pockets of gas in the building kept flaring up; the firemen were there well beyond midnight that day."

He grabbed Jacob by shoulders, and with joy, he shook the young man back-and-forth. "Don't you know what this means?"

"No." Jacob looked confused.

"Ciara and Colin are in that building, somewhere."

"How? We're in Dr. Miller's offices now?" Jacob said.

"Don't you understand? The doctor's business card doesn't state a building number; it only contains the street address. Ciara has never been in the downtown office. She's always gone to the suburban office close to our home in Oak Valley and didn't know the correct office is in this new building. She entered the wrong building, and the explosion happened while she was in there." He looked excited.

Jacob looked sad. "But, if, if that's true, they died in the explosion. The explosive concussion destroyed the elevator shaft all the way to the roof. I'm sorry; I don't see how they could have survived."

"No — they're alive. I have two friends who have helped me all along, and they wouldn't have helped me if there was no hope to save my family, but there is little time left to find them, and I should have thought of searching for fires in buildings much sooner. I'm risking their lives by wasting time in this tower."

"No, Mr. O'Beirne, you don't know the path, or the steps required to find your family. If you try to avoid taking any of those steps, you might not reach your final location and destiny."

"That's fair, Jacob," Aedan grinned; his demeanor had risen to near euphoria as he stared at the charred building through the window. He pulled out his cell phone, sent a coded numerical text message to Eddie. It was 10:40pm on Friday. He had eighty moments left.

Aedan walked to the suite entrance, where he would leave the offices. He turned back to Jacob. "Well, my move to break the keys inside the exit door locks doesn't matter anymore." He laughed. "Come on, join me, you don't want to miss this. I have to give myself up to the police so I can rescue my family before it's too late."

CHAPTER TWENTY-NINE

DESIRING ARREST

Aedan entered the stairwell and found a large contingent of Chicago Police Officers, in full protective gear, their weapons aimed at him. He laughed and stretched his arms well above his head. "Hi fellas, I'm the man you're after. I'm not armed, and I *will* cooperate." He beamed; his mood had risen since seeing building number one. He looked hopeful, which was a near-miraculous change in a brief period.

"Don't move," Officer Wilson said. He aimed his weapon at Aedan.

"I won't run. I understand the situation." He pointed at the doorway. "This is Jacob Schultz; he's the night guard; he's not to blame for me getting into the building. I forced him to join my search to find my wife and son."

Bellson made his way through the armored police.

"Hello, Detective, I was wondering where you were. I knew you wouldn't miss the fun of arresting me." Aedan laughed.

"I see you haven't found your family, as I expected," Bellson said.

Aedan's demeanor became stern. "Bellson you're a piece of work. You know I've been working almost non-stop to find them. They weren't here in this tower, but I know where they are."

"How many times have you said that in the last two days? I've heard enough, O'Beirne," Bellson said. He looked at Officer Wilson. "Cuff him."

Officer Wilson pulled Aedan's arms behind his back, cuffed him.

The stairwell power returned, flooding the group with bright light.

"Hey, Ghost got the lights on," Bellson said. He looked at Aedan. "You've been a real pain, O'Beirne. Breaking into this building and then taking the guard hostage will not end well for you. I don't get it, you seemed rational enough; why did you crack and do something so stupid?"

"Detective, don't you understand I'm trying to find my family and that I've been running on empty for the last couple days? There's little time left to find them, and I don't want you holding me back. I know where they are, and you don't seem the least interested in helping me — over-and-over I've told you that my wife and son are missing. When are you going to accept they're missing?"

"Oh, we believe you. Your family is missing. We've worked hard digging into your background, and we've talked to almost everyone you know. We also called Metric & Inch where you work," Bellson said.

"Glad you're earning your salary." Aedan flashed a sarcastic grin. "I'd hate to think you were wasting taxpayer dollars. What good does it all do if it doesn't help me find my family? All your work has proved worthless."

"We'll see," Bellson said. He glared at Jacob. "You, idiot guard, get out of the way so we can enter the floor."

Jacob stepped through the door and onto the main floor, clearing the path for the police.

Bellson pushed Aedan through the exit door and onto the twentieth floor. He looked back at Officer Wilson. "Now that the power is back, have them release the elevators, so we can get back down without taking the stairs."

"Detective — why won't you consider what I'm telling you?" He glared at him. "I want to find my family."

Aedan groaned, as Officer Wilson pulled him across the lobby to the exit door on the south side.

"Sir, I have a car waiting on the plaza," Officer Wilson said. "Should I put him in the car?"

"No," Bellson said. "Put him in the south conference room."

"Why?" Aedan shouted. "What do you want from me?" His concern swelled; every minute mattered. It was 10:50pm, seventy moments left. His mind flooded with worry; he didn't notice Bellson shoving him into a chair with high force. His left arm ached, but he no longer cared about the pain; he had to get into the burned building.

"Sir, can we take the cuffs off?" Officer Wilson said. "He's in pain, he's bleeding, and he's in lousy shape."

"Take them off but watch him. He might run."

"I'm not going anywhere you fool," Aedan shouted; it sounded like a growl, his anger boiling. "Don't you understand this complex is where I want to be?" He said with increasing impatience. "I'll save us time; I won't answer questions until you've processed me and after I've spoken with my lawyer. We can sit here all night, but I will not answer a single question."

"Why are you demanding a lawyer now?" Bellson said.

"Because, as you know, and as you can see, this has been a rough time for me, and I still haven't found my family. You're supposed to help law-abiding citizens, and I'm tired of you treating me this way."

Bellson glared at him. "I'm supposed to help a citizen who forced his way into an empty building?"

He took calming breaths to quiet his anger and frustration. "Detective, can I at least appeal to your humanity? I'm convinced my wife and son are in the older building behind us. Let me go into that structure to find them — "

Bellson grunted, cutting him off. "Shut up, O'Beirne."

"Detective, please, you're a human being, try to imagine how you'd act if your family were missing. You have nothing to lose because I have nowhere to run. You have an army of officers covering this complex, and if you let me go into that building, I might get hurt crawling around searching for them. There's no risk to you." Aedan looked hopeful.

"I told you to shut — "

Aedan stood and stepped toward Bellson. "No, listen to me. I have hurt no one but myself in this search; think about that. I have no weapons, and I plan to pay for the damage I did to the building's doors. Ask the night guard about me paying for his busted cell phone." He clenched his jaw in defiance. "I want my family back. Again, if you were in my situation, what would you do? Has it ever occurred to you I'm telling the truth? How will it be for your career if my family dies in the burned-out building and you were the one stopping me from getting to them in time?"

Aedan watched Bellson fall into a mental conflict.

Bellson grimaced. "I don't care — "

Jacob interrupted by leaping into the conversation. "Sir, I spent time with O'Beirne, and for what it's worth, I believe the guy is on the level, and he paid for the cell phone he crushed."

"Why should I care what a college-age night guard thinks?" Bellson said. "Get out of here now before I have you arrested. And, Wilson, get O'Beirne out of my sight, he makes me sick, do it now."

"Yes, Sir," Officer Wilson said. He yanked Aedan to the exit.

"Hey, be careful with my left arm." Aedan winced in pain.

"Cuff him. I don't want him running away," Bellson said.

Officer Wilson pulled Aedan's arms around his back, where he cuffed him. He used excessive force while leading him to the south exit. With vigor, he dragged him to the squad, with Aedan yelling at him all the way.

Jacob followed them outside. He approached them. "Mr. O'Beirne, do you want me to go into number one for you?"

"You would do that for me?"

"Yes," Jacob said. "I believe you, and I fear for your family, and I worry about you if something bad were to happen to them. I'm not sure what I could do in there, but I'm willing to try."

He grinned. "Thank you, Jacob. You're a good man. You need not go into the building for me. I will do it myself."

"How are you going to do that? You're under arrest."

"My best friend Eddie, wait, I mean Officer Wilson, will release me to do it myself." He looked at Eddie dressed in full police gear, including a helmet. "I like the tinted glasses," Aedan said.

"They add a nice touch, don't you think?" Eddie said. His hearty laugh echoed off the building. He placed Aedan in the squad car, making everything appear normal from a distance. He removed the cuffs.

Jacob grimaced. "Don't leave me out of this, I want to help."

"No, the building can fall down anytime. I'm doing this myself."

"Hey, Wyoming, I didn't risk jail to let you do this alone," Eddie said. "What happens to Ciara and Colin matters to me too, you're like family."

"Okay, Eddie you can come with, but Jacob I need you to stay out. I don't want to worry about you while I'm searching for them," Aedan said, as Eddie closed the squad door.

"I'm going with you," Jacob said. "You can't stop me."

Aedan sighed, knowing he did not have time to argue with the guard,. The squad pulled away and headed toward Asher Avenue, lights flashing.

Bellson saw the activity. "What's the guard doing?"

Jacob was running after the squad.

"I don't know," Genswolt said, with confusion.

Bellson looked at the squad slowing at Asher Avenue. He watched as the vehicle turned right, its brake lights glowed. "Oh man, they plan to enter. I'll have Wilson's badge for this." He ran toward Asher Avenue.

Aedan looked back and saw Bellson running toward them. He looked at Eddie. "He's coming at us in a hurry."

Eddie stopped the squad. Aedan left the car and ran to the west entrance. He looked back and saw Bellson and Genswolt running around the corner toward them.

"Stop, O'Beirne, stop," shouted Bellson.

Eddie pulled off his glasses and his helmet. He glared at Bellson. "Gerry, stop this, give the guy a break, he's trying to find his family."

"Eddie? Eddie? What are you doing here?" Bellson said.

"I'm helping my friend find his family. You can shoot us or join us. I thought you were a good guy. Maybe I was wrong about you," Eddie said.

"Detective, I'm not listening to anyone now," Aedan shouted. "My wife and son are in this building, and I'm running out of time. I must find them by midnight. Do me a favor and leave me alone," he shouted as he ran into the building. Eddie and Jacob followed close behind.

Bellson sighed as he looked at Genswolt. "Hand me your flashlight. Get the fire guys to bring a couple more trucks in case this nut job requires extraction from the building though I doubt the trucks can get close with all this wreckage still lying around. Have your team stand farther back in case something goes wrong. This place looks as if it can fall down at any moment." He turned and ran into the building.

CHAPTER THIRTY

ALARMING DEVASTATION

Aedan walked into the water-soaked, pitch-black, and material filled lobby. The explosion caused the devastation, along with the water cascading down from the higher levels after the Chicago Fire Department battled the blaze for over sixteen hours.

"Hand me a flashlight." Aedan looked at Jacob; the young security guard was visible in the darkness.

He shined the light on the floor. He observed, in debris-free locations, that marble tiles formed the surface. Most of the lobby contained mounds of plaster that had flowed away from the rushing water. The material had set-up in small rock-hard hills, which offered an appearance like the moon's surface, gray, white, and dark matter formed indentations and craters in the mounds.

"I'm sorry to say this, but no one in the higher levels could have survived the fire and ensuing explosion," Bellson shouted as he approached carrying his flashlight. "O'Beirne, are you sure you still want to do this?"

"What are you doing here, Bellson? Don't think about trying to stop me. They're in this building, and I won't stop until I find them," Aedan shouted.

"I won't try to stop you. But now that you've seen how bad it is in here do you still want to do this?"

"What a stupid question; my family's in this building. I must find them before it's too late. They're on the twentieth floor because that's where Ciara would've gone for the consult with Dr. Miller."

"But what if they didn't make it to the twentieth floor? Maybe the explosion trapped them somewhere lower," Eddie said as he entered the building.

"I don't have enough time to check every floor; she made it to twenty. Ciara's a determined and strong woman; she lets nothing get in her way once she sets her mind. She thought the doctor was on twenty, which is where she'd go." His harsh tone announced to them he wanted no additional arguments. "I have one chance left to find them and will not doubt my plan. I'll get to twenty because that is where she would have gone, no more discussion."

"O'Beirne, I'll check the other floors while you work your way up to the twentieth. How does that sound?" Bellson said.

"You're offering to help?"

"Yes. I want to make sure your family's not in the building, or else I'll never stop hearing it from you. If they're here, I don't want to prevent you from finding them. We have you surrounded, which means I can arrest you later if your mission doesn't get us killed." He laughed.

"Excellent. Let's find the stairwells because there is no other way, the explosion destroyed the elevators, which isn't surprising since I've experienced nothing but roadblocks." Aedan said.

The structure rested upon a steel girder system. It had vertical pillars installed in the outer walls, and similar posts running throughout all four corners of the elevator shaft system. Wrapped steel posts positioned with precision throughout each floor provided critical mid-floor load-bearing support. The elevator shaft created a twenty-foot-wide rectangle at the center of the structure, an overpowering sight when people walked into the classic tower.

They remodeled the building in 1957, including installing a fire suppression system. The massive Wednesday morning gas explosion destroyed the elevator shaft, and with that, it demolished the sprinkler system, which made it more difficult to put out the blaze.

The lobby appeared stark, businesslike, though the debris-filled marble floor surrounded the elevator shaft. A welcome desk, positioned about ten feet from the doors, lay in ruins with a crack running through its center, the result of falling rubble. The overhead lighting had all crashed to the floor, and much of the ceiling plaster came down with the deluge. Occupant listing boards had collapsed to the floor along the east wall.

Light gray marble panels formed the walls. A substantial analog clock, using the marble wall panels as a background, still hung untouched on the south wall. The clock's time remained fixed at 08:15, the time the fire department had the power to the building cut on Wednesday morning, after the explosion.

He faced the group. "We have to move fast. It's eleven-o-five; we have fifty-five minutes to find them."

"I still don't get the midnight connection," Bellson said.

"There's no time to explain. Trust me when I say we have to find Ciara and Colin by midnight." Aedan said. He looked at the east wall, which faced the new tower. He saw exit doors that opened into a cross tunnel extending to building number two.

Now I know why the tower has rear exit doors.

He saw an impassable blockage in the southeast stairwell — wood, plaster, and all manners of garbage that had rushed down from the higher floors. The obstructions were another result of the cascading water from fire hoses and water cannons, with random wreckage distribution. Several locations filled with debris while other areas seemed untouched by the carnage. "We have to find a clear path," he shouted.

He moved around the elevator shaft and shined his light at the stairwell installed at the northwest corner. "They're clear, let's go." He climbed to the second floor without incident.

"You guys go on. I'll check out this level." Bellson ran to a nearby office.

Aedan looked at the northwest corner where the rushing water had washed away much of the plaster covering the vertical steel support beams. Several steel water pipes extended through the walls, a result of the massive explosion that had sent powerful shock waves through the structure. He moved around the pipes and continued climbing the stairs to the third floor, with the others following close behind.

Wintry wind gusts blew through the stairwell from an unseen structural breach above, chilling him as he climbed. He arrived at the third level, where material covered the floor. He filled with fear as he surveyed the landscape; the damage was so extensive that it no longer looked like an office building. "Let's keep moving."

He climbed to the fourth floor and then on to the fifth floor where the situation was much worse. His sad expression revealed his concern.

I can't ever get a break.

"Where do we go now?" Jacob said.

Aedan stared at the blocked northwest stairwell. A massive plug of office desks, plaster, wall studs, paintings, pieces of steel, and various other materials blocked his path. "We have to try the other stairs." Aedan looked to the southeast.

Eddie ran to the stairs for a closer look. "Hey, Wyoming, get over here." He pointed. "We can crawl through the gaps in that junk."

Bellson sprinted to them. "The first five floors are all clear."

Aedan ran to the southeast stairs and began moving sharp pieces of metal from the path, he slipped on a still damp plaster clump, fell and hit his head on the edge of a steel desk. Blood ran from his forehead. "Give me a break," he yelled as he pulled his jacket off, ripped a sleeve from his shirt and wrapped it around his head to slow the bleeding.

He turned back to the wreckage and began crawling onto a desk that had landed on its side, hopped onto a steel bookcase embedded in a plaster pool. Foot-by-foot he scraped and crawled through the wreckage as the others watched him complete his ascent to the sixth floor.

"I made it," he shouted. "Be careful, the wreckage can't be from water alone, it looks as if a bomb exploded."

"I was in the new tower when it happened. The lobby shook like a bomb went off," Jacob said. "It was terrible."

Eddie grabbed Jacob by the arm and pulled the guard back, anger filled his eyes. "He's already scared out of his head, and you say things like that? What's wrong with you?"

"I'm sorry, I wasn't thinking," Jacob whispered.

Eddie grabbed him by both arms and moved close to his face. "Keep the unwelcome news to yourself, or I'll pound you. He's my best friend, and he needs to keep moving so he can find his family. Say nothing but positive comments from now on. Do you understand?" Eddie glared at him.

Jacob squirmed under Eddie's rebuking eyes. "Yes, I meant no harm."

"Calm down fellas, let's not rip one another apart," Bellson said.

"Knock it off — we have to keep moving," Aedan shouted. He walked across the sixth floor. "Ciara, Colin, are you here?"

"We can't get through the blocked stairwells," Jacob said.

"I know." Aedan ran to the northwest corner where he began crawling through the wreckage. He looked at the group. "Hurry, we have no time to waste." He turned from them and began climbing through pipes and debris that had fallen from the higher floors. Water puddles and wet material caused him to slip as he climbed the steps. With the others close behind, he made steady progress.

Aedan found good fortune all the way to the tenth floor. He heard Jacob's labored breathing — the robust man was struggling. He looked at the guard. "Are you okay?"

Jacob took deep breaths. "I've got to exercise and diet."

Aedan smiled with warmth. "Let's keep going."

Evidence of the explosion and the fire surrounded Aedan. The elevator shaft revealed gaping holes above. Pieces of brick and rock had blown outward through the offices and toward the outer walls. Large mounds of material had formed along the building's outer edges, inches from the outside.

Aedan's expression revealed his heightened concern as his senses filled with the smell of burned wood and plaster. He knew that before the explosion and fire, the building provided space for employees, patients, doctors, and pharmaceutical companies. "It was all wiped away," he said.

He shivered when a wintry gust blew through the floor. Nothing stopped or slowed the cold winds. He saw a down jacket fluttering in the air; held tight on a jagged piece of glass in a destroyed window. He looked at the others. "Come on, we have to keep moving." Anxiety caused him to clench his jaws; his eyes squinted. The floor presented an obstacle course for him. He crawled through and around the carnage seeking a way to climb to eleven.

"Hey, Mr. O'Beirne, the corners received the least amount of damage. The explosion swirled and reversed, creating more energy as it plunged outward through the offices," Jacob said.

Eddie glared at him with anger.

"Okay, I understand, I'll stop," Jacob said.

"Don't be careful about what you say around me. I'm not a china doll." Aedan frowned. "I need your help, not your protection."

"I was just trying to — "

Aedan turned away from Eddie. He swept the flashlight's beams back-and-forth across the floor. "If you haven't noticed, the bathrooms are in the corners on every floor. They seem to have survived intact. The women's restroom is in the northwest corner, and the men's restroom is in the southeast, duplicated on every floor. I hope that's a useful design for Ciara and Colin."

"How can that help?" Bellson said.

"I'm not sure, but Jacob's correct, it seems like the restrooms are the strongest locations on each floor." He sighed. Just then, as Aedan looked through the wreckage, excitement overtook him when an external light reflection caught his attention. He ran through debris to the west wall. Despite his fear of heights, he ignored the drop to the ground as he looked down at the parking garage across Asher Avenue. He turned back to the group. "She's here. She's here somewhere. I told you," Aedan shouted. Ignoring the pain in his left leg, he jumped up-and-down in excitement.

"Hey, Wyoming, what's going on?"

"Look!" Aedan pointed. "That's the top floor of the parking garage on Asher Avenue. That lone car parked at the center is Ciara's." He looked at Bellson. "Now, do you believe me?"

The detective looked stunned. "Yes."

"Ciara, Colin," he shouted. "We have to make noise, so they know we're searching for them."

"We have another problem — we can't make it through the blocked stairwells," Jacob said with a somber tone.

Aedan looked at the stairs. He sighed. "I need to catch a break."

CHAPTER THIRTY-ONE

CIRCUMVENTING

Aedan paced back-and-forth. He was trying to determine how to circumvent the blocked stairwells.

"Hey, Wyoming, let's try using the elevator shaft. It runs all the way to the roof; it might have a ladder for maintenance workers. Many older buildings have them. Maybe there's still a remnant we can climb," Eddie said.

Aedan grinned. "That's an excellent idea." He approached the shaft at the location where the entrance to the elevators used to lie; all units had blown away. The force from the gas explosion had reached its peak on the tenth floor, discharging its energy in all directions from there and sweeping straight through the roof.

Using the flashlights, he and the others stared into the shaft.

Aedan stepped back; he fell into a violent shiver. The shaft offered a frightening open space with a terrifying drop. He inched to the edge and shined his flashlight into the darkness, saw pipes jutting upward through a material pile on the lobby level, knew a fall into that mess would end in a painful death.

"Are you okay," Jacob said.

"No, I'm not okay. I don't like heights, at all."

"After everything you've been through, your fear of heights will stop you from finding your family?" Bellson said.

He glared at him. "No chance of that." With caution, he walked to the shaft's edge; he shined the light across the vertical space. "There's a utility ladder on the back wall close to the center point, ten feet away. I've no idea how we'll get there."

"I do," Eddie said. His hearty laugh filled their ears. He ran to the southeast stairwell where he began pulling at the wreckage, yanked a long six-inch board from the pile, tossed it toward the elevator shaft.

The others ran to help him. The group pulled two more boards from the wreckage. Just then, several tons of material moved downward sliding on steel pipes. The full blockage dropped four feet in an instant. A steel tube, under stress created by the fast-moving obstruction, jettisoned from the pile, slamming Eddie in the right knee. He rolled onto the floor while screaming in agony; his voice carried through the windows.

Aedan went to Eddie. He tried to help his friend stand, yet the slightest movement caused waves of intense pain to course through his friend's body.

Eddie stammered, "You're … going … have to … go on without me. Wyoming go retrieve your family. Don't forget about me waiting for you here at this fancy bar and grill on the tenth floor." He made a weak attempt at a hearty laugh. He failed.

"Detective, do you think your men can help him?" Aedan said.

"The firemen can help," Bellson said. He scrambled to the outer west wall. He pressed the transmit button on his radio. "Genswolt, we have a man down, with a possible broken leg, it's a knee injury. He can't move. The Fire Department should try to work a ladder up to him, on the tenth floor. I'll leave the flashlight on so they can locate him." He pressed end.

Aedan heard Bellson's radio as Genswolt answered.

"The trucks can't get close enough; there is too much debris surrounding the building. We're working on clearing it now," Genswolt said.

"Do the best you can," Bellson said. He looked at Aedan. "It might take some time to reach Eddie."

"I understand," Aedan said. He helped Eddie into an intact office chair. "I'm this far because of you, and I wouldn't be in this building if you didn't help. I owe you a month of pub stops for this."

"That's a deal, buddy," Eddie said. "Now get moving up to the twentieth, time is short."

Aedan helped drag the boards to the elevator shaft, where they formed a wood bridge to the back wall, resting on a slight ledge formed from the brick and level with the tenth floor. He looked at the others. He laughed. "Ciara won't believe me when I tell her I walked across an elevator shaft on some charred planks," Aedan said as he took in deep, nervous breaths, turned back to the task and began inching across the wood bridge toward the steel maintenance ladder.

He climbed the ladder, with Bellson in the middle and Jacob last. At first, Aedan allowed his fears to slow his ascent to a near crawl, stopping many times, clinging to the ladder and forcing himself to not look down and refusing to look upward more than a few feet, knowing that if he put too much stress on the ladder, it might break away, causing them all to fall to painful deaths. Aedan grimaced knowing there was no other choice, he had to take risks, or would not find them in time — he began climbing with renewed energy.

Aedan made fast work of the climb. He managed, in a few minutes, to reach the fifteenth floor where the ladder ceased four feet above the level. "We can't keep climbing, there's no ladder above us."

"What do you want to do?" Bellson said.

"We have to find a way out of the shaft." Aedan placed a firm grip on the ladder. He made a slight rotation and shined the light on the walls, which revealed a four-foot-wide gap in the wall along the shaft's western side, ten feet to his left. "Can we get to that hole?"

"It won't be easy; we must leave the ladder and walk along the brick edge. We'll have about four inches to walk on," Bellson said.

"What else can we do?" Aedan said.

"Hey, I'm not a skinny guy; I don't know if I can make it across a four-inch ridge," shouted Jacob. "Maybe we should go back down to a lower floor and see if there is a better path there."

"No," shouted Aedan. "I am going forward; there's no time to backtrack, they are counting on me to get to them. You can go back down. I'll move onto the ledge and inch toward the hole. I hope the stairs on this level will be useable. This is an all-or-nothing time for me, yet it's understandable if either of you wants to avoid the risk. It's not your family, they're my responsibility."

"I'm going with you," Bellson said. "I doubted you every step of the way, it's time for me to step up and help you retrieve your family."

"Man, you guys are such a pain," Jacob said. "You might have to help me get across the ridge. Let's go."

Aedan sighed with worry for Jacob and Bellson, not wanting to lead them to injury. He set his mind to the task, climbed one ladder step, placing his feet above the brick shelf, shined his light at old empty pipe brackets bolted to the wall. Years in the past, the building ran water pipes, and wires, to the higher floors through the shaft and used the brackets as hold-downs.

Ignoring the throbbing pain in his left arm, he used his left hand to grasp a nearby pipe bracket, about one foot above him. He stepped onto the brick ridge, testing its solidity.

While maintaining a firm grasp on the bracket, he slid his left foot sideways along the ridge toward the gap in the wall. With caution, he moved his right hand to the bracket and then he moved his right foot to the brick ledge. A shiver ran through him as he stood on the brick shelf at a frightening height above the ground.

"You've got it, Mr. O'Beirne, you can do this," Bellson said.

In an intense mental effort, he ignored the shivers. While maintaining a firm hold with his right hand, he pulled his left hand free. He began sliding to the gap. After moving two feet, with his left hand, he grabbed a nearby pipe bracket. He repeated the steps with his right hand and foot.

Detective Bellson observed Aedan's moves. "Hey, Jake, are you watching this?" he shouted down to the guard.

"My name is Jacob, not Jake. I'm watching you."

"Excuse me, pal," Bellson said.

"My name is Jacob."

Aedan stopped. He sighed with anger. "Will you guys shut up? I'm trying to focus here, and you sound like two children." He moved his left foot to a position in front of the gap in the wall. Using his left hand, he grabbed an exposed vertical beam; he slid his right hand and foot toward the hole. In a flash, he dove through the opening. He stood on fifteen, close to the shaft. He looked at them. "Follow my technique but be careful."

Bellson moved his left hand and foot off the ladder; he released his right hand and leg. With confidence, he used one hand to hold the bracket while he made aggressive slides toward the hole. He repeated those moves twice. Seconds later, he leaped through the gap and rolled onto the floor.

"Show-off." Aedan laughed.

Jacob released his hand from the ladder — followed by his left foot. "This isn't any fun," he complained. He slid his left foot while removing his right hand and foot from the ladder. His body weight caused him to lean a little toward the shaft's dark abyss, yet he maintained a left-handed grip on the bracket. He inched along the ridge and came to the last bracket. As he shifted his weight to move his left hand, the old bracket pulled free from the wall, he began falling backward. He shrieked in fright.

Bellson grabbed Jacob's left arm and pulled him tight toward the gap. Jacob did his best to shift his weight toward the opening, but a ridge brick under his left foot broke free. He fell backward toward the shaft despite the firm grip Bellson had on him. This time, he kept falling and took Bellson with him. The detective, as he rotated his body to maintain his grip, slammed into the steel vertical beam at the edge of the opening, breaking his left arm and several ribs. Like a stubborn bull, he fought through the pain while maintaining a firm grip on the falling night guard. "O'Beirne," he screamed. "Help." Waves of agony crossed his body, but he maintained his grasp.

Aedan raced to them; he dove onto the floor and grabbed Jacob's right arm. The night guard hung in the open air, maintained by the strong grips by the other men. While bracing against the vertical beam, they began pulling the guard to the floor. Jacob used his legs to help climb the wall toward them. Soon, his head came up over the top, and he squirmed his way through the opening. They pulled him well away from the hole.

Jacob took in deep breaths.

Bellson sat on the floor, a flood of pain revealed to him the damage done to his left arm and ribcage. He strained for regular breaths; his broken ribs made it difficult. He could not stand; his pain and dizziness consumed him. "O'Beirne, get going, find them. I'll call my men on the radio and tell them I'm on the fifteenth floor in need of help, can't go farther, and will slow you down if I tried. Move now."

Aedan looked at him. "Thank you, detective. You were a stand-up man when I needed it most."

"Call me, Gerry." He smiled. His forehead covered in sweat.

"Thank you, Gerry." Aedan grinned. He turned and ran to the southeast stairwell; found it debris free. He ran up the stairs taking three steps at a time, passing the sixteenth and seventeenth floors in a minute.

Jacob found extra strength as he maintained pace with Aedan.

After reaching the eighteenth floor, Aedan's shoulders slumped in defeat after he viewed massive material piles blocking both stairwells leading to nineteen. "Oh, man!"

CHAPTER THIRTY-TWO

DUCTWORK

Aedan sprinted to the elevator shaft; he found no means to climb inside the vertical space. He was at a dead-end two floors below his goal. "No, we're so close; there must be a path."

"I know of a way," Jacob said. He looked at the ceiling which held no plaster, and all overhead lighting had swept away in the explosive onslaught. "But you will have to go alone; I'm too heavy."

"Tell me what you're thinking, now," Aedan shouted.

"Every high-rise building holds a similar dilemma for its architects during the development stage," Jacob said.

"I know that from working for Metric & Inch. Large building architects and systems designers have to work out where they will place the mechanicals for each building they design while keeping them safe from everyone, except building maintenance crews."

"Yes, designers include mechanical floors and areas. Those locations house all the building's needs for heat, cooling, air handling, water and plumbing processing, modern electronics, telephone and data services, and all the rest," Jacob said.

"Get to your point; we have to reach twenty."

Jacob ignored him. "In the past, many architects divided their buildings into ten-floor segments. They treated each section as a separate unit when accounting for utility needs. They placed a mechanical room every ten floors, so all occupants received similar treatment, and in taller buildings, they had to do that to carry water and other needs to the higher levels."

"Hurry — get to your point," Aedan said.

"It's likely that this building has two mechanical floors, one in the basement that serves the first ten floors, which the maintenance crew would have accessed through a private lobby office. I'm sure a second mechanical room is on the twenty-first floor, which would serve the eleventh through the twentieth floors. I'm positive the public elevators in this building did not have a call button for the highest level. It's probable that access to that level was by special elevator keys carried by building management and maintenance personnel."

"Jacob, what's wrong with you? My family is waiting. Stop wasting time. Tell me, tell me now," shouted Aedan.

"The mechanical room is three floors above us." Jacob ran to the elevator shaft. "Look close, the ducts take a turn upward to the next level, walls used to hide the ducts. We can still see pieces of the old studs and beams. It looks as if they're still usable."

"So? Come on, hurry, get to the point," Aedan said.

"The ducts run along the elevator shaft, and I'm sure there are others that run along the stairwells, maybe through the bathroom spaces, repeated each level until they reach their source in the mechanical room on twenty-one."

"So, what?" Aedan glared at the guard.

"You will get into the duct. The ducts are twenty-four inches square, which is more than enough for you, but not for me. We are fortunate because they have been in this building since the time of its full remodel. They have sturdy tie-down straps because back in those days, the engineers did not have access to the same lightweight and streamlined building materials we have today."

"So?" he shouted. His patience evaporated, but he understood that he had to listen to him because they had no other way to get to twenty, and he had to get there soon.

Jacob looked frustrated. "Time is short. I'm providing you with information so you will feel confident about what you must do and because you will have to do this without me. You have a fear of heights, and you dislike enclosed spaces so this will not be easy for you. You'll use the vertical ducts to crawl up to the twentieth floor."

"Oh man, Jacob, is that all you have for me? You've seen too many movies. Those things can't handle our weight, and inside they're filthy, greasy tunnels designed to move air throughout the building, nothing else." He glared at the night guard.

"Do you have any other ideas on how to get up to the twentieth floor?" Jacob said. "The ducts run to the highest level. What else can you do to access twenty? Tell me that, and I'll be on your side." Jacob shrugged his shoulders in defiance.

Aedan took on a pale white appearance as he glared at Jacob. "How am I supposed to climb to twenty using those?"

"I don't know, but the ducts offer you a path to twenty."

He pounded his right leg over-and-over as he thought it through. "How thick is the steel used for those ducts?"

"I'm not sure, it can go down to hundredths of an inch," Jacob said.

"And that's supposed to hold me when I crawl through?"

"You're skinny, you weigh little, and in the old days, they used robust strapping when they installed the ducts. Let go of your fears and trust," Jacob said.

Aedan looked at the vertical air passageway; he inspected the elevator shaft and the remnant of the wall that had encased it before the explosion rocked the building. His eyes followed the duct as it rose to the nineteenth floor; he inspected the girder systems. "I won't crawl through the ducts because I have a better idea. We have to find something to use as a hammer and a pipe, maybe four feet long."

"Will a hammer do?" Jacob laughed. He handed the tool Aedan.

"Where did you get this?"

"I found it on ten when we built the wood bridge across the elevator shaft. I figured it might come in handy." Jacob smiled.

"Nice find," Aedan said. "Let's get to work and find that pipe."
He found a small breach in the vertical duct that hugged the elevator shaft, about three feet above the floor. He hammered the opening, working the tool's claw into the hole until he created a wide flange.

Using the pipe, Jacob peeled back and rolled the steel apart beginning at the flange.

Aedan continued hammering and clawing the opening around the square duct. Soon, with Jacob's help, he had created two detached sections. He climbed onto a cross stud along the elevator shaft, where he hammered the hold-down straps off the duct, scaled the wall to nine feet above the floor, repeating the steps along the way, and scrambled back down.

He grabbed the duct and began to swing it back-and-forth with intense force until the section broke free from the horizontal seam ten feet above them. The metal casing came crashing down, the sound echoed across eighteen and through the windows. He placed the hammer into one of his belt loops while stuffing his flashlight in his shirt, so light poked through the top and lit his way. He took the pipe from Jacob and began scaling the wall along the elevator shaft.

"You have created a brilliant plan. Climbing through the cleared duct holes will get you to twenty in a hurry."

"Thank you, Jacob. I'm glad you know so much about buildings and their mechanical systems. I work for an engineering firm, and I don't hold as much information." He grinned.

"Thanks, I'm not the dumb rock many people believe I am."

"You're a good man, Jacob," Aedan said,

"Thank you, and don't forget about me down here after you find them. I'd don't want to remain stuck on this floor." Jacob laughed.

"How could I ever forget you, Jacob?"

"Just don't forget about me down here on eighteen."

He laughed. "Okay, Jacob. I won't forget about you." He understood that he would not have made it that far if the three men had not helped. If he had driven along Asher Avenue first, he would have entered the burned-out building alone, and he would not have gained help from Jacob, Bellson, and Eddie. Each man played a critical role in getting him to eighteen. The rest was up to him.

Aedan reached the top of the eighteenth floor, with the underside of the next floor inches above. He held on to a steel vertical beam that ran alongside the elevator shaft, rotated away from the shaft, inched his legs farther up the cross studs to position himself to crawl across a steel horizontal tie bar between the girders.

He moved with caution onto the tie bar and inched himself to below the hole, created after he had ripped the vertical duct from the connecting seam. As he stood, he pushed the pipe against the square metal casing hanging over his head; the metal tunnel hung five inches above the nineteenth floor. Aedan shoved the duct away, which created easy access to the next level through the pass-through hole. He crawled through the opening and rolled onto nineteen. "I made it to the next floor," he shouted.

"Keep moving as fast as you can, and you will get there."

"I hope and pray I do," Aedan said.

CHAPTER THIRTY-THREE

BONE BREAKING EFFORT

Aedan ran to the southeast stairwell which he found blocked, sprinted around the elevator chute and found the northwest stairwell in the same condition, moved to the duct along the elevator shaft, climbed the shaft wall, as he did on eighteen. He pounded away the horizontal straps holding the metal casing to the steel beam hugging the shaft, worked to the top, where he stopped beneath the twentieth floor.

He broke the final strap on the duct where it extended through the pass-through hole to the next level, climbed down the shaft wall, using the old lath and horizontal crossbars as steps.

Once back on the floor, he grabbed the vertical duct at its lowest point, where it hung about five inches above the level. He used as much force as he could muster to move it back-and-forth until it began to break free from the connecting seam overhead at twenty.

In a swift and powerful move, he drove his legs away from the elevator shaft while maintaining a firm grasp on the duct. He leaped away as the metal air-moving tunnel pulled away from its overhead seam and came crashing down to the floor.

Aedan scaled the elevator shaft wall with prompt speed, he inched to the horizontal tie bar between the girders, he pushed the long pipe against the metal tunnel hanging five inches above the twentieth floor. After crawling through the pass-through hole, he rolled onto the twentieth floor. He took deep breaths. "Okay, I made it to twenty. Now, I have to find them."

His work had weakened the duct seams and the straps extending to the mechanical room on twenty-one. The fastenings holding the metal tunnel to the elevator shaft beam could not take the stress, they tore away from the brackets. As Aedan began to stand, a ten-foot duct section pulled away from the upper horizontal seam and came hurtling down on him. The metallic screeching sound warned him of the looming contact; he rotated away, but the duct made a substantial impact on his back, knocking him off his feet. He twisted to stop his fall with his hands; however, as he contacted the floor, he screamed as his left wrist broke. He groaned as the metal tunnel collapsed over him. The twentieth floor filled with reverberations of his painful howls, mixed with the ear-piercing sound of metal crashing to the level's concrete surface.

Are you kidding me?

He crawled from under the duct and moved into a standing position. He ignored the pain emanating from his left wrist.

At least I made it to twenty.

He looked at his watch, it was 11:46pm; he had fourteen minutes left.

I must get to them before Christmas Day begins.

He viewed the floor using a flashlight. He saw massive air handling units, along with several steel beams, had fallen onto the floor from twenty-one.

The explosion must have weakened the girder system above.

Aedan ran across the floor, checking what little remained of the offices, searched the areas where equipment had fallen. He halted at a massive air handler, shocked the floor withstood the stress of it crashing onto the level.

Frigid winds rushed through the structure. The building seemed to shake from the force of the wind, unstable, feeling almost as if it could topple over. He continued moving from one ruined office to another.

Where can they be? I know they're here somewhere, but where?

He looked to the northwest; the elevator shaft blocked his view.

The women's bathroom, I knew there was a reason I noticed those rooms on ten.

He ran around the elevator shaft. He stopped after seeing the area around the women's restroom. The stairwell had a full blockage of equipment having dropped onto the steps, crushing the upper portions, ice, and snow-covered the units. Bright stars were shining through open gaps in the roof. A large hill of inner building and office materials blocked the bathroom door. It was 11:49pm. Eleven moments left.

Now I need to get through that mess.

Aedan ran to the material hill. With frantic intensity, he grabbed at everything he could, pipes, plaster, a small desk, several computers, and reams of printer paper. He worked with desperation; his fingers and hands began to bleed as adrenalin coursed through him — he noticed some material remained warm, residual heat from the explosive onslaught.

Aedan forced his broken left wrist to work, despite the pain waves it sent to him. He no longer cared about himself; instead, he focused on getting into the bathroom and finding his family. He worked himself into a frenzy, clearing a path to the door at incredible speed. Soon, he had enough material removed to make it to the door which opened inward. He pushed the door; something blocked it, shoved harder; it moved about three inches, not enough. He shined the light into the room. A two-by-four, embedded in the bathroom wall, blocked the door.

I can't believe this, even here, at the last location, I must push through roadblocks.

With steel-like resolve, he pulled the metal door to the closed position; in a fast move, he drove the door with great violence into the wood stud; it moved a couple inches. He repeated the movement and gained several additional inches, took in huge breaths, pushed the door while driving his legs, moving the door another eight inches.

Aedan squeezed through the opening, looked at the stud, he pulled on it, but it would not budge, climbed on top of the board, several feet off the floor. He jumped up-and-down on the wood until it snapped, allowing him to open the door.

He shined the light at a long, and narrow, entrance hallway, with the main restroom, positioned to the left. With his flashlight cutting through the darkness, he took slow, anxious steps forward. His heart sank when he saw two massive steel girders from the mechanical room floor had collapsed into the bathroom. He hesitated, knowing he had to move forward, yet fearing what he might find around the corner.

Realizing he had little time left, he renewed his resolve and stepped into the main restroom with the light illuminating his way. Scattered across the tiled floor lay ceiling materials and pieces of the ducts that used to run to the mechanical room above. He shined the light across the room; he jumped at rustling noises emanating from the rear outer corner.

"Dad," shouted Colin.

Aedan ran to his son. He grabbed him and lifted him well into the air, not noticing the pain in his left wrist. "Are you okay? I was so worried about you — I love you so much."

"Nothing hit me, Dad, but it was really, really scary."

Aedan hugged him tight, kissed him, and put him down. He turned back to the room, looking for Ciara. He moved with frantic speed, knowing time had to be short.

"Dad, Mom's over there." He pointed to the rear outer wall corner.

He ran to Ciara. "Colin, what happened to her?"

"One of those big steel pole things hit her in the head right after the big boom. Mom asked me to get help, but … but I couldn't make it through the door. I'm really, really, sorry, Dad. I'm not strong like you."

He looked at his son. He beamed. "You did great, Colin. I'm proud of you." He leaned down to check Ciara. He found her taking shallow breaths. She had a steady pulse. A large dried-up wound on the left side of her forehead revealed the blow she received as the girder fell into the room. With caution, he lifted her off the floor, cradling her in his arms and holding her head in a stable position. Tears flowed from his eyes, creating ugly-looking little rivers in the grime covering his skin as the fluid ran down his cheeks.

Ciara opened her eyes and looked at him, her face filled with confusion. "Who is that?" She said in a weak voice, as she looked at him, the dim light conditions compounding her uncertainty. "Aedan, is that you? What happened to you? Are you okay? You're a mess. Is Colin all right? How did you find us?" Tears flowed from her eyes as an outpouring of love, and relief struck her. "I knew you'd find us. I love you so much."

"And I love you." He stared at her; a sight he had feared he would never see again. He beamed as he held her close.

I found them alive. Thank God, I found them.

He leaned down to her and kissed her cheek. "You're my soul mate, and my best friend and I'll prove that to you every day from now on," he whispered into her right ear.

She smiled and drifted to sleep. Her breathing was regular.

He looked at Colin. "We have to leave, right now. You're my little man, and I need your help. Take my flashlight and lead the way — hurry."

He looked at the floor. Ciara's cell phone laid in pieces next to her dark green backpack and purse, the girder had crushed the phone. "Grab mom's pack, and her purse put them on her belly." He turned and ran to the door.

"Dad?" Colin said as they approached the bathroom exit door.

"Yes?"

"I'm hungry, and I'm really, really, thirsty. I really, really thought I would die from thirstation."

Aedan laughed at the word Colin created. "We'll get you something to drink and eat, but right now we have to get you and Mom out of here."

"Pop, can I have a bottle of pop?"

"You can have a case of pop." He laughed.

Colin grinned. "Dad?"

"Yes?"

"I missed you. I love you, Dad." Tears flowed from his eyes.

Aedan's expression revealed his deep love for his son. "I love you too, you're my little man. Come on, we have to get out of this room."

He moved them through the wreckage and the fallen ducts, and then well away from the bathroom.

He stopped at the southeast corner, outside the men's restroom, where he laid Ciara on the floor, and then he helped her into a seated position leaning her back against the wall.

A horrible crashing sound knocked Aedan to his knees. As he stood, he stared at the northwest corner where two massive air handlers had crashed into the women's bathroom in the same location where he had found Ciara lying unconscious moments earlier.

He jumped at the sound of his watch alarm chiming. He looked at his timepiece. It was **12:00 Midnight, Christmas Day**.

"I did it." He smiled with relief and joy — his eyes watered. He looked skyward through the open roof. "Thank you, Lord."

CHAPTER THIRTY-FOUR

REUNITED

Aedan approached the elevator shaft with Colin walking close behind. He leaned into the shaft while holding an exposed vertical beam, and shouted, "I found them, they're alive, and they are out of harm's way, for now."

Aedan looked at the 21st floor with concern.

I wonder how much time we have before the rest of twenty-one crashes down on us. By the looks of things, it won't take long.

On the eighteenth floor, Jacob danced and shouted with joy.

From the 15th floor, Bellson roared, "Congratulations, O'Beirne."

From the tenth floor, Eddie shouted, "Way to go Wyoming."

Aedan laughed as he pulled his cell phone from his pocket. He dialed a number. "Gerry, do you still have your radio?"

"Sure, I do."

"Can you let your people know I've found my family? They're safe, but my wife has taken a blow to her head, and we are waiting on twenty for help. Also, several substantial units on twenty-one fell onto twenty, the explosion weakened the girder structure. I believe that floor is close to critical, so please get the crews to hurry."

"They won't be able to get a ladder to you on twenty, debris is preventing the fire trucks from getting close enough to the building, and you're too high for their equipment. I will let them know your situation. They'll get on it right away, they have several other options," Bellson said.

He returned to Ciara, opened her backpack, and found two bottles of water, opened the bottles, and handed one to Colin, who began gulping it down. "Hey, slow down, I don't want you getting sick."

He gave the second bottle to Ciara.

"How did you find us?" she said.

"The better question is: how did you end up in this building? Doctor Miller's office is in the tower to the east, it runs along Franklin Street."

She stopped sipping the water. "I didn't realize there were two buildings at the same address. The doctor's business card doesn't make that clear but working in a downtown office is something new for her, and mistakes happen. I parked in the garage, and this was the closest building. When we got to this floor, I realized right away the doctor's office was not here, so, I took Colin to the bathroom, and the massive explosion occurred. What happened to the building? What caused the detonation?"

"A gas leak caused the explosion which destroyed the top ten floors, and it wreaked havoc on the lower levels too, plus it took out the elevators. Taking Colin to the bathroom saved your lives."

"We were alone up here, which was another sign we were in the wrong place. The floor was empty when we entered."

"Why did you agree to come down here? The consult could have waited; it didn't have to get done before Christmas."

"Doctor Miller scheduled a long vacation. Considering how many problems I had when I was pregnant with Colin, I didn't want to wait to make sure the baby's healthy." She paused. Her face reddened and filled with worry lines. "I hope — "

He interrupted her. "No, don't do that. Our baby will be beautiful and healthy. Put that out of your mind, we will get you and Colin out of here, and we'll have a great Christmas. Our new baby will be unharmed."

She smiled. "Anyway, the doctor had several cancellations. She called me from her cell and asked me if I could make an eight o'clock here on Franklin Street. I rushed out of the house, hoping to give you a great Christmas surprise by taking care of the consult myself since you didn't want to go to the afternoon appointment. I planned to shop a little after seeing the doctor, and then surprise you in your office and ask you to take us out to an early lunch."

"Oh man, I wish that would've happened. It would have been an incredible surprise."

"How could you know what we were going through?" She smiled. "Anyway, about two minutes after the explosion, the roof above the bathroom made terrifying sounds. I pushed Colin into the corner, and then one of the steel beams hit me in the head."

"That beam could have killed you," Aedan said.

"Yes, but it knocked me out. I was unconscious for at least an hour. Poor Colin had to lie next to me the entire time, waiting for me to wake. It was terrible the first day because the fire department worked for hours-and-hours to put out the fire, we could hear all the activity, and we listened to them pumping water into the building. It was awful laying here sealed off from everything. I didn't know if we'd live or die. Our screams for help never made it through the walls, and after a while, we started getting tired and cold."

Aedan's expression filled with pain. "Oh, Cia, it's my fault. I acted like such a fool Wednesday morning, you jumped at the chance to make the early appointment. If I had stayed home, I would've talked you out of going to the downtown office, and none of this would have happened."

"No, don't blame yourself, going to the Loop was my plan to surprise you. I love you and work has you stressed." Her tears flowed again.

He looked at her. "None of this is your fault. I'm to blame; if only I had not been such a fool." His voiced faded.

"No, you had no way to know the explosion would happen."

"Still — "

She interrupted him. "No, you couldn't know the explosion cut us off from the world. With my cell phone destroyed, I couldn't call you or anyone, a blockage stopped us from leaving the bathroom, and I was too dizzy and weak from the blow to my head to clear the wood blocking the door. We tried pounding the exterior walls, but no one heard us. I fell in-and-out of consciousness and knew that might be a sign of a concussion; so, I forced myself to remain awake despite my exhaustion. And Colin had to endure everything." She sighed. "Poor kid, I didn't remember I had water bottles in my purse. He's been complaining of thirst for the last day."

"You were trying to give me a loving surprise." His voice trembled. "It's been a freaky time for us all. I still can't believe I found you both, it makes me happy beyond words. You've no idea how I feel."

"I was looking forward to surprising you." Her voice faded. "And, poor Colin, this is not something a five-year-old kid should experience."

"I had fun, Mom. I built a fort in the corner; it was really, really fun. I knew Dad would find us." Colin ran circles around them.

Aedan grinned. He grabbed Colin and pulled him close. "Okay, I'll be the first one to say it, Merry Christmas."

"What?" Her face revealed her surprise.

"It's twelve-twenty in the morning on Christmas Day, Merry Christmas."

Colin began crying.

Aedan looked at him. "What's wrong, little man?"

"Santa doesn't know I'm here. He won't bring any presents."

He pulled Colin into a warm embrace between him and Ciara. "That's not true. Santa will still leave your gifts at our house, and I'll prove it when I go home to get them after we get both of you to the hospital."

"Are you really, really sure?"

"Yes, my little man. I'll get the presents from Santa for you, don't worry." He pulled Ciara close. He wrapped his sleeveless left arm around her shoulder, causing him to groan from the pain, his broken wrist sent throbbing waves through his body.

"What's wrong? What did you do?" Ciara said.

"When I was climbing through the wreckage in this building to get to you and Colin, I fell and broke my wrist, or at least it feels like it's broken."

"What?" Her voice cracked with surprise. "How were you able to get through the blocked door and carry me out of there?

"I've been searching for you and Colin since Wednesday and ignored the pain throughout my search." He pulled her tighter to him. "I had no choice."

"How did you fall?"

He laughed. "That's an interesting story. Do you see the duct on the floor over there?" He pointed.

"Yes." Ciara looked confused.

"That duct fell on me after I climbed through the hole over there." He pointed to the location. "It hit me so hard that I fell to the floor, and when I put out my hands to soften my landing, my left wrist broke. It sure didn't feel good, but I had to find you and Colin fast."

"So, that was the crashing and screaming sounds we heard. I thought I was dreaming again," Ciara said. "Colin told me he heard you, but I didn't believe it could be you, it felt more like a dream. I thought the roof and the floor above us would collapse and crush us to death."

"I shudder at the thought of what would've happened to you and Colin if I were a few minutes later getting to you. Michael and Máire warned me many times I had to find you by midnight."

"Who are they?" she said. "And, how could they guess that we were in danger? You've never mentioned them before."

He laughed. "That's a story that will take a long time to tell." He leaned close to her; he kissed her.

She could not let her surprise go. "I still can't picture this. You climbed through that hole for us, but you detest heights. I feel so lost and confused."

He grinned. "To find you and Colin, I climbed through holes and up the elevator shaft, and through many troubles and roadblocks."

"How, how'd you do that?"

"I realized something bad had happened to you, and either help came from me, or you'd die. I could sense it from the beginning and have searched for you non-stop for hours-upon-hours. This situation lasted sixty-six hours from beginning to end, but it took me a while at first to realize you were missing." He kissed her.

"Oh yuck," Colin said. He continued running circles around them.

As they kissed again, the floor filled with the roar of a helicopter approaching. As Aedan kissed her, the dirt and grime on his face transferred to her. They took on a similar appearance as they hugged in joy and relief.

CHAPTER THIRTY-FIVE

SURVIVING EXTRACTION

The roar of the emergency helicopter drew Aedan's attention. He watched two Flight Paramedics, one male, and one female, in full gear; drop on steel cables through a gaping hole in the roof where several jagged steel supports threatened their descent. He viewed them with concern as they moved around the dangerous steel.

Talk about threading a needle.

He approached the paramedics. "Thank you for helping us."

"Glad to help, Sir, it's our job. But this will not be easy," the female flight paramedic said. "We won't be able to extract you through the roof; it's too dangerous going through the wreckage up top." She looked at the other paramedic. "Tell them to hold while we find another way."

The male flight paramedic pressed the microphone button on his vest; he relayed the order to the helicopter crew.

"I do not understand how you'll get us out." Aedan looked at Ciara and Colin huddling close together in the southeast corner.

"Sir, my name is Sofia. My partner's name is Owen. We'll get you out."

Carrying a field bag, Owen left to examine Ciara and Colin.

"Can we go through the windows?" Aedan said.

Sofia ignored him as she walked around the floor, looking for exit points. She walked to the elevator shaft; she shined her high-wattage halogen light downward as she looked at Aedan. "You entered the building to get to your family, correct?"

"Yes, but several others helped; there's a person on eighteen, fifteen, and ten. You need to remove them too."

"I see the elevator shaft on the first floor filled with material and pipes. Are the stairs to the second floor clear?" Sofia said.

"Yes, from the first to second floors, the northwest stairs are clear, but a blockage prevents the use of the southeast stairwell," Aedan said.

Owen approached. "The female patient — "

Aedan interrupted. "Her name is Ciara."

Owen grinned. "Ciara appears to have a concussion, and she's dehydrated. We'll extract her using a stretcher. The boy — "

"My name is Aedan, and my son's name is Colin."

"Colin appears unharmed. He's also dehydrated," Owen said.

Sofia pressed the transmit button on her vest. "Have a team go to the second floor. They're to use the northwest stairwell from the lobby. Drop a cable, two harnesses, and the airlift stretcher. We'll lower the patients through the shaft to the second floor, where our team will get them out from there. There are three others to extract. One person is on eighteen, one on fifteen and one on ten. How are the winds?"

Aedan heard their radios squawk. A man on the other end said, "Winds are holding at under ten miles per hour. We are one-hundred-percent operational."

Sofia pressed the transmit button. "We have to make this quick, the upper floor might collapse."

The radio squawked. "We are lowering the equipment now."

Sofia pressed the button. "Stand ready for further instructions."

Aedan watched as a cable, with two harnesses and a stretcher, dropped through the wreckage. He ran to Ciara. "They're getting us out of here soon."

He watched the paramedics place Ciara in the airlift stretcher, which was an oval-shaped aluminum cage, with wide heavy-duty nylon straps holding her in place. It had a full diameter hook for helicopter extraction. Ciara appeared in significant pain.

Aedan leaned close to her; they kissed. "See you on the ground with Colin in a few minutes. I love you."

"No — Colin should go first," she said.

"No, you need medical attention. We must get you out and to the hospital. I will be right here with Colin. I will go down with him."

"No, Sir, you will not," Sofia said. "Owen will take the boy."

Aedan pulled Colin into his arms. "I have gone through more than you would believe searching for my family. I will take him down, or no-one does."

Sofia pressed the transmit button. "Send the second cable." She looked at Aedan. "We will deal with Colin after we get Ciara down."

Owen fastened a lead cable to the stretcher. Sofia helped him carry it to the elevator shaft, allowing it to hang over the edge by two feet. They hooked on to the main cable. She pressed the transmit button. "Pull eight feet of the cable back."

The cable to the helicopter tightened. The crew pushed the stretcher into the shaft where it hovered one foot above the twentieth floor.

Owen, wearing a harness, hooked on to the second cable; he leaped into the shaft, dropping about five feet below the twentieth floor. He pressed the transmit button. "Take back about six feet of cable on line two." He rose and hooked on to the airlift stretcher.

Sofia pressed the transmit button. "Lower them now."

Aedan, while still holding Colin, looked at Ciara as they dropped her to the second floor. Portable high-wattage halogen lights illuminated the shaft. Shouts and cheers came from the eighteenth, fifteenth, and tenth floors as Ciara descended to the second floor. As they reached the second level, two paramedics snatched the stretcher and pulled it from the shaft.

Aedan looked at the upper girders, not trusting their structural integrity, and knowing the twenty-first floor could crash down on them any moment.

Aedan stood at the edge of the shaft wearing a harness around his body from his upper thighs to his shoulders, attached to the drop cable. He had Colin strapped to him and into the harness. Owen waited in the shaft.

Sofia looked at Aedan. "Sir, this is the only way we will let you do this. Owen will connect onto both of you, and he will guide you down."

"I understand." Aedan looked in the shaft, not wanting to drop into the open space; his fear of heights had returned. He hesitated, amazed that after everything he had been through, his fears still maintained a firm grip on him.

Sofia sensed his reluctance. "If you can't do this, we'll do it for you."

He looked at her and back at Colin. "No. Let's do it." He pushed off from the twentieth floor. He fell into a sharp shiver as Owen hooked on to their harness. They began lowering.

On the eighteenth floor, Jacob waited for them at the shaft's edge. "Way to go Mr. O'Beirne."

"You're next," Aedan said.

They continued lowering and came upon the fifteenth floor, where Bellson sat — his face revealed his pain. "Great work up there, O'Beirne."

"They'll get you out soon, Gerry," Aedan said.

They continued lowering. Colin laughed; he loved the ride which made Aedan feel less threatened by the height. They came upon the tenth floor, where Eddie sat on the office chair, his damaged leg propped up on a second chair.

"You look like you're on vacation," Aedan said.

"Oh yeah, sure, this is a wonderful place to rest," Eddie said. His hearty laugh filled the shaft.

They stopped at the second level, where two paramedics pulled them onto the floor and removed the harnesses. Seconds later, Owen moved up the shaft to extract Jacob.

"It's about time you guys joined me," Ciara said. She smiled. She sat in a regular ambulance gurney with wheels.

Aedan glared at her. "You should be on the way to the hospital."

"I'm not going anywhere without you two." She frowned.

Colin ran to her, climbed onto her lap. "This is fun, mom."

She pulled him into a tight hug.

Aedan turned to sounds coming from the shaft. He watched Owen lower Jacob to the floor.

"We will need the airlift stretcher now, the next two patients have injuries," Owen said. The other paramedics helped him hook the cable to the stretcher. They lifted it into the shaft and Owen elevated to the fifteenth floor, where Sofia waited to load-up Bellson.

Despite the pleas and shouts coming from the Fire Department's crew ordering him to exit the destroyed building, Aedan refused to leave as he waited for the remaining men.

Filled with gratitude, Aedan looked at Eddie and Bellson resting in regular ambulance gurneys, with Jacob standing close by. "I found my family because of you. If I did not go into the tower, and if you men did not volunteer to help me, I would not have found them. From my heart, thank you."

"What are you talking about?" Bellson said. "I slowed you down for hours and didn't believe your story until you showed us your wife's car on the top level of the parking garage. I could have dispatched personnel to locate your family; instead, you had to find them yourself. You should not thank me."

Aedan grinned. "You believed me at the right time, and you suffered bad injuries helping me." He looked at Jacob. "I wouldn't have thought of that duct removal plan on my own — thank you."

"Wyoming, stop with the gushing gratitude; it doesn't fit your personality." Eddie's hearty laugh filled the air. "What happened at midnight? Why'd you have to get them out by then?"

"At the stroke of midnight, after we were clear of the bathroom, several girders on twenty-one collapsed, sending massive air-handling units into the women's restroom space," Aedan said. "If it were not for Michael and Máire, and all of you, I might not have found them in time. You're all heroes in my book; thank you again and again."

"That comes from us too," Ciara said, as two paramedics lifted her gurney and began walking her down the stairs.

"Merry Christmas," Aedan said with joy.
One-by-one the gurneys left the building, with medical crews bringing them to waiting ambulances. Aedan was last to leave the building — he held Colin by the hand. They laughed all the way to the ambulance, waiting along Asher Avenue. Chicago news media vans and personnel covered the area, their bright lights illuminating the entire campus.

Aedan stopped; he looked at the sky and saw the emergency helicopter leave the scene, with the flight paramedics, Sofia, and Owen, onboard. The craft moved out-of-sight.

As he stepped into the ambulance, Aedan turned to an enormous crashing sound emanating from above, as the old building's roof and the mechanicals on twenty-one, collapsed onto the twentieth floors. He sat next to Colin, with Ciara on the gurney across from them. He shook his head in disbelief, he knew that they had escaped. His mind filled with images of Michael, Máire, Charlie, and Jacob. He knew his family would not be alive if not for their help.

How did they know it would take place at midnight? Who are they?

The ambulance driver looked at Aedan. "We are taking you to the Saint John Hospital Emergency Room," she said.

Aedan laughed.

Where else would we go?

He pulled out his cell phone. He dialed a number. "Detective, this is Aedan O'Beirne, may I ask a favor?"

"Yes, anything," Bellson said.

"Will you have someone drive my car over to Saint John Hospital's Erie Street parking garage? I left the keys in the glove box."

"Yes we'll place it in a reserved space on the first level, waiting for you and your family," Bellson said. "I'm glad I can help."

"Thank you for everything." Aedan beamed as he looked at his family. Sirens filled the air, little Colin giggled.

CHAPTER THIRTY-SIX

DAMAGE REPAIR

A sense of déjà consumed Aedan when the ambulance pulled into Saint John Hospital's Emergency Room garage. They stopped at the entrance doors. Two paramedics pulled Ciara from the rear; they extended the wheels and pushed her into the building. "My son should remain with her. He only needs fluids."

The female nurse grinned. "We have already planned for that." She rolled Ciara into a cubicle with two empty beds. A second nurse directed Colin into the same cubicle. The nurses pulled drapes around the area.

As Aedan entered the ER cubicle to join his family, familiar profiles of a man and a woman standing thirty feet away, drew his attention. He grinned.

Why are they here?

He walked to Ciara. "I'll be right back."

"Where are you going? Don't leave now."

"I have to talk to a couple people, Michael and Máire. I mentioned them when we were still in the building."

"But who are they?" Ciara said.

"I will explain everything later, it's a long story. I'll be right back." He left them and walked to Michael and Máire; they remained standing where he had seen them. He grinned as he approached. "My good friends, thank you so much. I can't find the words to express my gratitude. I thought you were my enemies for most of this painful journey, and it turns out you worked non-stop to help me find my family."

Michael smiled. "We are proud of you. You faced the daunting task of finding the people you love, which required a change of heart, and that change did not come with ease. Your rapid transformation opened your mind, which helped prove your love for them meant more to you than your own well-being. You became a new person."

"That is an extraordinary change in fewer than three days," Máire said. "We are happy for you and your family." She flashed a smile filled with warmth.

"We have a Christmas gift for you." Michael handed a small unwrapped box to Aedan.

He took the box, opened it and inside he found the glass angel ornament he destroyed Wednesday morning in their home's kitchen. "I don't understand. How? How did you do this?"

"That is not important," Máire said. "It is time for us to leave." They did not wait for a response; they turned and walked through the exit door.

Aedan grinned as he returned to Ciara and Colin. Intravenous bags hung close to their beds; fluids dripped into their bodies through their arms, restoring their levels. "I have our first Christmas gift. It comes from my two friends, Michael and Máire." He pulled the angel ornament from the box.

"You fixed it," Colin said. "You fixed it, Dad, you fixed it." He reached for the ornament.

"How did you do that?" Ciara said.

"It wasn't me; my friends did this. All thanks go to them."

A female nurse walked into the enclosure. "Mr. O'Beirne, please come with me, and we will get an x-ray of your wrist, and fix those wounds."

"But how did you know — "

Ciara interrupted. "I told them to look at your wrist and at your wounds, you might need stitches." She frowned. "And, Aedan, you need a shower, you stink." She laughed.

"But I need to get home to get the presents from Santa."

"Yeah, Dad, go home. Santa doesn't know I'm in the hosapul."

"Hospital, Colin, not *hosapul*," Ciara said. She looked at Aedan. "Why don't you go home after they take care of your wrist? Take a shower before you come back with the gifts from Santa. You stink."

"Yeah Dad, you're really, really, stinky."

He grinned. He leaned close to Ciara, kissed her. "I will do that." He walked to Colin, kissed him on the head. He walked from the enclosure and followed the nurse.

Several hours later, Aedan walked into a Saint John Hospital regular room where Ciara and Colin rested as intravenous drips continued to raise their bodily fluid levels. He carried the large Santa bag and a small suitcase with fresh clothes and shoes for them. A hard cast surrounded his left wrist, which extended to his elbow. New, clean, bandages covered his face and right arm —

fifty stitches required to repair both locations. He had showered and changed clothes; he looked like a different person from the one who had left the hospital earlier.

"Dad," shouted Colin. "Santa came to our house?"

"Yes, he did. I brought gifts Santa left." He placed the Santa bag at the foot of the boy's bed.

Colin began extracting gift-after-gift, many marked from Santa Claus to him, while some were from Ciara and Aedan. The boy's face filled with joy. Soon, his many unwrapped toys covered the bed; he squealed with glee after opening each gift. "This is really, really the best Christmas ever."

Doctor Stephanie Miller entered the room.

Surprise filled Ciara's face. "How did you know I was here?"

The doctor walked to Ciara, took her right hand. "The hospital provided a full report. You didn't show for the consult, which surprised me. I did not know that you were in building one behind us. You had me worried. I came here to check on you in person."

"Thank you, doctor. What about your vacation?" Ciara said.

"I wanted to visit you before I left. I delayed our trip."

Ciara's expression revealed her concern. "How's our baby?"

"The hospital will release you in an hour," Doctor Miller said. "It's Christmas, and you will go home. Your fluid levels are close to normal, and so are Colin's. They will pull the IV lines in a few minutes. You have recovered well from the blow to your head. You should get plenty of rest over the next week or two; however, the best news of all is your baby is healthy and is not in any trouble."

Aedan sat on the bed next to Ciara as her tears flowed. She sighed and smiled with relief. She took in deep breaths. "Thank you, thank you from my heart." A river of tears flowed from her eyes. "That news is a tremendous Christmas gift."

The doctor grinned. "I want to examine you in my Oak Valley office in three weeks." She smiled and walked from the room.

Aedan kissed her. "Maybe we can name the baby *Edward*."

She laughed. "Eddie's still trying to get his name in there, huh?"

"I promised him, and he risked his life helping me find you."

She laughed. "I have no argument this time."

He grinned as he opened the clothes bag and pulled out a wrapped gift. He handed it to Ciara. "This one is from me, not from Santa."

Aedan watched Ciara tear into the wrapping, unveiling the Pantec K10 35mm film camera he found for sale on the internet, a brand new in-the-box piece dating back to the 1970s. She hugged him.

"I can't believe you remembered the camera," Ciara said.

"I remembered. We also need to sit down when you're back to full strength and plan your darkroom."

"What?"

"You want to develop your own 35mm film, so I'll help by building you a dark room. I don't understand why you want to do all that work in a digital camera age, but because you want it, I will help," Aedan said.

"What's going on with you?"

"Nothing at all, I love you, and I will help." He grinned.

"I want to use and develop film because it's better."

"No, today's digital cameras create as good or better results than the old 35mm cameras," Aedan said. "And they can store hundreds of pictures, and the images are easy to place on the net and share with family, much better than film."

"That's not how you feel about your music." She countered, smiling.

"What does that mean?"

"Music in digital format is much easier to use than old-fashioned vinyl albums, but you love vinyl." She responded with a resolved smile.

"That's not the same; music is much deeper and far warmer when played from well-mastered vinyl albums," Aedan said.

"You're using similar arguments." She smiled and laughed. "Digital photos are more convenient, but film photography has much more warmth and depth, and when done well, it becomes an art form."

Aedan frowned as he remembered the black-and-white picture of Colin and him, recalled thinking the photo appeared alive and full of warmth, but he did not want to admit she was correct. He laughed. "Okay, okay, whatever — "

She cut him off and smiled. "Film is better."

"Wait, I'll only concede your point if you concede my point that printed books and vinyl albums remain superior to other formats."

She laughed. "You're so stubborn."

They broke into a long, cleansing laugh, a laugh that released hours of worry, anxiety, and pain. He kissed her.

"Oh yuck," Colin said as he opened his last gift from Santa.

They laughed again.

"I have a second gift … I saved it for last because it means so much to me." He handed a medium-sized envelope to Ciara.

"What's this?" she said.

"Open it."

Surprise overcame her as she extracted the pink heart-shaped note that Aedan had straightened and laminated. "How did you?"

"That note started everything. In the beginning, it sparked my anger but not anymore. I want us to keep it to celebrate and recall how much we overcame together. That note was with me everywhere I went during my journey to find you and Colin. I read it many times to help renew my strength. Each time I saw it, my heart ached to be with you both — it's an important piece of O'Beirne family history," Aedan said.

She had nothing to say — her face revealed her thoughts.

They kissed and hugged.

"Hey, I almost forgot, wait until you see what else I bought. You'll see it in a little while when we leave the hospital."

"What's with you?" she said.

He smiled. He kissed Ciara again.

Aedan entered the vehicle and drove it to the lower hospital doors. He left the car and walked to the garage side entrance. The doors opened, and two attendants pushed Ciara and Colin, sitting in wheelchairs, into the garage.

He walked to them and helped Ciara stand. He looked at her. "Here's the other surprise I promised you, this is our new car." He pointed at the X5.

"No way," Ciara said with surprise. "This belongs to us?"

"I bought it after totaling my car in an accident on Congress Parkway. You've been after me to get a new car — here it is." He laughed while opening the door for them, helped them into the vehicle, made sure Colin sat in the car seat positioned at the center of the second row.

"This is not like you." She viewed the luxurious interior.

"I know." He grinned.

She leaned over and kissed him. "It's perfect."

"We'll get you a new car too, something better to haul around Colin and his baby brother or sister."

She looked at him with a stunned expression. "This week has changed you."

"Wait, I have even bigger things in store; something that will bring me closer to my family." Aedan laughed.

"What does that mean?"

"That's for later."

"You can't say something like that, and not tell me," Ciara said.

He grinned and put the X5 into gear. He pulled away from the garage. Minutes later, he entered the interstate and aimed the vehicle to their home in Oak Valley.

CHAPTER THIRTY-SEVEN

A NEW FUTURE

Aedan pulled onto Ohio Street. It was Tuesday morning, December 28th. Traffic remained light three days after Christmas.

He parked in his usual garage location and left the X5.

Aedan entered the Prescot Hotel and walked to the elevator that would take him to the top floor, and to the private ballroom where he hoped to find Michael and Máire. He presented the exclusive card to Jonathan, and soon, the unit carried him to the building's highest floor. The door opened; he walked to the ballroom entrance, passing the picture frames along the way. He slowed at the last frame and noticed it was no longer empty.

That's a photo of Jacob … I should have known. He has the same smile and the same mystifying personality as the others.

He entered the ballroom. Michael, Máire, and Jacob sat in high-backed chairs. They appeared to be waiting for him.

Michael approached Aedan. "It gladdens me to see you, son."

Máire and Jacob embraced him.

Aedan looked at Jacob. "How?"

Jacob smiled. "You never know who will offer a special hand in your life when you most need the help."

Aedan smiled. "I need information about the school you attend so I can pay for your final semester. I will do it this week."

Jacob laughed. "No, Mr. O'Beirne, that is unnecessary. I will not return to school, I have far more pressing matters to attend to."

Aedan looked doubtful. "Are you sure? I have no problem fulfilling my promise—happy to do it."

"Please, Mr. O'Beirne, keep the money for your family," Jacob said.

"I won't argue." He laughed. "I came here to extend my gratitude for the support I received, and see I owe appreciation to three people."

Máire smiled. "There is a fourth."

"I understand, and I have that covered." He looked at them. "I need to ask this question one last time: Who are you?"

"We help, we can say no more," Michael said. His brilliant smile filled his face with joy.

Aedan looked at Máire. "Explain Millennium Park."

She smiled. "What do you want to know?"

"I am still confused about your attitude when we sat close to the Bean. You pressed me hard, and you worked to have me see or understand different actions fathers took. What did you want from me?" He looked hopeful.

"Aedan, there is a difference between being with your family because you must, versus wanting, aching to involve yourself in their lives because you love them. We did not witness forced participants in the park; each person we observed wanted to be with their children. They considered fatherhood a blessing, not a burden." She smiled.

He smiled. "Thank you."

"We need to take the guest card," Michael said.

Aedan handed him the card. "Thank you again, to everyone." He walked from the ballroom with a somber expression realizing that he would miss them.

Despite his injuries, Aedan had a happy spring in his step. After walking through the Grand Lobby, he saw a large sign notifying guests the hotel planned to begin a complete remodel of the highest floor, following the holiday season. The hotel planned to convert the upper level to high-end suites.

He grinned as he walked from the Prescot and into the crisp, winter air.

Aedan entered the pub and strolled to the kitchen. "Hey, Eddie," he shouted. "I stopped in to find out how you're doing."

"Hey Wyoming, it's great seeing you, but go home to Ciara and Colin. My leg will heal." Eddie's hearty laugh echoed across the pub.

"You came through for me. I can't thank you enough."

"That's what friends are for," Eddie said.

"Well, as a thank you, I kept my promise. If our newest baby is a boy, we will name him after you," Aedan said.

"That's fantastic news; now go home to your family, or I'll kick your butt."

Aedan laughed. "You can't kick me wearing that cast."

"I'll find a way if you don't leave and get back to your family."

"I'm going, I'm going. Take care of your leg." He left the pub and walked across the street. He strode toward Charlie's newsstand.

I know he'll be there; he never misses a day at his business.

He approached his friend. "Good morning, Charlie."

"Mr. O'Beirne, it is splendid to see you. But why are you here?" His deep voice echoed off the buildings.

He handed him an envelope. "Merry Christmas."

"That is most kind. What is it?" Charlie said.

"It's a little something to help you rebuild your newsstand." He grinned. "I must go to Metric & Inch for a meeting."

Charlie opened the card which read:

THANK YOU FOR BEING AN EXCELLENT
FRIEND - MERRY CHRISTMAS

Inside the card, Charlie found a $10,000 check written to cash. He looked at his friend already well down the street. "Mr. O'Beirne, stop," he shouted. "What is this?"

Aedan turned to Charlie and shouted, "A gift, and I hope it helps." He walked away, not allowing his friend to respond.

Aedan strode through the lobby. All elevators sat open and unused. He grinned and walked into the left unit; the same one he had spent so much time in with Michael. He took it to the thirty-ninth floor where he walked into Metric & Inch. He grinned as he walked into the office. "Good morning, Mr. Williamson."

James extended his right hand to him. "With all that's happened to you and your family, it surprised me to receive your call earlier."

"Those troubles are over. No thanks to you."

James frowned. "What does that mean?"

Aedan opened his briefcase; he extracted a letter and slid it across the desk.

James read the letter. He scowled. "You're resigning?"

"Yes, effective immediately. I'll make myself available for phone calls to help transition my work to my successor."

"But why?" James said. "I don't understand."

"Mr. Williamson, you did not hesitate to berate because I showed no interest in a partnership. But when you learned I was under enormous stress while looking for my family, you had no real support to offer." He grinned. "You scolded me for calling my new baby number two, but you offered little help and compassion for my family when you learned they were missing. You know Ciara and Colin, you've eaten dinner in our home, their lives were in danger, and you didn't care when you learned they were missing. I will *not* work for someone who held such a cold attitude toward me during the most trying time of my life."

James glared at him. "I was not sure what was going on with your family. There was no value in getting involved. Though, I remain of the opinion that you should be more ambitious."

Aedan frowned. "But you perceived value in lecturing me, and you perceived value in rebuking me."

"That's true, and I stand by the statements I made."

"Mr. Williamson, I was not the most ambitious person in this firm, and I apologize for having disappointed you; however, I helped make our clients happy, was loyal to the firm and hard working. You come from a dedicated and influential family, and you have worked hard to remain true to the role handed down to you. But my affection and trust go to your grandfather, Michael Williamson."

"I don't understand. You've never met my grandfather."

Aedan grinned.

A knock on the door interrupted them. An employee walked into the office. He was carrying a delivery box. "I'm sorry to interrupt. I was leaving for the day, and I noticed this came in for Mr. O'Beirne." He approached Aedan and handed him the box.

Aedan opened the container. He beamed as he extracted a black fedora; the same one Michael wore. He pulled a small card from the bottom, it read:

I AM PROUD OF YOU, AEDAN. I THOUGHT YOU MIGHT ENJOY THIS. WEAR IT WITH HEALTH AND JOY — MW

As he stood, he placed the fedora on his head. He looked at James. "It was a pleasure working for Metric & Inch. I'll look back on my time here with fond thoughts. I developed friendships and learned lessons I will hold for the rest of my life."

"What will you do next?" James said.

"Ciara and I plan to create a new future together." He placed the card from Michael on the desk. Aedan O'Beirne walked from the office, smiling and wearing the fedora.

THE END

*** Please read a note from the author on the following page.

Dear Reader,

Thank you for reading my novel, **39 SIXTY**. Please leave a five-star review online. You can learn more about my work at the publisher's website: https://kephapress.com.

I hope you read many great novels.

Thomas Johnson

CPSIA information can be obtained
at www.ICGtesting.com
Printed in the USA
LVHW111948210819
628455LV00007BA/76/P